I0742550

THE ONE PERCENT

A NOVEL

RICK COULOMBE

The One Percent
©2018 by Rick Coulombe
All rights reserved

For more information write: theonepercentnovel@gmail.com

ISBN: 978-1-7753087-0-6

THE ONE PERCENT

I

"Forgive me Father for I have sinned."

Of course you did. Personally, I think God holds us to impossible standards. He came in every Wednesday. He always wore a red tie. I can see it through the thin mesh divider that separates us. On the other side, he waits patiently. Waits for me to act out my part. Like I did every week. Every Wednesday at two o'clock sharp. I speak slowly. Softly. Like I'm trying to lull a baby to sleep. Like I'm trying to talk a kitten off a ledge. I push the tips of my fingers together. He can't see my hands but it's become ritual. It helps me get into character.

"Confess your sins," I say.

"I have committed fornication."

I used to have a list. Something that I could reference quickly. It covered everything from drinking binges to jealousy to any kind of dealings with the occult. Virtually anything that God wasn't happy with anyone doing. A mortal sins checklist. This was under the sixth commandment. Fornication. Sex before marriage. Personally, I didn't think it was a big deal. To this day though, I still can't figure out why it's listed under adultery. But there it was, right next to onanism and withdrawal for contraceptive purposes. I don't think that someone deserves an eternity of fire and brimstone for that either. But I don't make up the rules.

"Say three Hail Marys my son," I say.

He was horny but he was devout. Every week asking forgiveness for giving into the depraved animalistic tendencies that God had so callously given him. A cruel joke that you're stuck with forever. Every week he waits patiently for his punishment. His atonement. Atonement doesn't sound as harsh. He knows it's coming. He knows exactly what's coming. He's just waiting for me to come out and say it. To make it official. I take a slow, deep breath.

"Say three Hail Marys."

Three Hail Marys was the standard. From my research, three Hail Marys was the traditional devotional practice as a petition for purity and other virtues. It felt right. It worked with the whole Trinity thing too.

"I lied."

Three Hail Marys.

"I stole."

Three Hail Marys.

It only takes 16.61 seconds to recite Hail Mary at a reasonable pace. I timed it out one day. So, if you have 49.83 seconds to spare repenting, you can do whatever you want. It's a loophole. Sometimes I throw an Our Father into the mix. If I feel that they need a little more time to think about what they've done. 20.96 seconds.

Sitting there, in that tiny stuffy booth, I can't help but wonder why they don't put some sort of padding down on these hard wooden benches. A red velvet something would be nice. Gold trim. Tassels. Something to match my robe. A mini fridge. Some kind of snack. Maybe some of those crispy wafers.

The confessional curtain slides to one side and back and they kneel. A lattice divider separates us. It's dark and quiet. Like you imagine eternity might be. They would usually clasp their hands together like they've already started to pray. It's the ritual. But the praying comes later. Right now, they're here to say it out loud. To tell somebody. They have to. It's human nature. It's why your best friend will turn around and tell someone else your darkest secret the moment you turn your back.

They usually clear their throats. Run some fingers through their hair or adjust the collars on their shirts. "Forgive me Father for I have sinned," they say.

"How long since your last confession?"

It's a script. Three Hail Marys.

"I had impure thoughts."

Three Hail Marys.

"I lied."

Three Hail Marys. You get the idea.

"Father, God must know that I'm sorry for my sins. Why do I have to confess?"

I pause. Trying to think of something deep to say. Something about God's forgiveness. Something about showing God that you care about him. I stumble on my words and stop mid sentence. Shit. When in doubt, read the script. Stick to the script. "Just confess your sins to me my child." We're all infants in the eyes of the Lord. Children do what they're told.

"I have injured somebody."

Haven't we all?

I had hurt people too. It's human nature. But it wasn't until a few months later that I would really hurt people. Holding a gun and pointing it at someone's head. They're a lot heavier than I would have thought. It shakes slightly in my hand and I start to think that my outstretched arm might soon physically give out before Frosty finishes peeling the dynamite from this guy's chest. Someone said it would be counterproductive. To blow him up. The argument was that there'd be nothing left to identify the body with. Tomato soup was the analogy. Frosty wanted everybody to know who did it, and why. It wasn't even real dynamite. It was just tubes packed full of gunpowder. But I guess Frosty had put a lot of work into making it, so to not even use it would seem like a waste. Frosty hated waste. Can we blow something up? Anything? Okay, his car, we'll blow up his car. And maybe his house. Does he have any kids?

You can fill a drum with manure, stick a drain, valve, and filter at the bottom, piss into it, then top it off with water and dry it out in about ten months to get saltpeter. One of the main ingredients in gunpowder. That's what Birddog says he learned in basic. In case he was ever stranded behind enemy lines. According to Frosty we were always behind enemy lines. We were living there. And we had gotten comfortable living there. But it was time to plan our escape. It was going to happen now. We didn't have ten months to wait, so we just stole the gunpowder. Frosty could pretty much get his hands on anything he wanted. Including the gun I'm holding. And the one that pressed against my temple. My hand shakes.

"I don't think you can blow up a house with gun powder."

"Shut up," Frosty says, spitting.

Maybe we should have let Birddog make the nitroglycerin after all. He said it was pretty easy to do.

Russell didn't seem to mind that the duct tape Frosty was peeling off of him had ruined his suit. Even though it was probably worth more than a used car. He didn't even look down at the marks it left behind. He was probably more preoccupied with the fact that he was about to die.

That was why we were here. He was the mission of this particular cell. The CEO of some multimillion or multibillion dollar firm. He had a mansion, a few nice cars, a boat. Anything you could think of. Heated toilet seats and luxury, hand carved, perfectly square ice cubes. His annual bonuses alone were more money than any ten people would normally see in a lifetime. He was used to being called Mr. Howard and generally wouldn't stand for anything less. He was so rich, the money alone demanded respect. Regardless of the actual person.

On my checklist it was under the tenth commandment. Thou shall not covet thy neighbor's goods. Avarice or greed. There was an asterisk beside it denoting a deadly sin. All of that money was useless now as he sat, tied to a chair in a pool of his own piss, pleading for his life at the hands of the great equalizer.

Frosty tears the last tube from his chest. "Oh, thank God," Russell mumbles.

But God had nothing to do with this. I should know.

Frosty looks at his watch. "You know, at least you're going to die *for* something. Not a lot of people can say that. This is genuinely going to help people. You're kind of like a hero," he says. "Any last words?"

Russell opens his mouth and a mass of half coagulated blood stretches its way, like hot toffee, to his thigh. It doesn't seem to bother him. Concussions can leave you feeling disoriented. In some cases even euphoric.

"That's what I thought," Frosty says.

One of Russell's teeth falls out.

Forgive me Father for I have sinned. Those are the only words I can think of.

The pale yellow light flickers whenever a car drives by overhead. We're underneath the rest of the world. Hiding in a maze that most people don't even know exists, right under their feet. In a city this size there are unused service tunnels, sewer tunnels, abandoned subway tunnels, or forgotten bomb shelters all over the place.

Frosty had been living on the streets since he was twenty-four and knew practically all of them. He could almost get clear across the city without ever having to surface. Almost. There was only one place that I knew of, at the intersection of Main and Third, where he'd have to cross the street topside because of the new pipes that were installed for the water treatment plant. People naturally assumed he was stupid because of the way he looked. He followed me one day as I followed someone else. That's how we met.

After about an hour in the booth taking confessions, sitting on that hard wooden bench, my butt hurt and I was feeling pretty good about myself so I decided to leave. A good days work. It had been the usual stuff. Stealing, lying, lust. Those were the big three. The most common sins I'd hear confessed. Especially after a particularly good weekend. People tended to cut their morality loose on Fridays and Saturdays and start worrying about it again first thing on Sunday morning.

Three Hail Marys. Three Hail Marys and you'll be fine. I was a little surprised to find out that masturbating for a fertility test is a confessable sin. Or piercing your nipples. The subtleties of it all kept things interesting.

After everyone had gone, I peeked out of the curtain and thought I'd make my escape while there was no one around. That's when I heard them for the first time. Those high heels popping against the hard floor. They echoed across the vaulted ceiling as she crossed the nave. Marching between the rows of pews like a soldier. She had a goal. You could hear it in her walk. She was bridging the gap between her and absolution one step at a time. Then, the heels stopped and she stepped inside.

"Forgive me Father for I have sinned."

They were the first words those excessively red lips pushed out.

I stumbled on my own tongue. "How long has it been since your last confession?"

She was pressed up against the mesh screen that divided us. A faint hint of ammonia wafted through those tiny holes. Escaping her clothes and her skin. Making their way over to me. Bridging the gap between us.

She ran some fingers through her hair. Adjusted her collar. "Thirty three years," she said.

God holds us to impossible standards.

That's how I first met Rosalind. After that, I got to know her very well. She wore those same red heels every time she stepped inside the booth. She leaned in a little closer every time she started to run through her list. I could make out the hint of a smile stretched across her cheeks every time she finished her confession. I've seen it a lot of times now. Absolution. It makes a sound too. Kind of like a heavy sigh.

"I have injured somebody," she said.

Haven't we all?

Violence is a mortal sin. For a sin to be mortal, that is fatal to heaven, it must meet three standards on my check list simultaneously. First of all it has to be a serious matter. Second, before the sin, a person must have been mindful of the serious wrong, having reflected on the gravity of the situation. Sufficient reflection beforehand was written in bold. That meant it was important. A person must have freely chosen to commit the sin, in spite of possible coercion. So I guess having a gun pressed to your head might not clear you for pressing a gun against someone else's in the eyes of the Lord? Was God watching me? Forgiving me as I stand in the bowels of the city? Pointing a gun and watching the asbestos flakes flutter down from the ceiling every time a car passes overhead? Straining to keep my arm pointed out. A gun pressed to my temple. The smell of urine and a few people who haven't showered in over a month permeating the thick, stagnant air. I wonder if any of this was worth it. Part of me wishes that I had never met her. Either one of them. But I know that this would have happened anyway. It was all part of the divine plan. There was no escaping it.

"Forgive me father for I have sinned," she said.

There were one hundred eighty-seven mortal sins on my list. I'm aware of the irony now. Or the coincidence. Whatever.

She smiled and sighed. "Thank you Father." She has what she came here for. I heard her sit down, say her prayers, and then walk away. The sound of her heels faded. They're gone after the thunderclap of the oak door slamming shut dissipates. Contemplating buying a small inflatable pillow, I followed her out. Frosty followed me. The church bell rang. I forgave her every time she came in. Mondays, Wednesdays, and Fridays. Service on Sundays. Say three Hail Marys. She was afraid of going to hell. But if she really was on her way down there, confessing to me wasn't going to save her. I'm not really a priest.

2

I usually had paper cuts on the tips of my fingers. It was an occupational hazard of dealing with a lot of paperwork. So, my choice of finger foods was limited. Anything that was spicy or acidic would burn and cause them to swell. Nobody trusts an insurance salesman with swollen fingers. I learned that the hard way. So, I tried to handle the stack of paper carefully. Like it was a sleeping baby that I didn't want to wake. I would set it down softly in front of me in neat, tidy, color coded piles. Simple geometric shapes had the most impact on the client. The pyramid, the square. Stick to the basics. Once everything was signed, I would pick them up and smack them against the table to square them all up into a tight pile. The smack added gravity. A severity. Urgency. Hurry up, sign here. Before it's too late.

When asked to rank professions in terms of honesty or ethics, people generally placed insurance salesmen towards the bottom of the list. Someplace in the area between politicians and car salesmen. Equidistant from 'I did not have sexual relations...' and 'what do I have to do to put you in this car today?' Everybody has their scripts.

"The number one reason that a person re-marries after the death of a spouse is due to financial constraints," I would say. Fifty percent of all statistics are made up. They would look at me, look at each other, look back at me. Was the sweat on my forehead giving it away? I wasn't very good at my job. I had some sort of tell. Something involuntary like a facial tick or a heart palpitation just big enough to make my hand shake. Dilated pupils. Cotton mouth.

"May I have a glass of water?"

They exhale with conviction as they flip through the mountain of pages. "I think we're going to take some time and look things over. We'll call you." That was their script, what they would say when they were too polite to say 'no' outright. Okay. If you wake in the morning let me know, I say. Someone taught me that trick. Use the word 'if'. Your little parting dig. If. If you don't, it might be too late. It won't register with them immediately but their subconscious might grab a hold of it and rattle it around for a while. Fear might get the better of them. Your phone could ring in the middle of the night. Mine never did.

I got reprimanded by the manager of my division for not selling enough policies. He threatened to fire me. Adjusted his tie with the stripes at forty-five degree angles. Polished his cufflinks. They needed a shark, he said. Someone who could make the company money hand over fist. That was the goal of the corporate machine after all. So the district manager could get good results and maybe even a bonus, which, in turn, is good for the regional manager who, all potential bonuses aside, has his eye on the regional vice president job when Bob moves up the ladder and gets a sweet gig with huge incentives at corporate. Or something to that effect. I was busy looking at how well manicured his fingernails were. I bite mine. They're torn and uneven.

Could I be a shark? he asked. Where did I expect to be in five years? He had a picture of his wife and two kids on his desk. She was blonde. They were at the beach. Life was peachy.

Sharks don't even have fists. But I have bills to pay. The last thing I want is to end up living on the streets. That would be a lot harder than selling insurance. Not to mention more embarrassing. I needed to refine my technique. I needed a twist.

Right before handing them the pen I would look them in the eye. You hold their gaze until just before it becomes uncomfortable. They scratch the back of their necks. That's when you know they've had it. Skin flakes on the collar. I would talk fast so it wouldn't quite register and sink in. Try and slide the word 'extra' in there without anybody noticing. "We are going to be able to provide you with this protection, security, and peace of mind without having you spend much extra money out of your pocket on a monthly basis."

Provide, protection, security, without, much. These were all good words to use when trying to convince someone to sign.

They're soothing. Comforting. They put the client at ease. I learnt that in the introductory seminar on my first day. There were small paper coffee cups and tiny round doughnuts. A sign that read 'welcome aboard' with an exclamation mark at the end. They handed out blue binders. Shared some war stories and laughed. I remember like it was yesterday. I wish I could rewind the clock. Back to that day. Before I had to worry about making a sales quota. Before I had to worry about losing my job and going bankrupt.

People don't buy insurance, they said. People are sold insurance. It's a five trillion dollar industry worldwide. Hand over fist, they said. It's a nautical term. The best way to make money in insurance is to sell the policy for a bundle and then try to avoid paying out in case of a claim. Sharks have an average of five rows of teeth. And they use each and every one of them.

"I'm sorry Ms. Swanson but your husband's death cannot be ruled accidental if he willingly put on the parachute."

Things like that. They laughed. I had another doughnut and refilled my cup of coffee. God help us.

During the first church service that I ever attended, the preacher talked about the divine plan. He said that God had a whole life laid out for each of us. If that's true, then it's entirely possible that Mr. Swanson *had* to put that parachute on. That he *had* to jump. He might have had no choice in the matter. According to the preacher, you're really not in control of anything. At any time. We're all just puppets with a sadistic omnipotent being pulling the strings. So enjoy the ride and don't do anything bad. But then again, maybe God doesn't exist and you're free to do whatever you want. Either way, the company didn't pay out the claim. If there is an afterlife, someone's going to hell. Or at least to purgatory. That was harming someone. That had to be a sin, at least to a lesser extent. A lesser sin. A venial sin.

Venial sins are not as bad as mortal ones. They're not required to be confessed but you can lessen your time in purgatory if you do. It's the pious thing. At the bottom of the list, under the tenth, was failure to distance yourself from the world's wealth. Sign here and make out a check payable to cash. Don't forget to smile. I'm going to take it straight to the bank on my way home. Before the change of heart.

I stack the papers neatly, slicing the tip of my index finger. They're staring at the pile sitting in front of them. Trying not to make direct eye contact. I smile and hold my hand out. Palm up. Like I'm giving them something. Like I'm giving them hope. Someone taught me that trick too.

"And what you're doing is guaranteeing that no matter what happens, Julie is never put in the position where she is forced to re-marry just to make ends meet." He looks at her. She's wringing her hands.

Sign here. Is he thinking about his kids? Their future? Or is he picturing his wife having sex with the idiot from her office that keeps feeding her drinks every year at the company Christmas party? Can he afford it? Either way, who cares. Insurance is what keeps you poor so you can die rich. He signed, and I was a little closer to the world's wealth. Even if it was by a few degrees of separation. I put the check in my pocket. My first sale of the month. I didn't figure that I had that much time left before I got a high resolution scan of my pink slip emailed to me. The cubicle I occupied on the seventh floor of one-twenty-one Parkview Road was valuable real estate. It would be a sin to just waste it. Waste not, want not. That's the saying. I've heard that a lot of people go shopping when they feel depressed. Maybe coming home with a brand new shiny something, something was just what I needed.

I listen to the xylophone as it works its way up from a soft meandering melody into a crescendo. The gentle music coming from the speakers above the crowded shelf full of appliances and price tags is calming. There's something familiar about the melody but I can't quite put my finger on where I've heard this song before. Standing in the aisle of one of those stores that's so big and full of stuff you can never actually find what you're looking for, I listen to a young couple talk about a red coffee maker that reminded them of Christmas morning when they were kids. Then something hits me.

"Excuse me," I say, stepping towards them.

They step backwards. "We don't have any money to give. We're buying on credit."

I raise my hands slightly, to disarm myself. "No, no," I say, "I'm not looking for money. I just wanted to ask you a question."

They look at me with furrowed eyebrows and twisted mouths.

"You weren't even old enough to drink coffee then. On Christmas morning I mean, when you were a kid," I say. "What kid drinks coffee on Christmas morning before unwrapping a remote control car and a new pair of underwear?" I fake a hint of a smile. Just enough to show the tips of my teeth. Studies have shown that it makes you more approachable.

"Excuse me?" they say in unison.

"I'm just wondering, how does that remind you of Christmas? What is it about this thing? Did you start drinking coffee when you were six? Did your parents have one sitting on the counter or something? Is coffee the trigger? What is it? Is it the red cups that every chain of coffee shop puts out eight weeks before the holidays to increase the sales of gift cards and folk music digital downloads?"

"I don't know," she says, placing it back onto the shelf. "It just looks… Christmassy. It's red. You know, red like Christmas. And we kind of need a new coffee maker anyway." Shrugging their shoulders. Inverting their bottom lips. They walk away without saying anything else. He looks back over his shoulder to make sure I'm not following them.

That was just what I needed. I forget what I'm here to buy.

Remember the last time you were in an argument with a person that, even though you have all of the facts and an immaculately constructed logical stance, and all of the evidence in the world, won't budge? Something like forty percent of the population doesn't believe in evolution. They're emotionally tied to something else. It's comforting. Like a big red onesie with the built in feet and the butt flap. Christmassy. I realize, it's not logic that drives people. It's not a well constructed argument. It's emotion. It's how they feel about something. This is just as true in the way they spend their money. I can use this.

All people buy products based on emotion. Everyone makes the decision to purchase something based on some type of emotion that they have, then they justify it based on logic. That's how it works. That's why they play all of that sappy music during commercials. If they can get you to squeeze out a tear, they'll clear their entire inventory. Once I discovered this my sales soared. Uncovering what that emotion is will trigger a sale if you play your cards right. For some people, it's a deep love for their family. For others it's peace of mind. Security. Putting their kids through college. The thought of their spouse having sex with Neil from accounting. That one sold a lot of policies to middle aged men.

Could you imagine your wife marrying Neil? Could you imagine them sleeping together? I mean…Neil…he doesn't even have a chin and he always smells like deodorant.

Daddy needs a new pair of shoes.

You need to tie in all of the benefits of the product back to that emotion. I got good at it. Sign here. Hand them the pen and click the tip out for them. Take the sheet at the top of the pyramid. There's a bold black line at the bottom. He scribbles his name and then puts an arm around his wife and pulls her closer. That was my sixth sale this week. When do I get a key to the executive bathroom? Someone said it smells like potpourri and cinnamon in there.

I wasn't technically doing anything wrong. In fact, my boss said I must be doing something right. I was making a ton of money. Raking it in with my shark fists. I bought some new clothes and a premium cable subscription. I started buying the large specialty coffee instead of the medium. With extra whipped cream. Whatever I didn't drink, I could just throw away. I should have been flying high. My condo was becoming very respectable. My job was now secure. They even moved me into a bigger office. But every night as I lied in bed, trying to sleep, a knot slowly formed in my stomach until I found myself sitting on the toilet at four in the morning trying to push out a non-existent bowel obstruction. It would go away in the morning when I flashed my new gold card at the cashier while picking up breakfast at the gourmet bakery.

There's an old lady with an oxygen tank. She's on a fixed income, she says through the faint hissing coming out of her nasal cannula. Can't afford it. By the end of my speech she signs on the bold black line with a trembling hand. It's not four hundred dollars, I say, it's a cup of coffee a day. Wouldn't you like to leave something to your grandchildren when you're gone? Never ask them a question they can answer 'no' to. That's part of the script. It's only a cup of coffee a day.

The knot comes back at midnight. I'm going to hell. The bright white light in the bathroom hurts my eyes. I make a mental note to go shopping for some softer bulbs.

Dragging yourself out of bed in the morning is always the hardest part of the day when you feel like this. You end up sleeping in later and later. The air in your bedroom always seems a lot colder than it actually is. The floor too. I had all of the symptoms of depression. Hopelessness, I lost weight, no energy, loss of interest in daily activities, I couldn't concentrate. I had unexplained aches and pains. Self-loathing. At least that's what my new therapist tells me. I'm a classic case, she says. Textbook.

"Won't it go away?" I lie perfectly still on that little leather couch that sounds like a fart every time I move. "Or, is there some kind of pill that you can give me? Something fast? I have a ton of work to get to." I had just signed two new clients and was thinking about taking up golf.

"Depression usually doesn't just go away," the therapist says. She writes in her little book. Dog ears the page. What about a pill then? She'd rather pursue non-medicinal treatment options first. It's probably psychological. Let's explore the root of your unhappiness first. You have to start at the bottom and work your way up, she says. Really dig deep.

I started feeling this way when things got better at work. Was I afraid of success? Was I mistaking the excitement of it for anxiety? For some, the excitement of success can feel uncomfortably close to the feeling of sickness associated with traumatic events. Was I afraid that if I got my hopes up it would all come crashing down?

She ran through a list from a book that she pulled off the shelf.

"I just feel like I'm a bad person. I feel like the whole world would be a better place if I had never been born."

"Why do you feel bad? I mean, people need insurance right? You're providing peace of mind. Security. Right? I would even go so far as to say you're providing an essential service."

"Yeah right." She fell for it too.

Luckily there were more options that we could pursue. But it was going to take time. We had to really explore my feelings. Really dig deep. She pencils me in for another session later on in the week. "You can make the check payable to cash," she says. "Give it to reception on your way out. We're out of time for today."

I started spending a good portion of my take home pay on Dr. Caldwell. It eased the guilt a little bit. Of selling someone who was scared senseless a policy that they couldn't afford and that probably wouldn't be honored in the event that anything I was describing to them ever occurred. Talking about it helped. I needed someone to talk to. A conversation prostitute. Tell me what I want to hear.

She would roll her pen between her thumb and index finger. Have I tried meditation? Eliminate negative self-talk. Be positive. Keep a gratitude list. Create something. Exercise is good for the psyche. Put effort into a meaningful relationship. Are you seeing anybody?

No.

"Friends?"

Not really.

Finding yourself forty and single really puts a damper on your social life. After you get dumped you're relegated to the outskirts of social circles. With all of the other pathetic souls that will end up dying alone, while everybody else goes out in pairs. Couples. Tables were meant for even numbers. Two, four, six. I hadn't been out on a Saturday night in eight months, three weeks, four days. But who's counting? You're alone all the time. Forgotten. Invisible. It affords you too much time to think.

I'll probably get eaten by a houseful of cats when I die. I heard they did that.

The last conversation I had that wasn't work related was with the clerk at the convenience store three days ago. We both agreed that it was a nice day.

"Extracurricular activities?" she asks, still flipping her pen.

Nope.

"Helping someone out or lifting someone else's spirits can be a great way to feel better about yourself."

Funny how that's supposed to work.

"The point is," she says, tapping her little book, "to avoid the downward spiral. We need to find something to lift you up."

Don't despair. I later found out that not trusting that God will provide all material and spiritual needs is venial sin number one hundred and seventy-six.

"Tune out the shame," she says. "Shame is an emotion determined by society. When you feel shame, you're worried about what others think of you. Where's the value in that?" She takes off her glasses for effect. Tilts her head down and angles her eyes up. That's pretty good.

"What about my everlasting soul?"

Have you ever read that Chicken Soup book? You should. There are lots of good books on the subject. Let me tell you a story. It will make you feel better. I guarantee. She starts talking. Her voice fades away until it's just a low rumble in the back of my mind. I know exactly what she's doing. I do it all the time.

The most powerful way to really affect the emotions of whoever you're trying to manipulate is through story telling.

There are seven basic story plots.

Story telling has been engrained into our psyches. All that time spent sitting around the fire they say. The best stories are the simple ones. Rags to riches, the quest, voyage and return, comedy, tragedy, overcoming the monster, rebirth.

Seven.

I can tell my prospective buyer a positive story where the client bought the insurance, something tragic happened, but because of the coverage they were taken care of and able to grieve properly, without having to worry about money. Or I can tell the negative story. The client didn't buy the insurance, something tragic happened unexpectedly, and the family was decimated.

How to get to telling those stories is different in each circumstance. The key is that you use your salesmanship to weave it into the natural flow of conversation. Telling the negative story is harder but it will sell more, and bigger, policies. People will go to greater lengths to avoid loss then they will to gain something.

The regional manager got a bonus of two hundred and fifty thousand last year. Bought a big new car. Something imported from overseas. He was up seventeen percent from last year. He sent me a congratulatory e-mail on my birthday. Saw great things in my future. Keep up the good work, it said above his initials at the bottom. He was happy. Why shouldn't he be? The firm was doing well. Bonuses were just flying down the chain of command.

It's a real art. You buy a life insurance policy and say you don't smoke even though you might have one with your buddy at a bar every now and again. One day you get killed in a car accident. Your insurer finds out about your 'occasional indulgence' and they fight the claim.

Bonus. It's like Picasso or Dali.

Some of the time, they can spend less money fighting the claim in court for years than they would have had to pay out. In cases of car accident claims, adjusters can drag their feet on an investigation knowing there's a time limit to sue. They laughed about it standing around the water cooler drinking from small paper cones.

Bonus and bonus. Van Gogh. Modigliani.

You filled out the form incorrectly. You left that space blank. You signed outside of the box.

When your premium goes up for actually making a claim you're going to pay it all back anyway. It's the perfect scam.

Sign here.

They'll use every excuse in the book. That's what they told us secretly. Over drinks when they were sure that we could be trusted with this sensitive information.

"Use every excuse in the book."

"There's a book?"

He winks and takes a sip of his scotch.

It was a pre existing condition. I'm sure you've heard that one before. It doesn't matter if you knew about it or not. You have insufficient documentation. It was a suicide.

We aren't forced to provide statistics on what percentage of claims get rejected. We keep that little nugget to ourselves.

"See here, your address isn't up to date."

That's a good one. It's technically the fault of the insured for not offering the insurer the most up to date information. This can affect your policy rates. If you're paying an incorrect policy rate you are committing a type of fraud. You commit fraud, your claim gets denied. You'll be lucky to avoid a lawsuit.

And be very careful about how you word things. They had a lot of fun with that.

"He was all over the road. I had to swerve a number of times before I finally hit him."

That sounds premeditated to me. Denied.

"I told the police I wasn't injured but upon removing my hat I found that I had a fractured skull."

You can't make this stuff up.

"You told the police that you weren't injured. Had you not said anything at all I might be able to work with you. But it's right here in black and white. You weren't injured."

Denied.

I followed along. I got put in a higher tax bracket. Bob got that job at corporate. John lost his house.

Three-thirty in the morning. The soft yellow light in the bathroom does nothing to help as I clutch my stomach and lean forward. Staring down at the imported Italian marble doesn't seem to help either.

People say it's okay to hate your job. You have bills to pay, they say. You have to buy food. Cars. Save for that rainy day that everybody keeps talking about. What else are you supposed to do? What else am I supposed to do? You have to work. You have to fulfill your societal obligations. You have to fit in with everybody else. The fashion trend changes every year and clothes aren't cheap. There's a new smart phone coming out next month and you want to be the first one to get it. They say seventy percent of the population hate their jobs. That's why they call it work.

Dr. Caldwell exhales sharply. She's frustrated. For what I'm paying her she can be frustrated. "I don't know, quit your job then," the doc says.

"Great, then I'll be homeless."

The Bible says the meek shall inherit the Earth.

"Let's take a look at your gratitude journal," she says. I should have twenty-five entries by now but I don't have any. Get out, have some fun. What about spirituality? Oneness with the universe? The Ohm?

The pen spins. I can hear her foot tapping. She never used to do that. She had a picture of her and her husband on the desk. It was in the corner and angled outward so that you could see it from practically anywhere in the room. There was a waterfall behind them. A pink flower in her hair. Life was good. Why wouldn't it be?

The pen slips out of her hand. It did that when she started to lose it.

"I don't know, how about religion? It helps a lot of people through difficult times. Makes them feel better. It can be a good thing."

Sadness or anger at the good fortune of others was venial sin number one seventy-one. That's not what I ended up doing though. What I did was something different entirely. But I can honestly say that religion helped me.

"How about religion?"

How about religion?

3

Apparently, you're not supposed to drink the holy water right out of the little bowl at the front of the church. You're supposed to dip a couple of fingers in it and make the sign of the cross on your forehead and chest. But they don't tell you that. There's no instructions posted anywhere. A woman behind me corrected my etiquette. There's a lot to know. Stand, kneel, amen. And there are some rules. Some pretty weird rules. You're technically not allowed in a church if your genitals are damaged or missing. Check. But then again, I didn't know the names of my ancestors to ten generations so I was technically still not allowed in. Deuteronomy 23: 1-2. I figured they cancelled each other out, so I stayed for the Sunday show.

The preacher at the front of the church wore green and white robes. He spoke in a commanding voice and paused every now and then. Looking around the congregation for dramatic effect. "Man is not good and you need to mark that at the very beginning. Man is evil. His nature is bent on sin and given his prerogatives he will inevitably end up in the morass of immorality."

The words came out of his mouth slowly. Deliberately. Waving his hands around and pointing at people in the front row. The microphone pinned to his collar would pop every time he pronounced the letter 'P'. Painful, pestilent, penitent, perverse, pious, puny. Pop.

He confirmed everything I already thought. I'm a worthless sinner. I'm a terrible person. Maybe, it would have been better if I had never been born. Pathetic, pauper, powerless, pitiful. We're the cause of every bad thing that's ever happened on this whole planet. Ever.

He takes a breath and shrugs his shoulders. "But why is this so? Why has man always inevitably sunk to this condition? How is it that the infant life so lovely, so precious, so soft, so innocent will descend to the corrupted adulthood that inevitably awaits the human race? Why?"

Because human beings are awful things? Because we're born evil and it just takes a little while for it to show? Did it all go back to the original sin? That first bite from which all of us inherited our spiritual disease? Our defect? It's our natural inclination to disobey God. To hurt instead of help. I hope that was one hell of an apple. Prayer. Repentance. Pop. If we don't sin, then Jesus died for nothing.

This wasn't working out the way I had hoped. I felt worse halfway through the speech than I did coming in the first place. My head weighed twice as much as I was used to and I was starting to get hungry. My mind wanders back to the image of bacon and eggs. Not that thin floppy bacon either. That thick, crispy bacon that you can't cut with a knife and have to eat with your hands. It's Sunday morning after all. Time to treat yourself. Why isn't there any padding on these benches? I pick up a Bible and skim through a few pages looking for something I may have missed.

You shall not boil a young goat in its mother's milk.

Okay. I'll spread the word.

A woman must not wear men's clothing, nor a man wear woman's clothing, for the Lord your God detests anyone who does this.

Got it. I'll keep that in mind moving forward.

Do not wear clothes of wool and linen woven together. He hates that too.

From here on out. Wouldn't the almighty have something better to do? Anything? Doesn't he have a Professor Moriarty to take care of? Some guy with red skin and horns? The preacher was still talking. He has the whole congregation enthralled. Everybody except me. This wasn't helping. I started thinking about leaving. Slipping out when nobody was looking. There was a beggar outside of the church when I came in. I wondered if he was still there. If he would judge me for leaving early.

"Spare some change?" he said, when I was on my way in. Patting my pockets and holding my hands palm up, I stepped over his feet on my way up the stairs. Venial sin number seventy-nine. The oak door of the church was heavy and slammed shut behind me with the force of a lightning bolt. A forty day thunderstorm. I jumped. There was nothing particularly special about this church. It was just the first one I happened to walk by. How about religion? The people inside were quietly praying. I could see their lips moving ever so slightly. An old woman sitting in the front pew clutched her rosary so hard that it left little round bruises across her liver spotted hands. The old woman a few more pews down had shrouded herself in black. She lit a candle on her way in and made the sign of the cross. A single man gripped his bible so hard that his knuckles turned white. I got to know all of them. Especially the older members of the congregation.

Old people tended to confess more. Being closer to the end, I guess. When I tried to find out why, one of them said that they'd rather live their life believing there was a God and then find out there wasn't when they die, than live their life believing there wasn't and then find out there is.

Our Lord is a vengeful one.

They spent a lot of their last days in church. It was their final insurance policy. Sign here.

"Do you want to know why men are like they are? Why women are like they are?" The echo gives the sermon a severity. An authority. The architect had thought of everything. "Do you want to know why the fall of man is inevitably marked in every single life? The answer is here. It's because God gave them up."

Abandoned even by God. No, this wouldn't do at all. I shuffle along the bench whenever the priest addresses the other half of the congregation. Sliding closer to the edge until, when he's walking back to the altar, I slip off and head for the door. Looking over my shoulder the whole time to make sure that he didn't see me. If he didn't see me, maybe God wouldn't either. But he stopped mid stride. Before he could turn around completely I tuck myself behind a curtain. Into a small space. Like a wooden phone booth with another hard bench in it. I can hear the service continue. Bells ring. Amen. I'm too ashamed to step out, so I wait. In the dim box. Listening to the ritual take place outside. It's even worse waiting it out in here. There's even less to look at. I pick a spot and stare. How long was this going to take? How long does this usually last? My eyes start to feel like sandpaper and eventually, I fall asleep.

"Forgive me Father, for I have sinned." The voice wakes me up. Before I can react, the man starts talking. He tells me a story about how he lied to his neighbor to get out of feeding their dog while they were away. He hates that yappy mutt and wishes it would just die already. But he won't admit that to anyone else. On the other side of that thin mesh screen, he kneels and says he kept some money that he found at work, even though he knew who it belonged to. He bought a bunch of those scratcher lottery tickets with it and lost on every single one. Then, running his fingers through his hair and pulling at his collar, he stutters and says that he's masturbated while secretly watching the young woman across the street do yard work. He even thought about it while he was having sex with his wife. He exhales loudly once he's finished. The demons have been exorcised. "Thank you father," he says. But I can tell that he's still waiting for something. "Umm, Father?"

"Umm, yes?"

"Shouldn't I say some prayers or something?"

"Yeah, yeah right. Say some prayers. Lots of prayers."

He leaves disappointed. But as soon as he's gone someone else steps up. The curtain slides back and forth. They make the sign of the cross and kneel. "Forgive me Father for I have sinned."

That's how it started. Seven words.

It turns out that people will tell a priest anything. Like there's some sort of doctor patient confidentiality. Trading their darkest secrets for absolution like they were poker chips. He was a veteran confessor. It's been a month since my last confession, he says and then launches right into it and I can't believe my ears.

Behind a seemingly normal exterior there was something else. Not the pious people, devoted to God and the betterment of mankind, that they made themselves out to be. Pillars of the community. Loving wives, husbands, mothers and fathers. They were selfish, depraved, and perverted people who were afraid of ending up in hell for being who they were. For thinking what they did. For being made that way. So, they ask for forgiveness. They would repent. Here, in this booth. At confession. Spilling the beans to an all knowing God and wiping the slate clean. All you have to do is admit to it. It's that easy.

When he was done a woman took his place. Forgive me Father for I have sinned, she said. The mesh between us made it difficult to see her face. Like the others, she was ashamed, but that wasn't why she was here. She was afraid.

They poured their hearts out. Seven deadly sins. Ten commandments. One hundred and eighty-seven confessable mortal sins. One hundred and sixty-six venial. You can fit just about anything in the spectrum of human behavior somewhere in there. Our Lord is a watchful one. For the first time in, I couldn't even remember how long, I felt good about myself.

There's an awkward silence when she finishes.

"Well, what should I do Father?"

Shit.

"Ummm, look in the Bible," I say.

"Okay. Is there any passage in particular?"

"Forget that. Just…just pray. Say three Hail Marys, I guess."

"Thank you Father."

No, thank you. My lips turn up at the ends. Sitting in that tiny wooden phone booth listening, I realized something important. I was a saint compared to these people. The knot in my stomach went away and was replaced with butterflies. I couldn't wait to get back. To hear more. It was all I could think about. I would ride out the sermon in the back row and flip through the Bible to brush up. It's more convincing if you can rip off a few quotes. A parable here and there. In a deep voice. It sounds more official.

2 Kings 2:23-24. "From there Elisha went up to Bethel. While he was on the way some small boys came out of the city and jeered at him. 'Go up, baldhead,' they shouted, 'go up baldhead!

"The prophet turned and saw them, and he cursed them in the name of the Lord. Then two she-bears came out of the woods and tore forty-two of the children to pieces."

It was filled with this stuff. With this great stuff.

After the service finishes I sneak into the confession booth and wait for the curtain to slide open. To hear those seven words. The corners of my lips rise. They left feeling good. Forgiven for the crime of being born a lowly, flawed human in the eyes of the Lord. Free to start the process all over again. As for me, I've never felt better about myself in my entire life. It was win-win.

After a while I started to notice a pattern. People seemed to have the most trouble with the seventh commandment by far. I have viewed pornography. I dwelled on impure thoughts. I have had oral sex. I have engaged in impure acts with myself. I have allowed another to arouse me passionately who's not my spouse. I let a hooker ball gag me and whip my ass while I was tied to a chair and called her 'Mommy.' Adultery. There were forty-four possible mortal sins related to number seven. After adultery it was stealing and lying tied for second place. If we were made in God's image, that wasn't saying much.

I woke up brand new every morning, and I now had something to do all weekend. There were services on both days. The butterflies flew. I couldn't wait. It was getting harder to concentrate on my work. But I have bills to pay. A new client. Downtown in the financial district. In one of those big glass buildings.

People say that the giant glass towers downtown are phallic symbols. Whoever had the most money had the biggest dick by default. Take their word for it. They spent most of their days waving it around in everybody's faces. The money that is. Like sitting in a traffic jam in a hot red sports car with a top speed of 196 miles per hour just because you can. I'm here to see someone just like that. Someone who needed a fifty thousand dollar watch, not to actually tell the time, but to show everyone else that he could afford a fifty thousand dollar watch.

This was going to be my biggest account. I had to meet him in his office on the forty-second floor. He spent all of his time at work. He wasn't happy unless he was making money. He had more than he could ever spend, but he would trade it all for a little bit more. His kids were being raised by an Ecuadorian nanny that he paid minimum wage while his wife was god knows where. She came home drunk most of the time. He didn't care. He was here. Probably. There was a little mini bar in the corner. Some very old scotch. Rich guys like scotch. It's expensive. All single malts. It's expensive. Blended scotch might as well be the devil. It was the cause of all the world's misery. Child hunger. Poverty.

"Good morning Mr. Howard," I say. "It's my pleasure to meet you."

He was getting the works. My manager would get a nice bonus this year.

Flipping through the paperwork at the end of my presentation, he hums and haws. Takes off his glasses. He says he didn't get to where he was today by not being well informed. He wants to know every detail about what his money is buying. What it was doing. His Mercedes got 30.3 miles per gallon. Interest rates were going to go up. His secretary was a B cup. He knew everything about everything that was important to him. So he was going to ask questions.

"Is this policy transferrable?"

So, he also knows a little something about insurance too. All policies are transferable. We both know the game. You transfer an existing insurance policy to your corporation at little or no-tax cost in exchange for a payment from the corporation. When the shareholder dies, the death benefit may be paid tax-free to the corporation and you get your little bit more.

Insurance premiums are also generally paid with after tax dollars so it's desirable to fund a policy with the cheapest after-tax dollars available. If Mr. Howard here is subject to a personal tax rate of forty percent and the corporation only pays tax at a rate of twenty percent, the cheapest alternative is to simply have the corporation own and pay for the fund. A little bit more. It's that easy.

Buy it and sell it off on your way to the bank. While you're laughing. Get a new watch. The latest gadget that you can talk to instead of having to push those annoying little buttons. You'll be the envy of all your friends if you get it first. You deserve it after all. You work hard. You should have nice things.

Venial sin number one sixty-six.

Sign here.

He takes out his own pen and signs. It's gold and there's something engraved on it. "Have security escort you out of the building," he says. "We're having a little problem downstairs. Just a few malcontents. Nothing to worry about."

There was a small crowd protesting something. Standing in front of the doors and holding signs that said 'Main St. before Wall St.' and 'corporations aren't people.' They screamed at anyone coming in or out of the building. Security almost had to push me through. Mr. Howard says that they're just jealous of success. He says they'd have more money for themselves if they spent more time working and less time protesting other people's hard work. He snorts when he laughs. That snort of derision. Of smug pomposity. Self-satisfaction. I ask him what time it is. He pulls the cuff of his shirt back and looks at the diamond encrusted watch face. It's almost one o'clock. I can swing by the church just in time to take in a half hour of confessions before getting back to the office.

The homeless guy is sitting on the steps again. "Spare some change?"

Under my breath I mutter 'sorry', too quiet for anyone else to hear but me, and I step over his legs on my way up the stairs.

"Forgive me Father for I have sinned."

Of course you did.

"Tell me your sins…"

Best. Monday. Ever.

4

It was supposed to be his last big score. I guess he was tired of the game and wanted out. He couldn't go back to a Joe job though. That was beneath him now. So there was only one option. He had to set himself up for life with one last scheme. Bank fraud. It was a hot summer day. He walked into the bank dressed in a nice suit. Shiny shoes. Confidently walking straight up to the teller, he pulled a stylish leather billfold out of the inside pocket of his jacket. Then, tried to cash a check for a billion dollars.

I'm not even kidding. You can't make this stuff up. I cover my mouth to avoid making any kind of sound as I laugh. On the other side of the lattice, he keeps talking as though it's all perfectly normal. During a brief stint in jail he found God and now wants absolution for his sins. Oh, and he beat the hell out of another inmate who was trying to steal his apple cobbler once. But that was prison. God would understand. Wouldn't he?

"Does God forgive me Father? Are you laughing?"

Of course not my son.

"Say three Our Fathers."

I always left feeling as happy as any kid who could stay home and watch cartoons Sunday morning instead of putting on their best clothes and going down to the church. And I had the first entry in my gratitude journal. I showed it to Dr. Caldwell at our next session. She read it over while spinning her pen. Frowning, she looked at me and closed the book on her lap and placed her hands on top of it. She spoke softly.

"Why does the misery of others cheer you up?"

"It doesn't," I said. "It's not about their misery at all. It's something completely different."

"Then what is it about?"

They were confessing out of fear of retribution. That's it. Not out of some willingness to lead a better life. I was walking through a sea of liars, thieves, lunatics, adulterers, and murders. All asking for forgiveness so that they could start the cycle over again with a fresh conscience. I sold crappy insurance policies at inflated prices. I convinced people to pay more than they should. Told the occasional little white lie. I got a hooker once. Twice. In comparison, I was Mother Teresa. You should hear what I hear.

Anger, envy, gluttony, greed, pride, sloth, lust. There are as many deadly sins as there are stories. Pope Benedict XVI added excessive wealth as the eighth deadly sin a few years ago. It's generally not mentioned on the list.

Entry number one: I'm grateful that all the other people in the world are lying, stealing, perverts who only pretend to have any sort of moral backbone to maintain appearances and to maybe scoot around that whole hell thing.

"What you're doing is wrong," the doc said. "You're invading people's privacy. You're pretending to be something you're not. It's dishonest. You're lying."

I didn't see it that way. And I wasn't about to stop either. In fact, I stepped it up a notch. I get a priest's robe to complete the illusion. It's white and green and has gold trim. A classic style, the salesman told me. Good for everyday mass. This could get me through anything that wasn't Advent, Lent, or Christmas and Easter seasons. Tuck that in there, drape this over that. Maybe you need one size smaller. How does it feel Father?

"Good. It flows nice." It's designed to do that. He smiles. Like he was doing the whole planet a favor by helping out a priest. He presses his hands together and holds them up to his chin.

"Will you excuse me for a moment?" he says.

The yelling in the back room makes its way out to where I'm standing, admiring myself in the mirror. Someone forgot to make the coffee again. This was the third time this week. How the hell were they supposed to take over the business one day if they couldn't even get something as easy as coffee straight? Are you an idiot? Jesus Christ! Of all the stupid, irresponsible…

I turn around to see how the robe looks from behind. The salesman walks back in with the same blank expression on his face. His hands pressed together in mock prayer. A plastic smile glued to his face where his mouth was supposed to be. The only thing that betrayed him were the dilated capillaries in his face. "Can I offer you something else?" he says, in his best impression of Mr. Rogers. "A crucifix perhaps? This one's from Italy. Eighteen karat gold. Unfortunately, we're out of coffee."

I blend right into my environment. Camouflaged. Like a parasite waiting to climb up someone's nasal canal and lay eggs in their brain. People pour their hearts out to me. Beg me for my forgiveness.

One guy comes in to ask forgiveness for putting his parents in a home. Honor thy mother and father the Bible says. One because he became rich through a bullshit lawsuit. Thou shall not steal. Or Lie. Whatever. Someone else because they had sex with their husband's brother, who was also married. Double whammy. Thou shall not commit adultery, thou shall not covet thy neighbor's wife. But husband in this case. Are you sure you didn't work on Sunday? Three Hail Marys just to be on the safe side.

It was like a drug.

The more depraved, deranged or selfish the act, the happier I leave. I wake up refreshed. Reborn. I start going there three times a week. Whenever I feel that I need a little pick me up. It's especially necessary after seeing Mr. Howard. Knowing full well what he's intent on doing.

At the glass penis people yell something at me as I swing through the revolving door and step onto the Italian black marble floor in the foyer. I had been called back to Mr. Howard's office to conduct more business, there's more people protesting now than there had been before. They have signs and chant even louder. Someone might have thrown something at me as I push into the door. Whatever it is, it smells awful. I have a suit on and it smudged my shoulder. How embarrassing.

"I'm sorry about my appearance," I say. Mr. Howard gives me a once over.

"Clothes make the man," he says. "Maybe after today you'll be able to pick up something a little more…"

His shirt is double starched and white as the pure driven snow. It would probably stand on its own if you set it down just right. The rest of his suit probably costs more than a used car. His desk is clean. There's a magazine cover framed and hung up on the wall behind him. It's a picture of him in front of a giant house leaning against a red sports car. His jacket is slung over his shoulder as if it's no big deal. The sun is shining.

"I like the cut of your jib," he says, as he settles into a leather chair so soft it makes absolutely no sound whatsoever. It's a sailing reference. I can't afford a sail boat. "It's like we have something in common." He says he wants to take out more policies. A thousand to start. But there will be more down the road. Probably in the ballpark of fourteen.

"Why not just take the extra fourteen policies out now?" Remember to smile.

"Thousand. Another fourteen thousand," he says.

Move over Bob, guess who's coming to corporate. New car, new suit, new watch, new me. It's going to be a lot of work though. A lot of hours.

He sniffs, grins, and leans back in his chair looking at me as if he's my own personal Jesus Christ. Maybe he is. I know this game too.

Like hundreds of other companies this one, RDC Holdings, is going to take out life insurance policies on thousands of its employees with itself as the beneficiary. It happens more often than you think and most workers covered this way don't even know about it. Thousands of workers are worth a great deal alive or dead. Whatever. No big deal. It's a sunny day.

It's called broad-based insurance or corporate-owned life insurance. COLI for short. For years companies could only insure key people deemed essential to the business but a loosening of the rules in the 1980s allowed for an explosion in a new kind of COLI that covered rank-and-file workers. It's known in the industry as janitors insurance. In one instance: dead peasants insurance.

Companies can pour millions into COLI policies yielding tax-free income as their investment value rises, just like conventional whole life policies. They can even borrow against these policies to raise some extra cash if they need to.

Most companies say they use the money from the insurance to help pay for various employee benefits but they can spend it on whatever they want. Like executive compensation. Single malt scotch.

"Can I offer you a drink?" Mr. Howard says. "It's single malt."

Of course it is.

Young workers will generate anywhere between $400,000 to $500,000 in death benefits each whereas older workers will bring about $120,000 to $200,000 each. The document is called a death run. Each employee is listed by name, age, and how much money the company will receive after they die. Even if it's long after they've left the company.

A twenty-one thousand dollar a year administrative assistant dies at the age of sixty-three. The family receives a $21,000 benefit from an insurance policy provided to employees by RDC Holdings. RDC Holdings, on the other hand, receives a COLI payout of $180,000.

It's all perfectly legal.

It was this kind of thinking that eventually throws Frosty into a rage. That gives him his resolve. His purpose. That little bit more.

It's what sets him into action. Having nothing. Being left behind while the gap slowly gets bigger and bigger and bigger until the rich sail off the edge of the earth in their giant yachts. Man the braces. His rage is contagious. Even I'm all for it in the beginning. But, that doesn't happen till later.

I take the drink. The sharp smell in the glass meets my nose as I bring it up and take a sip. It's very smooth. "Of course I can take care of that for you. I'll start the paperwork immediately," I say, squaring up the pile. Hitting it against the table.

But not before I make one quick stop. Stepping over the beggar on the stairs. Putting on my new digs. The robe really does flow nicely. And the gold trim looks nice against the polished oak frame of the confessional. I exhale slowly. A calmness and serenity falls over me. Confess your sins.

"I told him not to mess with me!"

I shush her ever so slightly to calm her down. "Even so," I say, "you still have to make amends."

This woman had been married to her husband for eight years. During that time she's scrubbed the toilet with his toothbrush, blew her nose in his pillow, stuffed his dirty socks in his pillowcase, spit in his food, flicked cigarette ash into his coffee, and even peed in his shoes. Whenever she felt the least bit slighted she would get her revenge.

Venial sins number eighty-eight and eighty-nine. Seeking revenge and wishing evil. That's all I can find. I guess it's not that big a deal if you piss in your spouse's shoes or spit in their food in the eyes of God. Better not call anyone bald though. We all know what happens then. Watch out for bears.

I can't really find revenge anywhere on my list of mortal sins. Maybe it wasn't so bad after all. Giving people what they deserve. God does it too. That's what hell essentially is. Isn't it?

Our Lord is a vengeful one.

I've been taking confession for about an hour and my butt is starting to hurt from that hard wooden bench when I hear those heels echo through the vaulted ceiling of the church. They get closer and closer. The curtain slides open. The red lips part.

"Forgive me Father for I have sinned."

"How long has it been since your last confession?"

"Thirty-three years."

"Go on, my child."

She goes through the list. An extensive list. Delineating exactly what it was to be human in the world for thirty-three years. Every little thing, every little thought, every time. Every time she stole, every time she lied, every time she wished that someone would just keel over and die. She tells me all of these things. Lays all of her cards on the table. Then she smiles the smile of the absolved.

"Thank you Father."

Don't thank me.

The main service was on Sunday so you had to get your confessions in before then if you wanted to take communion. If one received the Eucharist without confessing their mortal sins they would be in danger of eating and drinking damnation unto themselves. The minimum was once a year. Cover your bases. Fire and brimstone, remember? Apparently He's always watching. Sure enough, Sunday morning she sits at the back of church. Holding a rosary to her chin. Her red lips trembling just a little bit. Like she's whispering something.

She confesses everything again the following week. Every little thing, every little thought. The week after that too. Then she sits in mass, at the back of the church. Whispering to the tiny crucified man dangling off the end of her rosary.

It's an indulgence. You come to know things.

The forgiveness of sin through confession entails the remission of the eternal punishment of sin but the temporal punishment of sin remains. You confess your mortal sin, you're forgiven, you can get into heaven. Okay. But when? Not before you spend some unspecified amount of time in purgatory for it. Waiting is the hardest part. Unless you indulge. Indulgence allows for the remission of the temporal punishment due at some point in life or after death. Recitation of the Rosary in a church is an indulgence.

You're allowed one indulgence per sinner per day. Get a fast track to the good afterlife.

She's making up for something. I know what it is. She told me in the privacy of the booth. She let it run through the stagnant air behind the curtain. She's scared too. I'm scared for her.

5

She never misses a week. Neither do I. I feel very close to those red lips after a couple of months of this. Sitting in the dark booth, listening to the steady drone of her voice. The cadence of the sinner. I always know what she's going to say next but I never rush her. This is our ritual. She's the closest thing to a best friend that I have. Even though she's never seen my face. The fornicator is gone. Either he'd come to terms with what he did or he'd gotten it out of his system. Maybe he was hit by a bus. But week after week she keeps coming in. Week after week telling me her life's story from the very beginning. Through her sins. I know her better than anybody else in the world. Doctor patient confidentiality.

"Thank you Father." She smiles. That gentle waft of ammonia.

Entry number two in my gratitude journal.

Listening to her walk away, I try to imagine where she's going. What kind of life she leads now. I know everything about her entire existence up to this point. When the echo of the heels fades and the thunderclap of the oak door passes, I duck out of the booth and follow her down the street.

She'd been forced to prostitute herself to make ends meet. It all happened one day when her boyfriend grabbed her by the neck and slammed her into a wall, displacing three vertebrae. The pain never went away, she said. No matter what. She got more and more prescriptions for higher and higher doses of painkillers. She grew a tolerance. To the point where there was nothing more she could take that would give her the relief she needed. It hurt all the time. It was crippling. One day a friend said he could help. Take the pain away. And he did.

She lost her job. Her house. Every dime she had ever saved. And no one wants to help a junkie. 'They did it to themselves.' 'It's their own fault.' 'Not my problem.' That's what people say to defer their help. To detach. We all do it too. It justifies inaction. It's not my fault. There's nothing I can do. It doesn't matter how you phrase it, the result is always the same.

She ended up at a homeless shelter. Desperate. Desperate for so many things, but most desperate for a hit. She started off performing sexual favors to the staff in the back room after hours. That way she could get what she needed and her laundry would move to the top of the pile. There was no help. Not even the police. There was no crime being committed, they said. "A staff member can solicit a guest for sex if they want to. It's unethical, inappropriate, and just plain wrong, but there's nothing we can do." It said 'to serve and protect' on the door of their cruiser as they pulled away.

She wipes tears from her cheeks. Through the screen I see the shadow of her hand move across her face. I know what she's going to say next but I let her compose herself and continue. She tries to justify it but she can't. She's lost faith. Despite everything she'd done, that was her greatest sin. I tell her to continue. Even though I'm ruining her chances for the afterlife. I'm taking her absolution away by pretending to give it to her. Damning her immortal soul for eternity.

After the overdose she got clean in a government funded rehab facility. Rented a room down the street at a place called the Waverly. She just appeared in the parish of the Holy Name one day. Out of nowhere. Nobody knew where she came from, and she kept that little tidbit between the two of us. She spent her time alone. I found out her name. Rosalind. She always wore red.

She had hurt somebody. Technically, she had hurt two people.

I follow her down the street. Keeping my distance so I'm not spotted. She opens the door to a crumbling building with grey paint flaking off the brick, and goes inside. Her face reappears in a second story window. I get a one second glimpse every time she passes in front of it. If she comes from the right I can see her face when she tucks her hair behind her left ear. If she comes from the left it's only the tip of her nose. She's carrying trays of food and smiling. Good work is an indulgence too.

"Spare some change mister?"

It's the beggar from the church steps. His clothes are stained. Ripped at the joints and frayed at the edges. He's holding out his hand and looking at me as if I owe him something. Like he's expecting it. He smells awful. Like something died underneath one of the seven layers of clothing he wore. He doesn't seem real to me. Kind of like a caricature.

"I don't really carry cash," I say, and pat my front pockets to make it seem more convincing.

"Yeah, nobody does," he says. "It's all credit cards, debit cards, gift cards. People don't even know how much money they actually have anymore. It's not good for a guy like me." His voice sounds as if the back of his throat is covered in scabs.

"Yeah."

He's still holding out his hand. There are black streaks across them and purple sores around his fingernails. It's getting dark. I turn to leave. Other homeless are starting to line up at the door for supper. It's first come first serve. Some of them yell. Some of them fight for their place in line. Some of them just stand there staring at the ground, defeated. All of them smell. He's still looking at me. A smile wrinkles his cheeks and accentuates the deep crow's feet next to his eyes. He doesn't blink.

"Are you sure you don't want to stick around? This is just your thing. Isn't it? Father?"

Hail Mary, full of grace.

The expression on his face never changes. "Yeah, I know your secret. Father. I know all about what you do at the church. Father. Will you listen to my sins Father?" The way he says *Father*. He lingers on the 'a' and the 'r'. Stretches them out like he doesn't want the word to end. "I know your secret." He spits on the ground. "Question you should ask yourself is: how much is it worth to you?"

"What do you mean?" I try to swallow but my throat constricts.

"What's it worth to you?" he says, and spits again. Making a dark gray streak on the pavement between us. "For me to not tell anybody about what you do in that little stuffy booth? Father. For me to keep your little secret? To tell you the truth, I could use a couple things."

Underneath the unkempt beard and the stained jacket was a real person, a normal, greedy person. I would find out just how real in the coming months. Especially after he kicks me in the stomach and slams the back of my head with the butt of a gun.

He calls himself Frosty.

He slept in a city maintenance hatchway near the church. It wasn't much but it was home, he said. There was a bag of things hidden in the pipes above. Dry socks, winter coat, a blanket. He used to frequent the church more often until the parishioners, one in particular, got thrown in jail for feeding the homeless. That was against the law. There was ban on public food sharing. A new city ordinance. They were trying to gentrify the neighborhood. To attract the next wave of young professionals with disposable income. The real estate market was hot. Cafes, fancy restaurants, and gastro pubs were springing up everywhere. Volunteers used to get dirty looks when they set up just outside of the church. Tables and hotplates. Styrofoam cups. You had to line up though. It was first come first served.

The cops walked up.

"Drop that plate right now," one of them said. He pulled it away from cracked and dirty hands and tossed it aside. "Get out of here." The other cops started picking up trays of food and throwing them right into the garbage, with lines of hungry people looking on. Then they dispersed the crowd. They didn't do it nicely either. The law is the law. The new ban on public food sharing was enacted on Halloween night. Right when millions of people with disposable incomes were out sharing candy all over the country. You can't make this stuff up.

Frosty still hung around the church begging for change though. Sitting there. Staring. Bored. Frosty saw me come in day after day. Knew how long I was inside cause the church bells ring every hour. He got curious. He didn't see me anywhere in the church and the priest, Father Price, had no idea who he was talking about. He eventually slid the curtain open and sat down next to me. People always thought he was dumb because of the way he looked.

"Forgive me Father for I have sinned."

He tells me that he followed me into the church simply because he didn't really have anything better to do. The worst part of being homeless was the isolation. Being ignored by the rest of the world.

I know how he feels.

People would avoid eye contact with him at all cost. It made them feel guilty. Like not picking up the phone and donating when you see those commercials with the puppies in slow motion. Or the little boy in Africa with the fly on his face. They stepped over Frosty without even looking down. It was like he didn't exist. The invisible man. You can only keep yourself occupied in solitude for so long. The boredom was suffocating.

I know how he feels.

No one else really knew that he existed even though Frosty stayed in plain sight, on the street, most of the time. You could usually find him in front of the church or someplace nearby. He knew of a few people who died and weren't discovered for days afterwards. After the insects and animals had claimed dibs. This way, he figured, if he died at least he'd be found. Buried face up. Or cremated. That was fine too. The church bells reminded him what time it was. And usually he could scrape a little change from pious parishioners looking to indulge. Birddog came around sometimes. He was a recovering addict so Frosty had to make sure he wouldn't have a relapse.

Frosty says that it's not Birddog's fault. Being an addict. Some addicts become homeless, some homeless become addicts. Your free time becomes your enemy. Make a list of how many of your leisure activities require having a place to live or disposable income. Take away an eight-hour work day on top of that. You have nowhere to go. Nothing to do. You start to lose your mind. The boredom is smothering. It holds a pillow over your face and pushes down hard until you stop struggling.

They sometimes go to the library. Parks. Eventually churches. But, with limited access to laundry and showers, you start to look worse every day. You start to smell worse too. You're not welcome anywhere in civilized society anymore. So you hang out on the street. Frosty says that the worst thing to do was to accidentally shit yourself. It didn't happen often, but it's happened, and it's a bitch to sort out. There's no way in hell you can land a job. You stop even dreaming about it. Having nothing to do and nowhere to go becomes a stress. Birddog didn't become homeless because he was an addict. He became an addict because he was homeless. One hit could kill a whole day.

Lather, rinse, repeat.

I ask Frosty why he didn't just go and stay with some friends or something?

"You lose your friends when you become homeless," he says. "After a while they start to avoid you. You're either a major fuck up or you're going to want something from them eventually. A couch for the night. Money. A ride. Turns out not many people are willing to give something to someone who they see as not being able to give back to them in return."

He spits on the ground. It's brown with a yellow particulate in it. He's still holding out his hand and looking at me. Grinning. Two moves away from checkmate and there's nothing I can do about it. "So what's it going to be Father?" I'm the only one with something left to lose in this exchange. The crowd gets bigger. The doors were going to open soon. Rosalind moves across the window. "I don't have all night," Frosty says. "I have to get back to my spot before someone else poaches it. That happens you know."

He would later tell me about his first night on the street. It was the loneliest feeling in the world. Like everything, everyone, and all you've ever known, had abandoned you. Forgotten or betrayed you. "It's scary, depressing, empowering, and humiliating. On the one hand you've hit rock bottom. There's nowhere to go but up. Finding the staircase is a bitch though." Hanging out on the street. People walk by. Avert their eyes. Look at their phones. Ignore you altogether. The nice ones will at least take the time to say 'sorry' and shrug. Pat their front pockets to make it look more convincing.

"Spare some change?"

That ends up being all he ever says. All day. After a while that stops too and he ends up just sitting there with a paper cup in front of him. You can jingle it from time to time for effect, he says, but eventually you stop doing that. You just sit and stare.

Sitting in front of the church staring, he saw me come in. He saw her come in. He saw her leave. He saw me follow. He followed me. He had a plan and nothing to lose. There was something that he wanted to do but he needed his strength back first.

I only get a one second glimpse over his shoulder before Rosalind moves away from the window again and I'm back on the street next to a homeless man holding out his hand and staring at me. Smiling. The doors open and people start to file into the building with gray flecks of paint peeling from the walls.

"What do you think would happen if people found out what you do in that church? Father. Would you be arrested? I honestly don't know. Or, if she found out that you follow her after she confesses all of her sins to a phony priest? Would you get arrested? I honestly don't know."

It's getting darker. Rosalind smiles as she hands a tray to someone. One second. She moves away from the window.

"I'm not following her," I say. It's transparent.

"Sure looked like it to me." He shrugs and eyes the door. "Look, I'm sure God already knows that you have problems, but how do you think the police would feel about it?"

I take out my wallet and pull out a couple of bills. He retracts his hand and closes it. "I don't want your money," he says. "I need something else."

He wants some food. Good food. Something healthy and nutritious. He's tired. Some fruit could do wonders. He couldn't remember the last time he had strawberries. Being exhausted was a normal part of life for Frosty. Even if you did manage to get a decent night's sleep. Which only really happened once in a while in the summertime. In a city this size food wasn't that hard to come by. Shelters, soup kitchens, dumpster diving. You could find food. You couldn't find good food. The food he was given at the shelter, or anyplace else he was lucky enough to score, wasn't necessarily meant to be nutritious. It was meant to fill him up. They'd give you rocks if they could, he says. Canned vegetables, iceberg lettuce, enriched white bread, pasta. Lots of pasta and potatoes and mounds of rice. You live off carbohydrates. Sticking the middle finger to Atkins. I tell him that's not a thing anymore anyways.

He snorts when he looks through the window of a fancy French restaurant. "It would be great to have the luxury to call yourself a foodie," he says. "Or invent another word for it. Something that doesn't make you sound like such a dickhole saying it. Foodie.

Dickhole." He spits on the sidewalk. Flakes of red betray his gingivitis. "Isn't everyone who eats food considered a foodie? Or is it just the people who can afford the really expensive stuff? They have the honor, eh? Must be nice."

His body had deteriorated. He had a fever, chills, body aches and barely enough strength to haul his bag around. He left it in the tunnels. Hidden in the pipes. Tucked away towards the back.

"Sometimes people give you food because they think if they give you money you'll just go and spend it on booze or crack. This lady once gave me a T-bone steak. Probably went home feeling pretty good about herself too."

That's nice. Isn't it?

"How was I supposed to cook the fucking thing? In my brand new, ceramic non stick pan or my convection self cleaning oven? I know, I'll throw it on my stainless steel grill and fire up the propane tank." It ended up making things worse for him. Now, he had to sit there and stare at his juicy piece of meat that he couldn't eat while his stomach collapsed in on itself.

The line behind us was moving well now, and one by one people filed inside. Frosty doesn't move to go in. He can see that I'm afraid of him. He's probably counting on it.

"Here," I say, holding out the bills. "Just take it. You can use it to buy your own food. Anything you want."

"Do you think they're going to let someone who looks like me into one of those fancy, gentrified grocery shops? I'll be out on my ass before I can make it to the produce section." He pulls something out of his nose with his thumb and index finger then holds his hands out. "Would you want me touching your nice, clean food?"

We make a deal but we don't shake on it. He slicks his oily hair back and reveals his caramel colored teeth. His tongue moves around them as he lists the different things he wants. Don't get the cheap cheese. He wants the good stuff. You can tell the difference. In exchange, he'll keep my secret. He won't go to the police or to the priest or to Rosalind. He backs off and takes a place in the line. "We'll meet by the church," he says. "I know you like that place." In a few minutes he slides through the front doors. Through the window Rosalind hands him a tray and smiles.

6

The curtain slides open. Tell me your sins.

"You're under arrest."

They're unnecessarily rough pulling me out of the confessional. My new robe tears when the hands punch through the curtain, grab a handful of material, and drag me out into the daylight that comes streaming in through the stain glass windows. The cop with the red hair seems especially put out when we get to the station. Slamming his fist against the table and storming out of the interrogation room swearing. His voice sounds familiar. I've heard it before. I'm sitting there, in a small cold room, answering their questions. Confessing it all.

"So what are you doing then?" one of them says, smacking his lips together as he chews on a stick of gum. A gold crucifix dangles from his neck. "Looking for a little blackmail material? Looking to make a few extra bucks?"

I tell them that I don't need money. That what I need is something else entirely. It makes the red haired cop even more angry. "There's something seriously wrong with you," he says. "You're fucked up in the head. You know that?"

Tell me something that I wasn't already aware of.

"Calm down Gary," the other one says.

The florescent lights above are bright and they never flicker. Not like you see in the movies. The two cops leave the room. I can see them pacing as they take turns passing in front of the small square window on the door. The red haired cop's voice gets louder. I hear him say, 'shit Carl!' Then they come back in. "What kind of person does this sort of thing? Preys on innocent people like that?" one of them says to himself.

Are they really innocent? They're just like me. Most are even worse. I think that. I don't say it, but that's what I think. Because I know it now.

The handcuffs come off and they leave deep red grooves in my skin. They can't hold me any longer. Technically no crime has been committed. The state has to separate itself from all religion so they don't adhere to the same rules as the church. They can't even get me on a trespassing charge. All are welcome. There's a sign there that even says so. Fraud would have been the punishable crime here, but I didn't ask for or take anyone's money. Or anything else except maybe their immortal soul. But the state doesn't recognize that as a tangible asset that can be bought, transferred, stolen, lost or leased. Impersonating a doctor can land you in the slammer though. Policemen too.

"It's unethical, inappropriate and just plain wrong, but there's nothing we can do about it."

But they want to know why, then. If not for money, then why? They have to know why. I tell them why.

"We ought to have you committed," they say. "Get the hell out of my sight."

I get pushed out of the front door. Unnecessarily rough. They're all appalled. What kind of person was I? Even the clerk frowns as I walk past. I start down the stairs. It's over. All of it. My therapy. My psychological well-being. My prescription has been torn up and scattered. The third entry in my gratitude journal is that I'm not in jail. But I'm angry. We had a deal. We didn't shake hands but we had a deal. And I was holding up my end of it. I should have never trusted those homeless guys. Our Lord is a vengeful one and we were made in his image. Why is it okay for God to take revenge but if we do it, it's venial sin number eighty-four? Either way. Venial sin number eighty-four was going to happen again. My hands are shaking. I ball them up into tight fists.

'In your anger do not sin. Do not let the sun go down while you are still angry, and do not give the devil a foothold.' It said that somewhere in the Bible. But giving people what they deserved wasn't on my list of mortal sins. God did it all the time.

Things had been going so well over the last couple of days too.

I handed in the first stack of policies to Mr. Howard. He was supposed to sign them all by hand but instead he got his secretary to stamp his signature at the bottom of each one with a big rubber mold. It gave her a repetitive stress disorder in her elbow. Injuries of that kind weren't covered under her corporate health insurance.

Stamp.

He wore suspenders to keep his pants up. How bourgeois. That little bit of grey at his temples. A tie pin.

"If I wanted to insure a worker at one of our plants in China, let's say. Could we do that?" He took a sip of his coffee and ran his tongue across his bottom lip.

Stamp.

"That's easy enough," I told him. The simplest way is to just take out a policy over there. The China Life Insurance Company is the largest life insurer in China. They have forty-five percent of the market. That would be a good place to start.

He adjusted his glasses and leaned in. Looked over his shoulder to make sure that nobody was standing at the door. Like they did in the boys club. In the private rooms with the high back leather chairs and expensive cigars.

Stamp.

"But if we wanted to do it from here? You know, through this company."

I told him that the last I heard, China's audit office uncovered over three billion Yuan in improper and illegal activities from some of its insurance companies. They were charged with the illegal sale of policies, improper claim settlements, illegal distribution of commissions, and what's called 'grey income.' Gains that are off the books. Probably pocketed by company officials. "I'm pretty sure we could figure something out," I said. Playing along. It's my biggest account. There's a way around everything if enough money is involved. That's human nature.

Stamp.

He smiled and leaned back in his chair. He had the exact same look on his face that he had in the picture hanging behind him. A cross between life is good and no big deal.

Stamp.

After leaving his office and pushing my way through the protesters I was feeling a little depleted so I thought I'd swing by the church for a cleanse. I carried a bag of things that Frosty said he wanted the day before. Apples, oatmeal, milk, tuna. When I get there Birddog and Tony are ready to fight. Tony was the new guy. He started hanging around the neighborhood on holidays at first. Then on Sundays too. Then, whenever he'd had a couple of bad days someplace else, or was told to move along. There was a service that evening so they had each claimed a spot somewhere near the exit to ask for change as the parishioners left. It was the best time. People were feeling good about themselves. All dressed up. Humble before the mercy of God and pious. Eager to show everyone else how much more generous they were. A guy could really clean up. If there wasn't competition five feet away.

Their unwritten code was that the first one to get there got the spot. They were usually pretty strict about that and everyone obeyed the rule. Maybe they arrived at the exact same time. Either way, there wasn't room enough for the two of them and neither one was backing down. Tony had his hand cocked back when Frosty threw himself in between them.

"F.O.A.D!" Birddog screamed at him.

That was how Birddog said 'fuck off and die' in the military. There was an acronym for everything in the military and he still hadn't adjusted to civilian life completely. In between them, Frosty placed a palm against each of their chests and pushed them back from each other. I was watching with the bag of food in the crux of my arm.

It's not worth it, Frosty said. What if you break your hand? You can't afford a hospital. You'll get gangrene and die. No one is looking out for us. We have to look out for each other, not fight each other. We have to stick together. Frosty could be convincing. He would have done well for himself selling insurance.

The fists slowly lowered. The fingers relaxed a bit.

Frosty suggested they make a pact. The three of them would split up, make their rounds separately, meet back up later on that evening, and pool everything together. Split everything equally. It solved the problem. But they had to trust one another. Could they trust each other?

"What if I make more than him?" Birddog asked. "What then?"

It didn't matter, Frosty said. They were going to share everything equally. "You'll be glad you agreed next time he rakes it in and you got squat. Trust me." They also agreed to rotate spots. It would keep everyone honest and no one person would get stuck in the same shitty place week after week. It was fair. Frosty said, they'd have a better shot together than they would individually. They'd be like a tribe. A collective. It was a deal.

I walked up and gave Frosty the bag of groceries. His first act of unity was to share it all with his new corporate. Make the first gesture. They passed it around, picking out the things they wanted most. Birddog wasn't a big fan of salami or granola but he dove in anyway. They stuffed so much food into their mouths so fast that I thought that they might die of asphyxiation before any nutrients even made it into their bloodstreams. Their mouths were a chorus of wet and spongy snaps.

Then, someone tapped me on the shoulder. "Excuse me?"

I turned around. Rosalind was standing there with her arms folded neatly over her abdomen. She had noticed me giving food to the group of homeless men. How selfless, she said. Not a lot of people would do that. I must be a good Christian. She tries to help out whenever she can too. She volunteers handing out food at a shelter a few blocks away. Maybe I've heard of it? It's not a very nice place though. The building is falling apart. Why doesn't the parish do something for the local needy? She wanted to talk to Father Price about that. I seem to be a compassionate guy. Would I be interested? It's very rewarding.

Funny how that's supposed to work.

I smiled and nodded my head. Too afraid to talk. She smiled back. I nodded some more.

Her eyes lit up. "Great! So, I'll work everything out and maybe we could talk about it again a little bit later?" She adjusted the flat red beret that was sitting on top of her head. "So, we'll talk later. I just got called into work so I have to go. It was very nice to meet you though." Her red glove waved. "God bless." She waved at Frosty, Birddog, and Tony as she left. Birddog had a mouthful of cheese and mayonnaise and held his stomach with one hand. Eating so fast had given him cramps but he didn't slow down one bit.

Nod, nod, smile, smile. I watched her walk away.

Frosty started to laugh. "Oh, so that's it. I get it," he said. "Guess who has a crush fellas?" They all started to laugh at me.

Spitting out crumbs of food into their hands when they couldn't control it.

Maybe he was more perceptive than I gave him credit for. That's what he did all day, after all. He watched.

"Most people would just ask her out. He pretends to be a priest and hides in there for months so he can talk to her." They laughed that laugh that let you know they had something on you and that they were in control now. And that they liked it. Frosty swallowed a big mouthful of sandwich meat and wiped his mouth with the sleeve of his jacket. "You know," he said, "you really shouldn't bother. Eyeing up that girl. It's a weakness. It's just one more thing that someone can go after if they want to get to you. Trust me."

The next day I brought an assortment of cold cuts and some fancy cheese and some canned soup. More strawberries. Pumpernickel. Dijon mustard. The good kind. The name brand. I gave it to Frosty before making my way into the church. He took it with a smile and a nod. Inside the confessional, I slipped the robe over my head and waited. The door to the church opened. Footsteps clacked on the hard floor. They got louder. They stopped in front of the curtain.

"You're under arrest."

And now I'm walking down the steps of the police station with red marks on my wrists and a crowd of people behind me frowning. They would probably spit if they could get away with it.

My feet scrape each step as the whole of my weight moves from foot to foot. I keep my head down as if it's camouflage. Like if I keep looking at the ground no one will be able to see me. The steps are full of chewed gum and cigarette butts. And a pair of black shoes. I stop and look up. It's Father Price from the parish.

"Forgive me father for I have sinned?" I say.

We walk. He asks me the same questions as the police did. It's strange. It's like he's not mad at all. He speaks softly and evenly. Makes good eye contact and even goes as far as smiling. He says he realized something was amok when members of the congregation started to complain to him about their atonements. They thought they were being treated terribly unfairly.

I had started to push it a bit more. I felt comfortable in that little booth and I thought I could make a difference. A real world difference.

Brandon came back with a black eye and bloody nose. He'd converted for the sake of his fiancé and really took a shinning to the religion. The pageantry of it all. He was in service every Sunday wearing a suit and tie. Got baptized. Read the Bible. Carried a rosary around his car keys. The works. Then he goes and cheats on her with the sales rep at a conference out of town. They had had too much to drink that night. It's not even original. Time for confession. What a great deal.

The only way to absolve yourself of this sin, a mortal one by the way my son, is to say three Hail Marys. And tell her.

I wanted to make an honest man out of him. Out of everyone that came in. I started making them do real world penance. Making them own up to it. Earn their forgiveness.

Give it back. Tell the truth. Return the money. Admit it.

My sheep would go out into the world and come back wolves, instead of the other way around. Or so I thought. Actually, I didn't even know what that really meant. I couldn't remember where I heard that anymore.

He frowned. I could tell because the silhouette of his forehead changed shape. The silk handkerchief came out of the pocket and he dabbed it a few times against his face. "Are you sure father? Isn't there another way? I mean, I'll do anything. But…"

"Do you believe in God my son?" I said. Deep voice. Pious.

"Of course Father."

"And do you believe in the afterlife? That God's servants will spend eternity in the bliss of heaven whereas his enemies will burn in the fires of hell?" Shakespeare has nothing on priests.

"Yes."

"Then you must. You must show God that you are sorry for your sin. You must show Him that you repent by making things right in the world."

"Are…are you sure?"

The divine plan technically says that God wants everything that happens to happen. It's been his plan all along. Right? A few billion years of cosmic whatever has been leading up to this point. So it's really not his fault. The whole thing is just riddled with holes.

"Goddamit," he says, with a heavy sigh. "I'm sorry father. What do I owe for that one?"

"Three Hail Marys." That makes six in total.

One guy stole from his best friend. Another wouldn't tell her neighbor that she dinged his car. A lot of them lied. To their spouse. To their friends. And as usual a few of them cheated. A few of them wanted to cheat. I sent them all out into the world to broadcast their indiscretions. To return their stolen property. To admit to it. And they were so afraid, that they did.

One Sunday Father Price wondered why one half of his congregation was injured and why the other half sat there wearing frowns. You always hurt the one you love, they say. Angry parishioners went to see him. Saying that he had ruined their lives. They cursed their punishments. What about the mercy of God? they said. He's filing for divorce now. Slapped me in the face. Took the kids and left. She yelled so much it woke up the neighbors. Father Price heard about all the fallout and had no idea what anybody was talking about.

He didn't know it then, but the root cause of his confusion was sitting in the congregation and listening to his sermon. And waiting for it to be over.

"Our Lord talks about the rulers of man, Matthew 15:14. 'Let them alone, they are blind leaders of the blind and if the blind lead the blind, both shall fall into the ditch.' The restraints are off. God is not restraining him and he has no capacity to restrain himself."

That's the truth. He really hit the nail right on the head. That didn't happen very often.

In ten thousand years when aliens land and they start digging around in the dirt they're going to find these trinkets. Crosses. Stars. Whatever. They won't know what it all means. What kind of species were these? they'll ask. What made them tick? They'll dust off the bones and display them in museums. At that point none of this will have made a difference. Our fashion, our gadgets, our forms filled out in triplicate. Neither will our sins.

7

"Helping others can often times help you feel better about yourself," Father Price says. I've heard that before. Funny how that's supposed to work. But you could argue that all giving is fundamentally selfish. We only do it to feel better about ourselves. Or make ourselves look good. Selfless good deeds don't exist. We see ourselves as altruistic or compassionate. It makes us feel confident or hopeful. Useful. It alters our brain chemistry. Squirts out some dopamine. Something to do with evolution. It's because humans are social animals. Like the monkeys. At the end of the day, we need one another.

Father Price stares at me, waiting for a response. There's a white ring of dead skin on his black shirt where his collar rubs against his neck. He leans in expectantly. Raises an eyebrow. He presses his hands together in mock prayer. Just like I used to do.

"What about a gratitude journal?"

"That's not what I was going to say but, okay," he says.

Mathew 24:11 – 'And many false prophets will appear and deceive many people.'

"Helping others. Not hurting them," he says. "Many of the people that you counseled," he makes quotation marks in the air with his fingers, "have had their lives irrevocably damaged." He looks at me. It's a stern flat stare. "Does that make you happy? Is that what you were trying to accomplish?"

I keep my eyes trained on the ground as we walk. "No," I say.

"Tell me this then, do you believe in God?"

I honestly don't know.

Well, God believes in you. God teaches us to forgive, he says. And he is going to forgive me. But why? Why would I perpetrate such a crime? It was the devil's doing. I remind him that it wasn't technically a crime. It was a crime in the eyes of our Lord, he says. I tell him everything. I confess.

He listens patiently and nods at the appropriate times.

"I see," he says. Scratches his head. Winces at the details. Widens his eyes. "I see. I must say, this is a very odd story." We walk for a few steps in silence. His laugh breaks it. "I was wondering why attendance seemed to be lower." It's amazing how devout people can be when it doesn't ask anything from them in return. "The mystery is now solved. That, and the cryptic remark uttered when Mr. Wilson burst in to thank me for having had him corn holed," he makes quotation marks in the air with his fingers, "by his soon to be ex-wife." He lets out a long deep breath. "I'm not proud of it," he says, "but I was angry at first." When he was angry, he turned to the Bible for solace. Not the genital mutilation part.

James 1: 19-20: "My dear brothers, take note of this: Everyone should be quick to listen, slow to speak, and slow to become angry, for man's anger does not bring about the righteous life that God desires."

"But life isn't about being angry," he says. "It's about forgiveness. I'm not angry with you anymore. And I forgive you." Forgiveness is mentioned one hundred and twenty-seven times in the Bible. It's important. "I want to help you. I want to help you to help yourself. God is here for you, if you can open your heart and let him in. Trust me."

Aren't we abandoned? His own words.

"If we come back and embrace God, he too will embrace us. But we cannot understand how great is our forgiveness unless we understand how deep is our sin." It looked as though he might have a lazy eye. "I forgive you. But I would also like something from you. I would like for you to atone for your sin. I would like for you to give back to those from whom you have taken." Nothing worth doing is easy, he says. Nothing worth having just falls into your lap. Including peace of mind. It comes from hard work. Resolve. A resolve to do good and to be good. To live in God's good graces. "Taking advantage of people to fulfill our own needs is simple. Helping people is hard." And in a strange twist of fate, helping others is supposed to make us feel better about ourselves. Give us worth. Value. Purpose. Because humans are social animals. If I don't want to take his word for it there were plenty of scientific studies that came to the same conclusion.

"It's about the work," he says. "The real world good that you do. Here and Now. On this world. That will define you as a man. The legacy that you leave, through the people that you help. Have you ever considered working for a charity?"

Those CEO's make millions of dollars a year. Literally. Big bonuses. Expense accounts. Italian suits. Private jets. Good will means good wages. And mansions. I've lined enough pockets already. I can tell you five major charities that give less than fifteen cents on the dollar towards actually helping people. But they have great add campaigns. Lots of slow motion. Flies landing on children's foreheads. John Lennon singing 'So This is Christmas' in the background even though it's July. The music rights alone must have cost a fortune. People don't just decide to give to charity. People are sold on charities. It's a cup of coffee a day. Can't you spare a cup of coffee a day? Wouldn't you like to help the children? Save their lives? Never ask a question that they can answer 'no' to. Especially one that they won't answer 'no' to in public. It's the same script. They wear bright t-shirts to attract attention and ask for money on street corners. Can you spare a moment for the children? Of course you can.

It's a business.

For some reason I think about the huge stack of paperwork I have to do.

"There's a member of my parish who's expressed interest in doing something for the neighborhood homeless."

You don't say?

"I'm not sure."

"Like begets like," he says. "The police are urging the church to pursue a civil suit. But we couldn't, in good conscience, prosecute a good, kind hearted member of our community. Could we?"

Atonement. Matthew 5:5, Blessed are the meek for they shall inherit the Earth. Good work was an indulgence. I have to make up for my sins. Three Hail Marys wouldn't cut it this time. What about Our Fathers? It would make me feel better about my life. He was sure of it.

"You have to make a real world atonement for what you have done," he says. "If you ever expect to get back into God's good graces." Better to live your life thinking there was a God and find out that there isn't when you die rather than live your life as if there wasn't and find out otherwise at the end. It's a good point. "Perhaps she can help you on your journey of spiritual healing. Shall I introduce you?"

I found myself missing the smell of ammonia.

"Amazing!" she says, clapping her hands together. The gloves she was wearing mute the sound but it still has the desired effect. Her eyes are wide. Her cheeks become a soft shade of pink. Capillaries in the skin expand when the flow of blood is increased. "We'll make a great team."

I stick my hand out to shake on it. "So where do we start?" She doesn't shake it.

"There's so much we can do." She'd been thinking about this moment for a while and has a lot of ideas. But we have to work within the rules. Spiritual and municipal. Her heels click against the floor as she paces back and forth. Working out the details in her head. Rosalind always wore heels. And lipstick. Red heels and red lipstick. Red gloves, red dress, red hat. It's to hide the stains should they occur, she says. If any of it got on her stuff. She talks a mile a minute. There's an authenticity to her. She's genuinely excited.

We aren't allowed to feed the homeless. Not on city property anyway. Gentrification and all that. So our first step is to collect some donations and get them some odds and ends. We have a bake sale at the church. A bazaar where people sell every breed of thing imaginable. We even play bingo. The first thing we buy is socks. Socks are a hot commodity. Frosty takes them with a smirk.

"I didn't turn you in," he says.

"I know."

"You thought it was me."

"I did."

"But it wasn't."

"I know."

I don't have much. I don't have anything, really. But I have my word, I promise you that. Well, now I have my word and some new socks."

That's one thing I got to know about Frosty. He meant the words that he spoke. To him, they weren't just random sounds made by the larynx designed to communicated basic wants and needs. They were tangible things. They were cement. They were all that he had left. When he said he was going to do something, he meant it. When he said I was like a brother to him, he meant it. When he said that he was going to wage a war, he meant it. When he said he was going to fuck me up, he meant it.

"But that was weird," he says and coughs into his hand.

I know.

"You're not right in the head."

I know.

"Don't sweat it. We're all fucked up. Fucked up people doing the same fucked up shit that the fucked up people before us used to do. We need to break the cycle." He spits on the ground. Flakes of red line the white bubbles at the edges.

"How do we do that?" I ask.

He winks his right eye. "I'll tell you later."

Rosalind dips her fingers into the holy water and makes the sign of the cross. Her heels echo through the empty church as we walk through the rows of pews. A giant faucet dripping. Each drop evaporating in the emptiness before a puddle can form. Leaving us parched. She's excited to show me something. A big idea. We pass by my old booth. I miss the comfort of it. Those polished wooden walls. The anonymity of that mesh screen. The darkness. Father Price doesn't take confession as much as he used to, she says. Yeah, I say. You go to confession too? She picks up the pace.

Rosalind wanted to teach the world to sing in perfect harmony. Like the song. She wanted to buy the world a cola. Like that commercial with the song in it. Standing on a hilltop, swaying from side to side, arms wrapped around scores of multinational orphans. Blue skies. Sunflowers. Slow motion. That kind of thing. If it were only that easy.

High fructose corn syrup gives you diabetes.

I know why she wants that. It's to make up for something. Good work is an indulgence. Indulgence is atonement.

She leads me through a small door, down a narrow and dark staircase, reaches up and pulls the string that hangs from the one bare bulb in the center of the room and stretches her arms out.

"Tada! What do you think? We'd have to clean it up a bit. But I think it could work. Don't you think it could work? There's plenty of room down here."

Old boxes occupy every corner. A few cases of expired Eucharist. Ancient Christmas decorations. Potato bugs roll themselves up on the floor whenever you move anything. Her eyes are glossy with anticipation. The tips of her front teeth rest against her bottom lip, marking them with red.

I look around the church basement. "I guess it could work. Wait, work for what exactly?"

"It's going to be cold outside soon, maybe they could stay down here. The three of them. At least for the winter."

"You want them to live here? In the church?" I say. "You want to start a homeless shelter?"

She takes off her hat and presses it against her chest. "They're the most vulnerable people in our parish. They need our help. And they're always at the church anyway. It would send out a good message. Set a good example." It's hard to say no to her. It's those wide eyes. Letting her down would be like choking one of the seven dwarves with a roll of barbed wire.

"That's a long shot," I say with a sigh. People's altruism is like their devotion. It tends to be a lot stronger when they don't really have to do anything about it. Most people anyway.

"But we have to at least try," she says. "If we don't try then we just give up without trying." She can barely keep her body still so I take her to talk to Father Price. He's in his office. Wringing his hands. Squinting and sucking short bursts of air through clenched teeth and stretched lips. Flakes of skin flutter down onto his lap. Some stay airborne. I've probably inhaled some. Most household dust is dead skin cells.

Rosalind leans forward. The tips of her fingers rest on the desk. Father Price wrings. The skin falls. Some of it stays airborne. Rosalind pleads some more. She casts hopeful glances at me in between the points of her argument. Father Price wrings some more. He casts furtive glances at me in between the points of her argument.

I shrug my shoulders. "W.W.J.D?"

"Huh?"

"What would Jesus do?"

"Yes. Indeed."

He raises the point that there are some designated shelters for the needy, that might be a more appropriate place for them to stay. With trained staff and resources. And more importantly, with insurance. There is a system in place to help these people that they can avail themselves of. He pulls at his collar. I'm waiting for him to say, 'Is it hot in here or is it just me?'

"I've talked to them about it already," Rosalind says, "they don't want to stay at that shelter."

"Oh dear," Father Price says. "Why not?"

Frosty, Birddog, and Tony all agreed that, most of the time, they'd rather stay on the street than in a shelter. Rosalind could relate to that but she never said so.

Frosty decides to hit a shelter. He has to line up mid afternoon so he can get a bed for the night. There are swarms of people. He's lucky and gets in. It's over crowded. If he gets out of bed to take a piss, or to try and pick the bedbugs or lice off of his body, it's gone. He can't use his own blanket either. They take everything away for the night. All personal possessions. They say it's for security. A lot of the times the items never come back. The last guy that slept in this bed had tuberculosis. You can't smoke. You better not be drunk. Or even smell like you were. Lights out at nine. He wakes up in the morning and his shoes have been stolen.

He spat when he told us the story. "Not having shoes or having a pair that don't fit good makes it hard to walk. You get blisters on your feet. They don't heal. It's just not worth it."

Tony has a bulldog. Gertrude. She's not allowed in. And he's not leaving her alone. She's his only real friend. The closest thing he has to a family. To unconditional love. They give away free bone shaped treats at the pet store sometimes. He grabs a couple and finds a good spot under the bridge. Someplace out of the wind. Away from the crazies. Sometimes people frown when they walk by him. They're looking at the dog wondering why he would have one when he couldn't even afford to take care of himself? He can tell. He can see the judgment. Sometimes they come back with a small bag of dog food to give him. He'd resorted to eating a handful or two himself a couple of times. "It's the company," he tells me. At least he's not invisible to something. There's one soul on the planet that will always be happy to see him. One is better than none.

"I see," says Father Price. "That's very unfortunate." He stares at his own hands resting next to a copy of the Holy Bible.

"We can take care of them here," Rosalind says, "at least make sure that they're fed and that they don't freeze to death. Give them someplace safe to sleep."

Father Price tears the cuticle from his finger. It starts to bleed. "One thing that you have to understand is that the church is ill equipped to house these people. There are many factors to consider when undertaking a task such as this. There could be damages, the church could be held liable should there be an injury of some sort." I keep my mouth shut.

Rosalind takes a crumpled piece of paper out of her pocket and flattens it out. "Whoever is generous to the poor," she says, "lends to the Lord, and he will repay him for his deed. That's from Proverbs." She folds it up neatly and puts the tiny square into her sleeve. "You can give us the means to do God's good work," she says. I sit next to her and nod. "We'll be with them every step of the way. We'll keep an eye on things. Right?" She looks over with those doe eyes. I can feel the rhythm of my own pulse. It's steady and strong in my head. I nod. "Good Christians take action. We don't take the easy road."

Maybe it's the ammonia that's making us light headed.

"Fine," he says exhaling, "we'll give it a try. We can hold services for them. Help them to find the righteous path. Bring God into their hearts and souls."

Rosalind claps her hands together. Her red gloves mute the sound. Crow's feet in the corners of her eyes make an appearance. She can hardly contain herself. If this works, that's some serious indulgence. It might just be enough for a ticket straight into paradise. I hold my palm up, waiting for inevitable the high five. "I can't wait to tell them the good news," she says, putting her hands in her pockets and skipping out of the room.

Frosty wipes the corner of his mouth with his sleeve. Dark vertical lines form in between his eyes. "No, we're not going to any services," he says. Frosty speaks for the rest of them too. "There's no way in hell."

I don't understand his resistance. Neither does Rosalind. She presses the issue too much though.

"What do you have against going to service?" she asks.

He raises his voice. "We're not attending any goddamn services. It's God's fault we're in this mess to begin with. I don't need to be forgiven. He should be asking me, for mine."

He had no faith in God. No trust. No love. Abandoned and pissed off about it. He wasn't going to go crawling back for any reason. Asking for forgiveness for something that was never his fault to begin with. He says, it'll be a cold day in hell before he kneels to anybody. All powerful or not.

Birddog is against it too. His moustache bounces when he talks. "Some churches used to set you up pretty good but they'd make you sit through a bunch of shit all day. Try and convert you. You can handle one or two days but… It's like being brainwashed. Like they do in the army. That's why I went AWOL."

Tony follows along. Together they are the abandoned. The forgotten. Weren't we all? They had to stick together. It's the only way they stand any chance. "All this church stuff, all this pageantry, it's all bullshit. That ain't the world. Not even close. When some asshole spits on you for asking for a quarter," Tony says, "that's when you know what the world is all about."

"It's when you're sleeping on a sewer grate in the middle of winter," Birddog says, "and some asshole steps on your shit with some nice soft Italian leather shoes. You know then too."

"It's when some asshole," Frosty says, "arrests you for not having enough money for a place to live. Or when they say that you have to sleep under a bridge because God is punishing you and you have to make amends. We're not going to any goddamn services."

The excitement in Rosalind's eyes fades, just a hint. Nobody would have even noticed it if they weren't looking for it. She lost faith for a while too. Her biggest sin. She was making up for it now. But she's worried that it won't be enough. She was blessed, she said. Born again. Saved. They could be too.

For her, it started when she got clean and answered an ad in the newspaper. It was going to be a hard job, they said. It wasn't for the faint of heart. She was nervous. She didn't trust anybody anymore. She couldn't fall any further though. She'd be lost forever if she did. She needed to get her life back on the righteous track. Whatever it took. "Not everyone can do this kind of job," they said to her. "Depressives are probably not great candidates. Empaths shouldn't apply either. Do you fall into one of those categories?"

"No. Not anymore."

She was unflinching. Staring at one tiny point in space with those glossy doe eyes. Focused on it. Oblivious to anything else.

He said that the company would also reject people who showed signs of voyeurism or an enthusiasm for gore. First, she had to go through the psychological tests. If she passed that, she could start training to be a crime and trauma scene decontamination specialist. CTS decon for short. Death is a messy business. Someone has to clean it up. That's going to be the tag line for the movie.

Saved. Praise Jesus. In the confessional she said that cleaning up blood helps make up for the blood she had spilt. She was helping people though difficult times. Good work and all that. Another indulgence. She was stacking up her chips like a poker player on a hot streak. It wasn't easy. It made her sick to her stomach at first.

Removing the evidence of a violent death is the responsibility of the victim's family. The cops take the body but usually there's a lot left behind. This can prove too difficult for the family to deal with. The shocked and grieving. If ever there were a situation begging for capitalism to step in, this was it. She started making decent money. A veritable fortune compared to her usual nothing. She bought high heel shoes. Red lip stick. She always wore red. To hide the stains should they occur, she said. She smelt like ammonia most of the time now.

That's what the church basement smells like now. My hands are raw and burning. All of the potato bugs are gone and the boxes are stacked up into neat piles in the corners, exposing a floor that was now so clean you could probably eat off it. The cream and green linoleum designed to look like real tile reflects the florescent light back up to its source. Except in those spots where it was gouged or had thick black marks leftover from the soles of dark shoes. Off to the side, the matching counter top in the kitchenette, surrounded by a bank of cupboards with a faux wood finish, has just as many nicks in it. So does the pale gray walls. But it's ready. Sterile.

Tiny fingers sprout from the corner of Rosalind's eyes and pull her cheeks upwards. The three of them would be warm and safe down here tucked away behind the 70s Jesus with the long hair and the sideburns. Rosalind told father Price that we'd take care of the place. Supervise. I nodded. The deal was they'd also spend time working in the church. Painting needed to be done. Pews needed repair. The hard to reach spots were caked in an inch of dust. The Virgin Mary had bags under her eyes.

"We're in this together, right?" she says. Eyes beaming. Cheeks flushed. Knees shaking. I nod. Chest pounding. Knees shaking. We're in this together. "Good. I couldn't have done this alone." She wipes some moisture from the corner of her eye with the back of her glove.

Frosty said that a lot too. They couldn't do it alone. They're in this together. He drilled it into Birddog and Tony's heads. They were stronger together. Even the most insignificant organism had strength in numbers. Look at what bacteria can do to you if they put their minds to it. "You could easily kill one ant but if you ever find yourself tied down on an African ant hill drenched in honey, watch out. That's the strength of the swarm."

"But there's only three of us," Birddog says.

"Five of us," Rosalind corrects him.

"Yeah…"

There are three mattress rolls on the ground and a little kitchenette. Almost like a real home. Their things are hung up on a rack and Rosalind cleaned the few dirty dishes that lingered in the sink. Frosty keeps Tony and Birddog coming back 'home' each night. Where they're warm and safe and fed. He says that he's finally starting to think straight. Finally starting to feel good. Almost like a real human being. He lays down some ground rules for everybody in the beginning. Everyone has to stay clean. No booze, no drugs. They're going to need their heads soon. Tony smoked crack. He didn't want to stop. Frosty promised him he would stop. And Frosty always kept his word.

If you give a mouse a hit of cocaine every time it presses a lever, it will do nothing else but press that lever. It won't stop for a minute to take a sip of water or a bite to eat. Eventually it will die from an overdose. The main thing that keeps people from overdosing are their bank accounts. Or lack thereof. The odd intervention or after school special.

Under two years ago Tony was what most people would call respectable. He had a job. An apartment. Credit cards. Now he sits shaking on the floor, pleading for a fix. Praying to a God that Frosty told him wasn't even listening. Willing to sell his soul for relief. Frosty, Birddog and Rosalind stay with him the whole time. I have to work during the day. There's a pile of paperwork that has to get done. I only watch in glimpses.

"It's all in your mind," Birddog says. He knows from experience. He dabs a moist cloth onto Tony's forehead. "It'll go away. As sure as shit stinks."

"Please…"

"Been there brotha. You'll get through this," Birddog says.

"It won't get better," Tony says, "please."

"It'll get better," Frosty says, "Trust me. I'm going to see to it."

Tony writhes on the floor. He's covered in sweat and shaking so hard they have to put pillows under him so that he doesn't hit the linoleum and crack his skull open. He pukes. Rosalind cleans the affected area with soap and water. Then disinfects with a 1:10 bleach solution for ten minutes. It has a proven effectiveness against non-enveloped viruses, she says. Take care not to contaminate other surfaces and always practice good hand hygiene.

He eventually gets through it. Entry number four. He has to. It's one of Frosty's stipulations for being part of the collective. They can't waste their minds, or their resources, on drugs or booze. There're more important things to be done, he says. Things to take care of that will require their strength and clarity of mind.

Each night, either Rosalind or I let them into the church basement through the back door using the spare key that Father Price gave us. We swap it back and forth depending on our work schedules. They're gone all day long. That's part of the deal too. Father Price didn't want them around while service or Bible camp was happening. The door automatically locked behind us when it closed.

The three of them spilt up. They each have different ways of going about things. Getting whatever money they could. The same thing that kept them down was what they wanted most in the world. You couldn't blame them though. You always want what you can't have. It's human nature. You only want it until you have it. Then you don't know what you have until it's gone. There are songs written about it. Stories too. The alien archeologists will never know that about us. That we never figured it out.

Birddog posted himself where the freeway exit ramps spill onto the surface streets. He held a sign. It's a popular technique. You didn't have much opportunity to plead your case though. You had to print words like 'homeless' or 'hungry' in big bold letters. 'God bless' suggests a certain humility that couldn't hurt either. 'Please help.' His first sign didn't have the desired effect. He sat next to the ramp for two days with a sign that read FUGAZI. Fucked up got ambushed zipped in. You wouldn't get it unless you had been in the army. People didn't even slow down.

Some guys tried jokes. 'Family kidnapped by ninjas, need money for karate lessons.' 'Too ugly to prostitute.' Some were brutally honest: 'Need money for beer.' Some offered a service: 'Kick me in the balls for $2.'

He categorized drivers who actually rolled down their windows. About one in a hundred. Feeders gave you food. Drinkers gave you beer. Johns propositioned the women for sex. They figured someone that close to the bottom probably wouldn't mind having a quickie in the back seat of the car for a few bucks or a foot long submarine sandwich. It had pickles and tomatoes on it.

Most people stared straight ahead. Didn't even acknowledge him. Locked their doors. The more compassionate would at least pretend to be talking on the phone. Some would play tricks, yell insults or throw things at him. Drivers in the shitty cars gave more money than the long, shiny luxury models. Black women gave the most. Old white men the least. Someone dropped a handful of pennies all over the road as he handed them to Birddog. Just to make him bend over and pick them all up. Humbled. Someone threw a doughnut at him before speeding away.

Six or seven dollars was a good day. N.F.G. No fucking good. He used to say that to his buddies when they were caught in a tight spot during combat missions. The same combat missions where he'd be the one in charge of fifteen lives and ten million dollars worth of high tech government equipment. Now he's staring down at the crevassed palm of his hand rubbing the dirt off of quarters. Standing with his back against the wind cause it was warmer that way.

Tony hit the streets with Gertrude. He had a system. You had to choose a place with a lot of foot traffic. Subway stops were good. Different people pass through every couple of minutes. Turnover is high. But competition is fierce. You have to get there first. It wasn't easy. You want to be downtown. A lot of these big box stores on the outskirts have security that will eventually send you packing. He said that he avoids rich neighborhoods and expensive restaurant districts. You'd figure that'd be the place to go, but the richest people give the least to panhandlers. They were afraid. He could see it in their eyes as they clutched their possessions to their chests and gave him a wide berth. They were more likely to call the police than anything else. That was the last thing they wanted to see on their streets. The last thing they wanted to smell too.

It was important to keep moving. Hitting up the same coffee shop everyday will get you in shit with the staff and the customers will quickly lose interest in your story. You had to be polite. You had to be believable. Be specific. Be funny. Be sympathetic. People are more willing to donate if they honestly think you're in a bad spot. Whether it's the truth or a lie. You had to be careful with elaborate lies though. Claiming to be a veteran and running into real soldiers with a bogus story could cause real problems.

Gertrude's puppy dog eyes helped out sometimes. A lot of people left more money to the dog than they would to him. The dog isn't the lazy one that won't get a job. It's not the dog's fault. The dog's the victim here. You can eat puppy treats in a pinch. They're designed to help clean your teeth too.

He always left himself a little bit dirty. Cleaning himself up too good would hurt his chances at a decent haul. There was a certain image to portray. He washed in the sink in the bathroom of the church basement. Just enough to maintain appearances and stay somewhat clean. One dark streak across his cheek.

Not trusting that God will provide all material and spiritual needs is venial sin number one hundred seventy-six.

Frosty was the most proactive of the three. He spent his days routing through garbage. Looking for anything he could sell. One man's trash…that whole thing. He had his usual spots that he checked every day. Favorite neighborhoods. A stack of old CDs could net you a couple of bucks at the pawnshop. But that was before digital downloads put an end to that. An old TV, VCR, left next to the dumpster in perfect working order. People want the thin flat televisions now. And tape is so 1980s. Water bottles. Soda cans. Once he found an old leather jacket. The guy at the second hand store gave him a couple of bucks for it then turned around and sold it as 'vintage' to some hipster for seventy-five. His friends were green with envy. Mortal sin number one eighty-five.

A particularly good haul was also stressful, he said.

"You run into a place to sell something and come back to find some shit gone. All that work for nothing. Nobody wants it when it's sittin' on the side of the road next to the garbage but as soon as you pick it up people are trying to steal it from you. You end up guarding the garbage." He said it would be best to work in pairs. There's power in numbers. That's what Frosty always said. So I ended up going with him whenever I could. Mostly on the weekends when the others were doing work around the church. They covered for us. You have to stick together. Have each other's backs. That's what ants do.

Pushing a rusted shopping cart with a dummy front wheel filled with empty wine bottles and crushed beer cans, Frosty says, "You know, one time some guy came running out of his house and accused me of stealing his trash. Can you believe that? Stealing his garbage."

"How the hell do you steal garbage? You're practically doing him a favor by getting rid of it." The cart pulls to the left but I tighten my grip and steady it.

"What the fuck is wrong with people? Does he run out of his house every week and chase the collection truck down the road waving his fist?" He laughs. He doesn't do that very often. "What an asshole."

"We should go back there one day and give it all back to him. See what he thinks of that." Now the cart pulls to the right. "So how much do you think we'll get for all this stuff anyway?"

"What?" Frosty says. Then he stops mid stride and turns to me. "What do you mean 'we'?" The smile fades from his face. "Oh, is that why you're doing this? Looking for a friend? What's the matter? All the yuppie assholes that you work with busy this weekend? They all checking out a restaurant that you've already been to? Is it to impress your boss? Part of some 'give back to the community' corporate policy? Or does it really give you a warm feeling down in the cockles or something? Let me tell you something, don't do me any favors."

I don't even know what cockles are. He starts walking again. I do my best to keep up but that stupid dummy wheel keeps pulling the cart to the side. The sound that the loose metal makes broadcasts our position to anyone within a five block radius. Frosty says something but I can't hear him over the clanging steel.

"What?"

He raises his voice. "She's doing it to save her own soul. How altruistic." Clang, clang, clang, what? "I said, but what about you? I haven't figured out that part yet." He looks at me as though I'm made of polyethylene. Stretched really tight and nailed to a wooden frame so that there's no wrinkles in it. He can see right through me. I pull the cart left but overcorrect and have to straighten it out with my shoulder. His mouth moves but the only thing that comes out of it is the sound of aluminum vibrating against tin. What? What did you say? "I said, there is no such thing as people who give selflessly. Everybody gets something in return. What are you getting?"

What are you getting?

I don't tell him that I'm selfish. I don't tell him that I'm looking for my own medicine. Avoiding a lawsuit. I don't tell him that I'm trying to make up for something or that I'm trying to make myself look good in the glossy doe eyes of someone else who genuinely is. I don't tell him that I want to be part of something good for once in my life. The only thing I say to him is: "I want to be part of the swarm." And he laughs in my face. The breath that wafts up my nose has six different layers of miasma.

"You? Part of the swarm?"

"Yeah. I'm an ant too."

"What?"

"I said, I'm an ant too."

He grabs the front of the cart and stops it dead. "Let me tell you something, you're nowhere near." The edge is back. "You're too worried about the resale value of your new condo or the crease in the pants of your new suit. You're dressed too nice. You're too clean. Look at your fingernails. You're still too worried about what everybody passing by will think of you. We're free from all that. You'll never be."

"Show me." I want to see it with my own eyes.

"You want to see it? You want to see the swarm? Fine. I'll show you. But remember, you asked for it."

But when we get there the swarm's gone. We stand on the edge of a smooth asphalt expanse that stretches out into infinity. Yellow and white lines divide every square inch of its surface into little rectangles of equal size. The black mass hangs there. Suffocating any insignificant organism that may have been unlucky enough to get caught underneath it. That life is gone now. Frosty crosses his arms and looks out at the urban wasteland.

"Shit," he says, spitting. "Should've known. Was only a matter of time I guess."

This is where Tent City used to be. He had even lived here once for almost a year. It was a vibrant community with its own economy and government. We found out later that the municipality had gone in and taken the whole place out. Bulldozers. Excavators. Lots of cops with clubs and stun guns. They rounded everybody up at the crack of dawn one day and shipped them off. There were over a hundred residents at its peak. They had been out of sight and out of mind for the longest time. Left to their own devices. That is, until the home improvement center next door bought up the land. Now, there was also plenty of free parking to advertise in the leaflet that they mailed out to everyone in the neighborhood. The residents were redistributed among the street corners and overpasses of the city. Begging everyone walking by with their long overcoats and leather briefcases for change for something to eat. Holding up signs. Pissing in the alley ways. Dying next to dumpsters.

"Yup," Frosty says, looking out, "seems about right."

Divided and conquered. That's how it's done.

He stands there, arms crossed, looking over the urban desert until the sun starts to burn the back of his neck and the heat coming off the asphalt forms small clear globules on his forehead. Not a word leaves his lips. The expression on his face is blank. I don't interrupt. I don't say a thing. Finally, he wipes his forehead with his sleeve and says, "Let's get the hell out of here."

When we get back to the church of the Holy Name, Father Price is making the rounds. Like some sort of military inspection. The guys are standing at attention in a row with Rosalind at the end. He runs his freshly exfoliated hand across the pew.

"This is really great," he says.

The church looks good with a fresh coat of paint. A few things refinished here and there. They've worked hard. This is working out. Thank you. No, thank you. It goes on like that for a few minutes. He pulls me and Rosalind aside. Out of earshot. He fidgets like a little kid who has to go to the bathroom but whose too afraid to ask.

"Perhaps I could join you downstairs one night? To spread the grace of God?"

Now it's our turn to wrings our hands. I look around absently. Frosty takes the guys downstairs. He looks back over his shoulder and shakes his head at me.

"I'm not sure. But I'll run it by them again," I say. It's a lie. Mortal sin number one sixty-seven.

Rosalind's voice is subdued. Reflective. A bit depressed. "It's important that we don't lose faith in them though."

I wasn't going to say anything. It would just bring up the same stale argument we've been having for days now. Frosty says that they don't need God. That if there even was a God, he's the one responsible for things turning out like this. Rosalind hates it. She says they should make amends and ask for forgiveness. I'm stuck right in the middle. When all of the eyes look up I have nothing to say. Part of me would like to believe in something. Sometimes.

"Fuck God," Frosty says.

"Don't say that! Please don't say that!" Rosalind says, and storms out. She's doing God's good work. Seeking God's forgiveness. Counting her blessings. Frosty would undermine all that at least once a day. I don't know if he's trying to convince her, the others, or himself. But Rosalind never let up. She wants to share the blessing from above that saved her with everyone else.

That blessing started out with a gross factor test. They needed to make sure she could handle the work without throwing up. You had to wear a respirator. If you puked in it, it wouldn't work. You'd either suffocate or risk being exposed to some disease. She was shown a graphic visual presentation of previous crime scene clean ups. It culminated with an actual clean up of animal remains. No animals were harmed in the training of this employee though. Not as a direct result anyway. She was numb by that point. It was just the beginning of her atonement. There was a middle and an end as well. She worked odd hours. Tragedy doesn't adhere to a strict schedule. We spent most of our free time at the church together. When it got late, we'd leave the basement and I kept her company on the walk home.

We make our way down the dim and quiet street. Her heels click on the sidewalk. My hand grazes her arm. She smiles. We've done good. Yes, we have. They were right. The doctor, the clergy and the scientists. Does that mean we're bad people? Who did we really do this for? Does it even matter? The ends justify the means.

I've got a lot of paperwork to finish. Six hundred and twelve policies.

"Do you think heaven really exists?" she says.

"I honestly don't know."

We stop under a street lamp. I feel closer to her than I have to anyone else. Her head cocks to the side. She has no idea that I know what I know about her. What I do know is beautiful. I want to put my hands on her hips and pull her into me. I want her glossy eyes to look deep into mine without judgment. We're not alone anymore. There's power in numbers. I lean in and kiss her softly on the cheek. She beats against the side of my head with the bottoms of her fists. Kicks me in the shin and screams.

8

Birddog has my arm bent around my back. As he applies pressure upwards it feels as though my elbow is going to explode. He kicks my knee out from behind and I'm on the ground. Twisted.

"Uncle!"

"There's no such thing as uncle in real life brother," he says.

Frosty agrees.

Birddog eases the pressure and helps me up. We're learning to defend ourselves. There are stories all over the news about the homeless being assaulted. Some people don't like them hanging around their streets. Other people do it just for fun. Birddog is our teacher. He passes along everything that they taught him in the army. Shows us all the soft spots. How to bend the human body in ways that it didn't want to be bent until it breaks. If you grind your head against your opponent's ear you can tear it. Or pop the eardrum by striking it hard with the palm of your hand. Stick to the basics. Eyes, throat, knees, temples. If someone grabs you from behind, the best thing to do is to push your hips out and hit them in the groin repeatedly using the blade edge of both hands. Works every time.

"Let me try," Frosty says. He grabs Birddog by the arm and twists. The trick is to practice it so often that it becomes muscle memory. To the point that your body will just do it out of pure habit. Frosty runs through the motions over and over again. Birddog shows us the variations he was taught as he moved up the military ladder.

Birddog has no love for the military since he went AWOL, spent some time in jail, was discharged and found out that there was no civilian equivalent occupation to going AWOL and spending some time in military prison. And while he was gone serving he'd been left behind by the next generation up and comers and didn't really qualify for anything except fighting. The kids that had developed their hand eye coordination by shooting people in virtual environments, as opposed to in real life, got all the cushy jobs now. Full benefits. Christmas bonuses. And nice offices with large windows and reclaimed wood surfaces.

Frosty reverses the hold and twists himself until he has Birddog on the ground in a contorted mass of lose limbs. He pulls a little too hard and Birddog screams in pain.

"Easy there brother!"

"I thought there was no uncle in real life."

"I said brother, not uncle."

Birddog shows us how to twist limbs. Break bones. How to take someone down fast and hard, and where to hit someone to have the most impact. Solar plexus, throat, jaw. Fish hook into the eye was good because your opponent would immediately start to water and wouldn't be able to see.

Frosty smiles and slaps Birddog and Tony on the back. "You have so much untapped potential. And we're gonna put it to good use." While we lather, rinse, repeat, he sets up two chairs to lie on and he's doing bench presses with the 70s Jesus and his sideburns.

One.

"Is that blasphemy?"

Two.

"I don't know. I don't think he cares either."

Three.

He pushes harder, until a glaze of sweat covers his skin and his arms start to shake. He lowers Jesus deliberately. Isolating his muscles. He squeezes upwards slowly. Feel the burn.

Four.

When Rosalind gets back Tony has Birddog's head wrapped in his arm and he's wringing and pulling as hard as he can. She drops her bag of things. "What's going on? What are you doing?" She kneels and tears Tony's arm away. "You're hurting him."

Five. "That's the whole point," Frosty says.

"But why? Why are you doing that?"

Frosty exhales as he pushes the 70s Jesus over his chest. "We can't rely on society to take care of us. So, we're learning to take care of ourselves."

"Amen to that brother," Birddog says. "Got your six."

"Yeah," Tony says.

Rosalind lowers here eyes. She exhales slowly. Like she has a terminal disease and only a few breaths left, so she wants to hang on to them a little bit longer. The back of her hand presses against the corner of her eye. She's fighting a losing battle. Rosalind the faithful. Rosalind the indulgent. Rosalind who would thank me for my help, kiss me on the cheek, and then slap me in the face and start to dry heave. She looks at us like a mother scolding her children. I'm not mad, I'm just disappointed. She tells us that life is short. That we should be shaking hands instead of making fists. That there was good in the world still. It's everywhere. She talks a lot about how life is short. Before you know it your time is up. The end comes faster than you can anticipate. And you'll never see it coming. Lead a good life. One that's worthwhile. Make the change now while you still have the time. Her eyes are half open. "I need to sit down," she says. "I'm very tired." Her fingers are trembling. Not enough to notice if you weren't looking for it. But still. She folds her arms and rests her head on them. "I'm going to invite Father Price down tonight. Maybe he can talk some sense to you."

"We don't need advice from a priest."

"He knows what it's like. He can help you."

Frosty sets the 70s Jesus down and sits up. A thin layer of sweat covers his face. "What does he know about what it's like to be one of us? All these priests live in palaces! Have you seen pictures of the Vatican? All that gold? The house of God, they say. Why does God need all of these houses anyway? He doesn't even have a body. I have to sleep on the goddamn street."

"You're staying in the house of God now," Rosalind says. He doesn't have a comeback. "The Bible teaches us to love one another. To treat each other with kindness and respect. Maybe you should read more of it."

"You know, priests also molest little kids," Birddog says. "That's why altar boys have their hair parted in the middle."

She peels the polish off of her thumb nail with her index finger. It leaves little red flakes all over the counter. Like the crime scene remains of a tiny murder victim. "That's a horrible thing to say." They're deliberately pushing her away. But Rosalind wouldn't give up on them. Good work was an indulgence. Life was short. Do it now while you still have the time.

"And another thing,"

"Leave it alone," I say.

"What? I'm not allowed to have an opinion? I'm not good enough?"

"Nobody said that. Just, leave it alone." I'm right in the middle. Frosty lives in a world devoid of compassion. One where it never stops raining. Rosalind is trying to see the silver lining that comes out every once in a while, when the clouds break and the sunshine sparkles off their edges. I sell insurance. Just in case. "You can invite him down tonight. If that's what you want. If it'll make you feel better." Frosty starts to open his mouth but catches himself. They owe her that much at least.

"Fine," he says.

She'd become their adoptive mother. Carol Brady or June Cleaver in the flesh. She cooked, cleaned, put just the right amount of dirt on Birddog's and Tony's faces so that they could garner some sympathy, but kept them clean enough to maintain their approachability. It's a fine balance. She wore an apron and she packed a snack for them in the morning before sending them off with a pat on the head and a peanut butter sandwich in a brown paper bag, with the top rolled over on itself to keep it closed.

"Good luck today boys. Be back for dinner."

They nod and smile. "Yes ma'am."

So they sit, while Father Price paces the room with a solemn expression on his face. He holds a Bible and rubs the palm of his hand over the gold cross on the cover. "I hear that there is some anger coming from all of you. I can understand that. You've been treated unfairly, I can see that. And your first instinct is to lash out.

What you have to understand is, the solution to the problem is to embrace your fellow man. Not to segregate yourselves from the world. 'Behold, how good and how pleasant it is for brothers to dwell together in unity.' Psalms 133:1-3. The Bible teaches us to cooperate with one another. To work together. In peace. For God."

Frosty's the delinquent student at the back of the class making spitballs and fart sounds. "Work for God you say? How about work for ourselves?"

The others nod together.

"We need it more than he does," they say.

Father Price waves his arms when he talks. Like he did to the congregation on Sundays. It's a script. He's holding the hard copy in his hands and referencing it. "But working for God is working for yourselves. We are all, all of us, a part of the divinity." His Adam's apple bobs up and down when he speaks. Like he's trying to swallow a thick mouthful of peanut butter.

"I ain't part of shit," Birddog says. "Just part shit."

Rosalind exhales. Exasperated. Her hand reaches up to her forehead and covers her eyes.

Birddog gets up. "The only thing I know for certain is that I've spent the better part of my fuckin' life fighting to stay alive against other parts of that same divinity." He made quotation marks with his fingers in the air when he said 'divinity'. "And let me tell you, they don't look so divine when they're pointing an automatic rifle at your face."

"I'm so sorry Father," Rosalind says.

Frosty watches. There's absolutely no evidence of it on his face, but he's smiling. "You can't convince us into thinking the world is all roses. We know firsthand that it's not. All of this kneeling, bread, wine. It doesn't change anything. It's just a brainwashing ritual."

"That's how they did it in the goddamn military. Structure and ritual," Birddog says. "They get you used to it. Get you to expect it. Hell, they get you to want it. Whole thing's FUBAR if you ask me. Before you know it you're part of the machine. You're that one little cog, that regulates the timing for the next step up, which turns the rotor, that swings the arm, that chops the head off of somebody twenty fuckin' miles away. You believe it. FIFO they say. Look where that got me."

FIFO was military for 'fit in or fuck off.' He ended up L.L.M.F. Lost like a motherfucker. To this day he still has the habit of constantly checking his gig line.

Father Price tucks the Bible under his arm. "I see," he says quietly. Tilts his eyes upwards.

Maybe Frosty should start a gratitude journal. Maybe they all should.

Father Price wasn't prepared for this resistance. He pictured coming down into the basement to talk with Frosty, Birddog, and Tony as a Sunday sermon. Complete with a noble message and a rapt audience. That wasn't what he got. He stumbles over his words and backtracks. "No, what I meant to say was…" He wipes his forehead with a small black handkerchief. "I'm sorry if you got that impression…" Finally, he closes the open Bible resting in his hands. The book sighs when the pages come together and the air in between them escapes. "I'm sorry you feel that way," he says. "Rosalind, may I have a word? I'm wondering if you might help me find something? They step away, into the corner and we can't hear what they're talking about. Rosalind looks over to us a couple of times, shakes her head once and nods. "But I'm sure it's nothing," Father Price says, just loud enough for everyone to hear, before climbing the stairs to the rectory. "It'll sort itself out. Good night." The lock slides into place.

There's absolutely no evidence of it on his face, but Frosty's smiling.

It's a Saturday. We should be helping in the church but Frosty and I are on the street. The others cover for us and tell Rosalind that we're out getting supplies. I'm watching Frosty's cart while he's in the pawnshop selling a flat screen TV that we found in the garbage. It had a frame. The new ones didn't have frames. Everyone wants one with no frame now. That's a sign that it's newer. Better and more expensive. A group of four loud teenagers in polo shirts and leather jackets walks by. One of them looks in the cart and stops. He reaches in.

"I'll take that," he says.

"Hey, what are you doing?" I say, pushing his hand away.

"I'm taking this." He looks to his friends. "We can throw it off the bridge. Or maybe we could toss the whole cart off the overpass. Maybe we'll hit someone's car." They all laugh. He starts to push the cart away. Doesn't even look my way. Like I'm invisible. Just a voice in his head. I grab the cart and pull. Now he sees me. He pulls harder. One of the others hits me in the ear from behind. I let go of the cart and cover myself. I can hear the cart rolling away. Before I can look up I get kicked in the stomach and stomped to the ground.

"Fucking creature!" they say, laughing. They spit in my hair. Laugh some more. "Nice clothes you fucking tramp, who did you steal those from?"

"He found them in the garbage."

For a second I think about how I should've changed before I left the church. My work clothes are spattered with paint and frayed at the edges. My jeans have a hole in them. I keep these clothes specifically so that I won't ruin anything new.

Their laughter recedes from me. The cart rolls and whatever's inside it vibrates. You can hear it from two blocks away. Frosty comes running out of the pawn shop and clocks the tallest one across the jaw. The sweet spot. He goes down hard. Instantly. Birddog said to clip the side of the chin for a knockout. And that's what he did. 70s Jesus made him stronger. Having strength gave him wrath. The tall one is the leader. When you cut the head off a snake the rest of it falls away, limp. The others don't even bother dragging their friend away with them. They just run and don't look back.

"See that?" Frosty says, "fucking cowards. You okay?"

"I think so," I say.

He grabs me by the bicep and pulls me to my feet. I'm angry. Furious. I'm mad at my own weakness. At my own insignificance. I'm pissed off that I've just been stomped on by some piss ass kids. It's embarrassing. I want to run after them. Attack them from behind. Return the favor. Frosty doesn't let go of my arm. "We're going to teach those people a lesson. Soon too. I'm going to show them that they can't do whatever they want." He spits. "It's a real class war now. These people think that your right to exist depends on the numbers in your bank account. Who your daddy is. What you're wearing. They think they can step on us to step over us. Yeah, right."

He starts clipping stories out of newspapers he finds on the streets. Stories of assaults. Mainly stories of assaults geared towards people living rough downtown. He pushes small pins into an old map of the city and circles the densest clusters. One story made the front page.

Three thirty a.m. Saturday. Two policemen breaking up a fight spot a man in his late twenties or early thirties running down the street in his underwear. He's being chased by about twenty kids. Youths, as they're referred to in police lingo. More and more youths join in the chase. Laughing and taunting him. The two officers catch up to the man near a subway station. He's now completely naked. The group chasing him has grown to over thirty. He's terrified. They shout at him. Fool. Idiot. He breaks away from the two officers and bolts into the station where he tries to grab someone's jacket, to cover himself. Humiliated. He runs onto the platform. Still naked. They laugh. He jumps onto the tracks to get away, and as the laughing mob watches his hand touches the electrified third rail. They don't stop laughing. They think it's a joke.

"You see? You see this? This is how the world sees us," Frosty says. "We're a joke to them."

What's the best part about dating a homeless girl? You can drop her off anywhere.

"Everyone just stood there and watched. Laughing. We're not even good enough to help anymore. We're not even human. You know why? Cause we don't pay taxes. Probably wouldn't even stop to piss on one of us if we were on fire."

About one percent of the country's population is homeless. They're the unseen. The stains on their clothes are urban camouflage. People walk by and don't even turn their heads anymore. One percent. It's so small it hardly seems significant. They blend into the brick and concrete. They meld into the spray painted tags along the walls. Being poor isn't just about being broke. Poverty is also being unwanted, unloved, and uncared for. It says so in the Bible.

"You know what his problem was?" Frosty rests his index finger on the black and white picture of the rail line. "He was alone." He looks at Birddog and Tony to let it sink in. "See what I mean?"

Frosty takes us under the Fourth Street bridge. It's cloudy and the sides of the gully act like a funnel that gathers up the wind and sends it tearing along the ground. A lot of people congregate under the Fourth Street Bridge after tent city was cleared out. To the surface dwellers they were trolls. Avoiding the sunlight. Spewing out at night to scavenge the remains of the day and slinking back before they turned to stone in the morning. It smells awful. A few people are arguing. A few more are passed out. We don't know it, but one is dead.

"Look at that," Frosty says, pointing towards the bridge. There's a lot of foot traffic across it but not even one person ever takes the time to look down. "Just a few feet above us people are walking by, talking on their brand new phones. The one that they just had to be the first of their friends to get. You know, so they can brag. They don't even care that it's making them sterile or giving them tumors. As long as it's new. You know, slick. One, just one, would feed everybody here for a couple of weeks." He spits.

The money that people piss away on status symbols the world over could effectively end poverty. All this new technology, more expensive cars, plastic corn cob holders so your fingers don't get any butter on them. People don't buy what they need. They buy what will make everyone else think they're more important. More important means having more money. Having something that other people want but don't have access to. Paint it red so everybody will notice.

My corn cob holders are yellow and they're shaped like little ears. Well, they were. I get rid of them that night.

"These people down here are alone. The rest of society abandoned them when they didn't fit into the mold. Out of sight, out of mind. But they're more alone than that even." He walks up to someone hunched over and sorting through a paper bag. "How's it going brother?" he says, and places his hand on their shoulder. The man jumps back and turns to face Frosty.

"Stay away from me," he says, clutching at his things.

Frosty raises his hands. Just like I used to do. It's disarming. "Alright, alright. No problem." He takes a few steps back. The man stares him down a long time before he turns and walks away.

Looking over his shoulder to make sure that no one's following him.

"See what I mean? Look at all the people here." They huddle individually to shield themselves from the dirt that blows around. They keep their belongings near to them. They watch for anyone that might get a little too close. The occasional argument breaks out over the best spots. It's usually first come, first served, but some people don't like the unwritten rule. "See what I mean," Frosty says. "They're alone even when they're together. They don't talk to each other. They don't share anything, and they don't work together. That's why they're taken advantage of. Individually, we're weak."

He starts talking like that a lot. Drilling into Tony and Birddog. "One bee sting is annoying but a whole hive working together can kill you," he says. "Remember that. It's important." The yellow jackets listen. "One time a swarm of mosquitoes killed more than forty cows in Texas. Sucked the blood right out of them. I shit you not." The swarm nods. "A school of piranhas can tear you to shreds in minutes. Because each of them bites a different spot. Takes a different piece. They don't fight over the same one. Get it?"

He spits. We start to walk away. Frosty keeps looking over his shoulder at the slumped over bodies obscured by the windswept dirt. "What can we do about it?" I say. There's something welling up inside my stomach. A nonexistent bowel obstruction.

He gives me a look. His cheeks are flush and his eyebrows are pushed together. "You'll see."

9

Frosty wants me to experience it firsthand, show me what it's like. He wants me to be the butt of it. He says that it's the only way that I'll ever really understand. So he takes me downtown and we stand on a corner holding out paper coffee cups. When someone walks by Frosty nudges my arm. "Here you go. Give it a try. Just give it a try."

My voice wants to stay in my throat but I force it out. It cracks. "Spare some change?" The person doesn't even acknowledge that I exist. He looks right through me, as if I were a window, and keeps on walking. So did the next one. And the next one.

"See? Nobody gives a fuck. All wrapped up in trying to make their little lives more comfortable. More convenient. Move up the ladder and get a bigger house or a faster car. That's all they care about. Society, my ass."

A bony old man with skin that looks like tree bark limps up to where we're standing. I can smell him from ten feet away. He doesn't say a word. He doesn't look at us either. When a man wearing a shiny gray suit walks by, the old man sticks out his hand. He only says, "Please." The suit walks right through him too. The old man retracts his hand and waits patiently for the next one to come along. I ask Frosty about the rule. We were here first. Who does this guy think he is?

His eyes drop. "That's the first thing that has to change," he says. "Out here, there's no sense of community. We're all in the same spot but we're not all in it together. There's only competition in a place like this. Human nature I guess. Limited resources." He takes the one coin that's in our cup and gives it to the old man. The old man smiles a toothless smile and nods. "Come on, let's get out of here."

Back at the church we all eat together. The clinking of silverware fills the basement. There's even a little laughter mixed in. Tony leans over and gives Gertrude a handful of food which she devours. The place is really shaping up. Rosalind put a fake fern in the corner. I brought a lamp from home. We had new blankets. The three guys looked better too. I bought them some new clothes out of my own pocket. Long underwear so they would be warmer. I'm making all of that extra money through RDC Holdings anyway. At least this way it's being put to good use. And it's also a tax write off. I can claim it as a charitable donation.

"You know," Frosty says with a mouthful of food, "the rich guys that you make money for don't pay taxes. Nobody cares who they take from. And nobody cares what results from it. They still get protection. They still get respect. It keeps you down and keeps them up." He's right. Things are hard to see from the inside. But I don't feel like I'm on the inside anymore. "They hold all the cards and you pay all the ante."

"Can we just have a nice dinner for once?" Rosalind says.

Frosty swallows. "I'm sorry ma'am, but how am I supposed to relax and enjoy all this when there're people all over this city starving or freezing to death?" A vagrant was found dead on Victoria Avenue. They estimated that he'd been dead for a day. The police were called when the owner of some hipster café complained that he was hurting business by hanging around, driving customers away. There's nothing kitsch about that guy. "Lucky me." He throws his fork down.

Okay, okay, I got one. What did the homeless guy get for Christmas? Nothing.

Rosalind stares down at her food. "We should be thankful for what we have."

But, tonight's dinner marked the last of the money from the donation box. These days the box at the front of the church is usually empty. The novelty has worn off. Rosalind scrapes the leftover food into a plastic container. Careful to get every last crumb. She places it in the fridge and then washes her hands and wipes down every surface. In the quiet spaces in between, there's a faint knock at the door. It's barely audible but it's there. Frosty gets up to answer it, like he's expecting it. The rusty metal door swings open and on the other side of it stands the old bony man from the street corner. Frosty puts a hand onto his shoulder and ushers him in.

Paddy lost everything when his house burned down with his family in it. He hit the bottle. Hit the bottle hard. Lost his job. Couldn't pay rent. Needed something to help him sleep. Sober a year now though. Three of his toes were gone from frostbite. His fingertips are black. Like he'd spent the day working under the hood of an old car. But he hadn't.

Frosty sits Paddy at his own spot at the table and gives him his own plate. "Don't eat too fast or you might throw it up. Okay?" You're not garbage, he says. Your life is worth something.

James, Lucas, Puppy, Gibbs, Brock, and Socks.

Night after night there's a weak knock on the rusty metal door of the church basement. Frosty tells them they can stay if they follow the rules. His rules. No drinking, no drugs. They agree. Frosty slaps them on the shoulder. Smiles a smile that spreads to the others. You'll be safe here. Rosalind doesn't have the heart to turn anyone away. W.W.J.D? He was in the corner cold chillin'. Groovy.

Father Price isn't going to like this. I know exactly how he's going to respond.

The Bible tucked under his arm falls to the floor when Father Price raises his hands over his head. "There are too many people.

We are not qualified to take care of this many needy. We have to consider the well being of the church. This could have unforeseen repercussions."

Frosty speaks steadily. "I'm just doing what it says in the Bible. We're helping the less fortunate. Isn't that what God tells us to do?" He picks up the book and turns the pages over.

"Yes, but you have to understand that we can't accommodate the entire population. There are other things that we have to take into account. Such as, what if there's an accident?"

Frosty stops on a page and starts to read. "Whoever has two tunics is to share with him who has none, and whoever has food is to do likewise."

That isn't exactly fair, Father Price says.

"Isn't it?"

Perhaps they'd be more comfortable at a shelter? Perhaps you'd all be more comfortable at a shelter? His lips tremble. His eyes move around the room.

Frosty's finger skims along the page as he reads. "Because I rescued the poor who cried for help, and the fatherless who had none to assist him."

The church cannot be held responsible for—

"Whoever oppresses a poor man insults his Maker." He closes the book with one hand. The pages slap together and echo throughout the basement.

The meek shall inherit the earth. It says that in there somewhere.

"This isn't about scripture!" Father Price yells, "this is about practicality." I've never heard him raise his voice before. He always speaks quietly and steadily. Rosalind and I are silent. Father Price blames us. I know this. I can tell by the way he looks over at us. He's given up on them and has to go straight to the source.

Frosty says that he needs to protect them. His flock. Like priests tend to a congregation. Nobody else cared enough to do it. People do their best to forget about them. Just like Father Price wants to do. Send them to a shelter. Out of sight, out of mind.

"That's not true," Father Price says.

"Prove it then."

I'm stuck in the middle again. Rosalind and I are both stuck there. Father Price has a point. Frosty has a point. They pull equally hard. The best way to influence someone is with a story. I can tell the negative story or the positive story. I open my mouth but no sound comes out.

"I'm sick of parables anyway," Frosty says.

"Punishing Father Price for helping you isn't going to accomplish anything." Rosalind starts to clean. She does that when she's nervous or excited

Father Price always says that nothing worth doing is easy.

"Yeah, well, all this talk is cheap. It's time to do something."

There'd been a series of assaults on homeless people. There's clusters all over Frosty's map. As if the upper classes are sick of all their gentrification being spoiled by the sullied. Their nice clean neighborhoods made dirty again. A constant reminder of how close to the edge they actually are. Spending more money on trying to look affluent than they actually had. New car. New clothes. That fancy dining room table made by some artist out of reclaimed wood. Corncob holders. The homeless are like someone constantly shaking them awake from their delusion of safety. Success. Prosperity. And the smell of urine is back. What a buzz kill.

A woman with two off-duty firefighters attacked a homeless man sleeping on a war memorial. She yelled at him for sleeping there. Said it was disrespectful. She kicked him. The firefighters joined in. One of them used a stick.

Someone else was spray painted and stomped on while he slept. One was beaten with a table leg. Another a baseball bat. One was found stabbed to death. His prosthetic leg missing. Another was doused in gasoline and set on fire. There were forty-three homeless killed this year. The experts say that's up twenty percent from last year. Everybody on the news analyzed the statistics.

"Laws and ordinances that criminalize behaviors associated with homelessness, sleeping outside, loitering, devalue homeless people and distance them from mainstream society. They're looked at as criminals. People are afraid. And yet, they're the most vulnerable to physical attacks."

Frosty watches the television. There's a round table of experts talking about the problem. They're all wearing suits and have really shiny hair and impossibly white teeth. Frosty turns up the volume.

"As the economy recovers from recession, empathy and sympathy for the homeless decline," one of them says. "During the recession many people reported that they had a friend lose a home, have to bunk with friends, or become homeless. This impacted people's perceptions."

I sit next to Frosty trying to catch up on some of my paperwork. Whenever I look up we don't make eye contact. He's glued to the screen. I fill out policy number 8737852.

They were actually calling them 'sport' killings. Drunken youths, the police said, were responsible for the majority. Ages fifteen to twenty-four. They called it bum bashing. Five points for a knockout. The highest score you could get was ten.

"I think it reflects a lack of respect for the homeless."

Looking down at the policy, I snort. "Lack of respect for the homeless," I say. "No shit, Sherlock. I wonder what fancy school he went to? What do you think? Harvard?"

Frosty laughs and looks over at me. "Yeah."

High paid experts stating the obvious for idiots who've gotten used to not having to think for themselves. Turn on and shut down. Have a name brand something. They're more expensive so they must be better. What a world.

The tin sounding speaker on the old television shakes. "It has reached such extreme proportions that homeless people aren't viewed as people anymore," one of them says.

Are knock-knock jokes wasted on the homeless? Because they don't have doors?

There's a fifteen minute segment that night on the news dedicated to addressing this 'growing issue.' The city estimates that there could be hundreds of people living on the streets. About one percent of the population is the statistic. They cite two trends as largely responsible. A growing shortage of affordable rental housing and a simultaneous increase in poverty. Children under the age of eighteen account for 30% of the homeless and 39% of that are children under five. Unaccompanied minors make up about 5%. 25% are ages twenty-five to thirty-four. 6% are fifty-five to sixty-four. That's as high as the infographic goes. It's all neatly divided. Color coded. 73% are male. Fifty percent of all statistics are made up.

They're studied, like bacteria in a Petri dish. The scientific method states that in order for a study to yield any useful information it must be unbiased. The observer is prohibited from interfering with the subject. Watch them starve and make a note of it on your clipboard. Check boxes B and C if the subject is complacent. Do you agree number 144? Attachment is also frowned upon. Jane Goodall was criticized for naming the chimps.

The moderator of the discussion adjusts his jacket and hits his microphone. Tries to look concerned. It doesn't work. We can see right through him. "I don't know what the solution is. But we'll be right back after this commercial break." They stare at the camera and smile in unison as the image fades away. It's replaced by teenagers on jet skis drinking some kind of soda or something.

I look up at Rosalind. She looks away.

"Al least we're safe tonight boys," Birddog says. "Can't say that for some people." He leans back and puts his feet up on the table. A couple of guys in the corner nod.

"Can't say that for a lot of people," Frosty repeats. Behind him, I see the dark outline on the wall where a crucifix used to hang. He took it down. Rosalind never gave up and had put it back. It was gone again. It was back up. It was gone again. She still doesn't give up.

"Amen to that," she says, and hangs it back on the wall. I look up from my paperwork and see him looking at her. They're both silent. He breaks the stare before she does. It's her first win.

I'm filling out policy number 7203612. I sign the bottom of the policy and slip it into my briefcase. The brass clips make a clicking sound when they latch and I place it by the door so that I don't forget it when I leave.

Nine are safe tonight. Nine are fed tonight. Ten if Frosty counts himself. Nine isn't enough. But the next night, at this same time, there's only seven. I'm finishing up my nights paperwork. Rosalind is cleaning. Some people are already asleep or playing cards or watching TV. Frosty paces the length of the basement. There's a knock on the door as I place my briefcase next to it, so that I don't forget. Frosty pushes me out of the way and opens it.

Gibbs pats Frosty on the shoulder as he and Brock walk in. The heavy metal door slams shut behind them.

"What?" Gibbs says, shrugging his shoulders. Around the room, all eyes are angled upwards towards them. You could cut the silence with a corn cob holder.

Brock looks around. People turn their eyes away from him. "Who died?"

"Where have you been?" Frosty says. He crosses his arms and speaks in a level voice. I know that voice now. It's a voice that's hiding something. The vein popping out of the middle of his forehead gives it away.

"You know, out," Gibbs says. "Should I have called first dad?" He laughs.

"You were supposed to be back an hour ago."

"Relax dad. Or should I say Father?" He makes the sign of the cross and giggles. Frosty doesn't. "What are you going to do?

Spank me? Eh dad?" You can smell the booze on the stinking laughter that's coming out of his mouth from across the room.

Without saying a word, or even changing the expression on his face, Frosty quietly opens the door. He grabs Gibbs by the collar, pushes him outside, and then closes the door behind him. The lock snaps into place like a judge's gavel hitting the hard wooden surface of the bench. Flakes of rust fall from the rotting frame. The door only opens from the inside. Unless you have the key. Rosalind or I usually have it. We trade it back and forth. One day we can't find it anywhere. It ends up in Frosty's pocket. Neither of us say anything. Everybody goes back to what they're doing. Gibbs sleeps outside for the night. His name doesn't even come up again until sometime the next morning. When we go outside to clean all of the junk that has been accumulating in the fence of the church yard for Father Price. Rosalind says it's the pious thing to do.

The surrounding streets have become more populated with baby carriages lately. Some people start crossing to the north side when they pass the church and the people hanging around it. They glance over their shoulders, quickening their pace. Not enough to be too noticeable though. That would imply some sort of prejudice. But just a little. Enough to notice a little. Organic smoothies are advertised in the windows of the dozen quaint lunch spots that spring up overnight. They're packed full of essential fish oils to help lower high triglycerides. Boutique art galleries and coffee shops. Coffee shop, after coffee shop, after coffee shop. Make sure to tip your barista. They draw little designs in the foam of your latte.

I have a fist full of take out coffee lids and dog crap in small plastic bags that were left behind to become someone else's problem. One resident has the guts to stop. He waves at us politely. A big smile on his face. "Howdy!" he says, and puts his hands on his hips. "Wow, looks great. I guess you can get a lot of work done with so many people chipping in."

I try to match his enthusiasm. We're all one big happy family. I smile. "Yeah, I guess so." But what I really want is for this guy to go away. I can see right through his teeth.

He looks around, taking in as much detail as he can. I can't see his eyes through the reflections on his glasses but I can tell where they're looking by the way he moves his head. "A lot of people here now," he says, stroking a bare chin. "What's going on?"

I tell him that we're helping out some of the neighborhood needy. Helping them back onto their feet. Making the whole neighborhood a better place for everyone.

He takes a sip of his coffee. There's some hazelnut in it or something. I can smell it. "There wasn't a homeless shelter here when I bought my house," he says. "I walked around the whole block to scope it out." He looks at me as though I'm supposed say something to placate him.

"It's not really a shelter," I say.

"Because I thought that the homeless shelter was a ways off. You know, not technically in this neighborhood."

"It's not really a shelter."

"There's families in this neighborhood."

"It's not really a shelter." I know what he's thinking. He can't hide it behind the reflections in his glasses anymore. I can tell by the way he's dressed, by the way he takes tiny sips out of a hazelnut smelling coffee and then presses his lips together to savor it. He's afraid for his property value. I want him to go away. Now. "Well, nice talking to you. I'd better get back to work. Lots to do."

"Huh," he says, and walks off staring intently at the screen of his cell phone. He doesn't look back at us either.

I gather everyone together and corral them back inside. Out of sight, where Frosty introduces us to the new arrivals. Violet and Colby.

Father Price is going to freak out and do that thing where he makes the sign of the cross and looks up and sighs. Pleading for patience or understanding to be rained down on him from above. For some kind of solution to be magically bestowed upon him. It never is, and Frosty just keeps on pushing. Something about an inch and taking a mile. I pull him aside. I tell him that maybe it wasn't such a good idea after the last conversation we had with

Father Price. Plus, we're running out of space. And, more importantly, we're out of money.

I'd been putting a lot of our expenses onto my own personal credit card. I'm afraid to even look at my statements. My credit rating must be down a few points.

He wrenches his arm free from my grip. "You sound just like the rest of em'. You know that? We're saving lives. What's more important than that? Money?"

"How are we going to feed them all? The donation box is empty."

"You'll figure something out," he says. "I have faith in you." He walks away.

I wonder if he's aware of the irony.

Rosalind is groaning from behind a pile of old boxes. I climb behind them to help her out. Taking the box from her hands, I place it on top. It's dark back here. Dark and quiet. A faint hint of ammonia. It reminds me of my confessional. Our own private universe that nobody else knows about. I look Rosalind in the eyes. Her pupils dilate, hiding the blue of her iris. She smiles and turns her head. I can't tell her why but I've never been so intimately close with anybody before in my life. I reach out. I try to touch her. Her arm, her shoulder, her cheek. Anything. She retracts. Takes a couple of steps backwards. The muscles in her face go limp. There's a sadness underneath them that wants to bleed out. She just can't, she whispers. The thought of me touching her makes her skin crawl.

"Don't be offended, the thought of any man touching me makes my skin crawl." That's something at least. I know why. A man had ruined her. A man had made her ruin herself. Her biggest sin. The one that she might not have enough time to atone for before the end. "There's only one person in my life now. I'm sorry." She means God. If God qualified as a person. But we're made in His image, right?

Maybe in time? Maybe we can work through it? There is no time, she says. She raises her hand. For a second I think she's going to brush it against me. Instead, she pushes the hair back behind her ear. The sadness leaves her face in an instant. She's smiling. "What are we going to do about dinner? We have a lot of mouths to feed."

I don't want to disappoint her. I don't want that look to spread across her face. So, I go down the street and the few things that I pick up get charged to my credit card again. But I can't afford to support this many people forever. I've tried everything to raise some extra money to accommodate our numbers. But it's not the giving season yet. Nobody's watching right now. People don't seem to remember what to be thankful for until you get in their face and remind them. I have one last option. The mouse cursor rolls over a button and turns into a little hand. Father Price wouldn't want me in the rectory using the church computer but he's out at the moment.

Givemesomemoney.com

You just click the link that says 'post a beg'. You then have the option to post a beg for free or you can sign up for the premium account for $9.95 a month. With the premium account you get a full page post that allows images and video. The beg will also feature no distracting advertisements. You can cancel anytime. It's called cyber begging. The website was organized nicely into different subcategories. Money for school. Money for travel. Help with the bills. Medical expenses. Entertainment. Unusual requests.

Feeding the poor wasn't on there.

A lot of people really want to take a vacation but can't afford one. Click and post a beg. Someone wants a new home entertainment system. Click and post a beg. Someone who wants to become a poet needs money to live while they write poems. Because you can't do that in your spare time. Obviously. The muse strikes when the muse strikes. Click and post a beg. Then there's the unusual requests. I leave that one to my imagination.

If you're lucky your beg will be featured under the beg spotlight. You can tweet it and like it on social media. E-begging gained momentum in 2002 with savekaryn.com. It was started by some girl named Karyn to have the internet public pay off her credit card which had been racked up due to her predilection for designer clothing and Starbucks coffee. It worked. She was on the news. The morning show. Not only did her card get paid off, she also got a book deal.

After all the information is entered I click and post a beg. You never know.

The account is joint between me and Frosty. I set it up and I give him the information to withdraw the money. If any comes. It seems like a long shot. I also find out that people beg using the chat function in online poker rooms, at the high stakes tables. But apparently that's frowned upon. People don't like to be bothered while they're pissing away their life savings.

So, tonight's meal is simple. It's designed to fill more than anything else. We eat in silence. Father Price comes down again looking for something. He says the neighborhood is petitioning the church to stop housing homeless people. There're families in the area. Kids. Think about the children. And property value. One resident is particularly vocal about the issue. If anything were to happen, the church could be held liable in a civil suit. Frosty won't listen to reason though. He's not going to stop. He says he's just getting started.

10

Rosalind is hitting me in the temples. Her fists bounce off my arms as I try to protect myself. She keeps swinging until she's out of breath.

"Don't fucking touch me!" she screams.

Her hands shake, lips tremble. She had kissed me. In one of those quiet moments when it was just the two of us and it was easy to forget about the rest of the world. She reached out. Put her finger tips against my chin. Leaned in really slow and closed her eyes. Her lips were cold against my skin. She only lingered for a second before her hands balled up and I felt the first blow land onto the side of my head.

"I'm sorry. Can you ever forgive me?" She wipes the corner of her eye with the back of her hand.

I have already forgiven her. More than once.

"I don't want to go to hell," she says.

"You're not going to go to hell. You're a good person. Good people don't go to hell."

"You don't understand."

But, I do. I can't tell her that I do. But I do.

She's repenting. The word 'repent' in its various forms occurs more than one hundred times throughout the Bible. It's very important. The church requires repentance from sin of its members. You have to do it to be saved. The first command that Jesus gave in the New Testament was to repent. It's important that you do. 'Repentance and remission of sins should be preached in His name to all nations.' That's what it says. So it's a good thing that God forgives all sins. Except one.

There are no limits to the mercy of God, but anyone who deliberately refuses His mercy by not repenting rejects the forgiveness of his sins and the salvation offered by the Holy Spirit. That hardness of heart leads to final impenitence and eternal loss. That's what it says. Blasphemy against the Holy Spirit. Eternal damnation.

God forgives all sins, except one. That's what she's worried about. That's what keeps her body moving day after day. That's the sin she always confessed last. Swallowing hard, like there's a lump of raw dough in her throat, before whispering it through the mesh that separated us. It wasn't the blood spilt. It wasn't the sex or the stealing. It was the time when she lost her faith. The time she renounced God.

"I just wish there was more time."

"Don't worry," I say, "you have time."

In a second, all expression is gone from her face. "Anyway," she says, straightening out her dress, "we have a lot to do. How much money is in the tin?"

We keep all the money that we can amass in an old tarnished can. People returning from a day of panhandling deposit most of what they manage to get into the can for the group as a whole. It never amounts to that much, but it's something. Frosty says that it keeps the group together and focuses them on a common goal. They are, each of them, a different cog in the same machine. It's good to get them used to thinking that way. To give them structure.

I shake the can. "Not much."

"It'll have to do." Rosalind digs the coins out of the bottom and slips them into her pocket. There's something of a smile on her face. Not a smile of genuine happiness though. It's not hard to tell the difference. "Don't worry, I'll make it work. Somehow."

I grab my briefcase and head downtown for my afternoon meeting. After I push my way through the protesters, security escorts me through the building and up to the forty-second floor. Mr. Howard flips through the paperwork as he sips his double ristretto large half-soy nonfat decaf organic chocolate brownie iced vanilla double-shot gingerbread frappuccino extra hot with foam whipped cream upside down double blended one Sweet'n low one Nutra sweet and ice. It's the longest order possible given all the choices on the board. He liked it because it took time. Making it was difficult. He wanted the lowly minimum wage worker to earn their money. It's character building, he said. And as for everyone waiting in line behind his assistant, they could bloody well wait.

"This all looks fine," he says, absently turning over pages. "So, how are we doing with the other thing we were talking about?"

"Well, I've been looking into it. Life insurance policies issued for Chinese workers have to be issued through a Chinese insurer unless the worker had been living here for at least ninety days prior to the start of their employment."

Stamp.

"So how do we get around it?" You can get around anything if enough money's involved. There's always someone that will sell themselves out for a big pile of it. Or even a small pile. Hell, one bill would do the trick most of the time. It's almost embarrassing.

The idea is to incorporate some sort of shell company over there, an independent subsidiary of RDC Holdings, with a Chinese CEO. He insures the workers with COLI policies through the shell with all assets returning to RDC Holdings when it's dissolved. When, not if. Then, just sit back and wait for them to start dying. A little bit more.

"Since all assets are technically owned by RDC Holdings, everything over there, might as well be here."

Stamp.

He nods his approval. Some kind of musk scented cologne wafts through the air. It makes me sneeze. "Good, good," he says to himself. "That's what we thought too. It's good to know that we're all on the same page." He takes a sip of his coffee and lets it linger in his mouth before he swallows. Then, he leans back in his chair. "Have you ever considered working for someone else? We could really use someone like you here. Someone who's really a team player."

"Well," I say surprised. "I'd be willing to consider all options."

"We offer very competitive salaries, among other incentives. I'd make it my business to make sure that you were personally, very well taken care of. I'm sure you know what I'm referring to. You could be a rich man." He smiles a smile that looks like it was taken off the assembly line in a mannequin factory.

"That sounds good." That's all I can think to say. "Thank you."

"We'll talk about it again soon then."

He looks at his Rolex with the diamond encrusted face. My boss has suspenders just like that. A pinstriped shirt too with the white collar. It's the uniform. "Have security escort you out." The protest is bigger now. Some of them have gotten violent. Speeches were made. He can hear them cheering through the unbreakable glass of his office that overlooks it.

Stamp.

It pisses him off to have to watch them all day. Sitting around, complaining about everything, not doing anything meaningful. While he works. While he's productive. He calls them freeloaders. He says that they're a drain on the system. A waste of his tax dollars. I don't say anything.

Security dumps me at the front doors and locks them behind me. The protesters yell and pull at my suit as I push my way through. Someone tries to grab my briefcase. I jerk it back then I swing it and clip them on the shoulder. One of them throws a tomato that bounces off my chest and stains my shirt. What a waste of food. Once I make it to the edge of the crowd I stop to catch my breath.

"You're starting to look more and more like one of us." I look up and find Frosty standing there. "You're nice pressed shirt is all stained. Tomato too. You can't get that out. Trust me, I've tried."

"What are you doing here?"

"I like it here," he says. "I like what these people stand for." He looks up the length of the glass tower. "Why should these rich assholes get to have all the fun while we're all stuck in the sewer?" He spits. "How'd the meeting go? Climbing up that corporate ladder are we?"

"He offered me a job."

"Oh, really? What does he get out of it?"

I don't know yet.

We walk through the crowded downtown streets. I can see people looking at us. I can see them looking at Frosty. At the stain on my shirt and the tear in my jacket. They look away when our eyes meet.

"Do you like it?" he says.

"Like what?"

"You know what I mean."

I look down at my briefcase that's filled with stacks of insurance policies. Selling people's lives away. Assigning dollar values to each minute that ticks away without them dropping dead. "Not really."

"It's a good thing you've devoted your life to it then. Pays the bills. Let's you buy nice things. It's worth it, I guess. How much did that fancy briefcase cost?"

It's a Porsche. Literally. They make briefcases too. Genuine leather with hand brushed aluminum hardware. It has an ergonomically designed handle, exterior zip pockets, and clasp closure. I got it when I was promoted. I figured I could afford to splurge a little bit. I deserved it.

"It looks expensive," he says.

"I don't remember. Either way, I need a briefcase."

"Yeah, but do you need one that could feed a family of four for three months?" We're stopped at a red light. The guy standing next to us keeps looking at his watch. Watching the seconds tick away individually. He paces back and forth. Sighs loud enough for everyone around him to know that he's not happy about the delay. He throws his hands in the air and says, 'Really!?' at no one in particular. Places to go, people to see. Time is money. That sort of thing. "You'll turn into that guy eventually. I guarantee." Frosty points out a woman in a power suit taking large strides down the sidewalk while reading something on her cell phone. She passes by two people asking for change without even looking up. The deep lines of her permanent frown never change. "She's probably playing that stupid candy game too. She just wants to look important. Gives her the right of way." All around the business district people have shiny hair, abnormally white smiles, expensive clothes, and polished shoes. They walk with purpose. "They all want the same thing. They want to be in that top one percent. And they'd probably kill to get there. They all wear the same uniform. They all have the same hairstyle and drive the same cars. They want to belong to it. And if they can't, they obsess about making themselves look like they could. Even if it ruins them." Most of the people swarming around the financial center never even look up from their cell phones. They're so caught up in their little worlds that they never even notice the real one around them. "Why do they bother to look so perfect anyway?" Frosty says. "They don't even look up at each other." He laughs. "These people are so entrenched in their day to day lives that they don't even know how to deal with anything outside of it. Here, I'll show you."

Frosty sprays water all over his crotch then stumbles over to some rich lady outside of the jewelry store. "Spare some change?" Her eyes widen. I can hear her gasp audibly. She digs into her purse, then throws the change as far away from her as she can so that Frosty has to step back to get to it. When he turns, she bolts. Walking as fast as she can. Looking back over her shoulder.

"See? She panicked. Didn't know what to do. She didn't want me to touch her. Get her coat dirty."

Some of them hold out their little windup toy dogs and hope that the incessant high pitched barking will drive him away. It doesn't. Someone gives him a fin. Just leave me alone. Get the hell away from me. They walk in the other direction at a brisk pace. Not fast enough to look like they're trying to get away, but fast enough to notice that they're trying to get away.

"If I were wearing a three piece suit do you think they'd be skipping away looking over their shoulder like that? All because I can't afford one, that makes me dangerous. They don't know anything about me."

"But they gave you a fin," I say.

Frosty holds up the bill. "They didn't give me this out of kindness or altruism. They gave me this because it did something for them. It got me the hell out of there. Not for any reason other than it suited them."

They say all giving is fundamentally selfish.

"There's no other reason for people to assume that I'm not trust worthy or straight up other than I'm poor," he says. Some kind of weird Stockholm syndrome. Emulate your oppressors. Blend in and they might not notice that you're out of place. Make that money. Get a little bit closer to that one percent. He points at my briefcase. "And that's just another step on your way to becoming the exact same thing. It's a symbol."

Frosty says that hunter-gatherer tribes had no police, no nobles, no kings. He says that several thousand years ago some societies moved from hunting and gathering to domesticating animals and growing crops. He read it at the library before he started to smell so bad that they asked him to leave. The people who produced the most food took control of the society's surplus. As the surplus grew, they could take some of the extra and use it to pay for specialists. Craftsmen, priests, servants or professional warriors. They eventually became kings.

The next day my briefcase is gone and my papers are laid out on the counter in a neat stack. I carry them to work in a plastic bag with bright blue lettering on it. People make fun of me all day. I look like an idiot. A kink in my camouflage.

"Class war must exist so long as society is divided into classes with opposing interests," Frosty says.

We're a little more even now, him and I. There's no reason for anyone to assume that I wasn't a good worker other than the fact that I didn't have a fancy briefcase. Or a briefcase, period. But they do. I can see it on their faces. Nobody takes my lunch order that day either. I have to go and get it myself. Then I ate it alone.

When we get back to the church, Rosalind's out of breath. "Thank God you're here," she says. "I didn't know what to do."

Brock is laughing hysterically and Gibbs is slumped at his feet in a semi conscious haze. Every now and then he looks up and laughs. The drool spills from the corners of his mouth. The only noise he makes is a broken groan. Brock and Gibbs hadn't been back to the church for two days before that. They smell of booze. Brock laughs. He points at anything and laughs. He points at Frosty and laughs. Frosty doesn't.

Frosty reaches into Brock's bag and finds a couple of blue pills. They're a mixture of MDMA, bath salts, and meth. You take one of those and the tooth fairy will come swinging in through your window in about an hour. That chick knows how to party. There's also a little heroin. Fentanyl. Frosty flushes it all down the toilet then grabs Brock by the neck and slams his head against the wall. Rosalind runs outside. She knows that sound intimately. It hits a little too close to home.

"What did I tell you?" Frosty says.

There's only one language that everybody in the world understands, and you don't use your mouth to speak it.

"What? It's harmless."

He slams Brock again and points at Gibbs. "Does that look harmless to you?" He squeezes Brock's cheeks together so that his lips look like a suckerfish about to scour a slimy rock. "Do you understand?" He kicks Brock's feet out from under him and starts pacing. He scratches his chin like he's thinking and runs his fingers through his greasy hair. "If anyone wants to leave, the door is right over there." He pauses for dramatic effect. Just like I would when I was selling an overinflated policy. "But if you decide to stay, then there are rules you have to follow." No drugs. No booze. "Everyone contributes equally. These things are non-negotiable." They look up at him like they're kids being chastised by their father. Or like sinners being chastised by an angry god. Frosty doesn't break his stare until everyone else in the room is beyond uncomfortable. Including me. "Someone help Gibbs," he says, and leaves.

I hear the lock on the basement door slide open slowly as we move Gibbs' limp body onto a bedroll. Father Price cracks the door open slightly and sticks his head through the small opening. "May I have a word?"

"Of course Father," I say. And quietly to the others around me, "Take care of Gibbs, and keep him hidden."

We talk in the dark stairwell, away from the others, where no one can hear us. I can tell he's nervous. He stutters a couple of times as he tries to choose the right words. Usually he has more time to prepare his sermons.

"What is going on down here?" There's an accusatory tone in his voice. The unwavering forgiveness has been pushed down and out of sight. He stumbles over what to say next. "Are they fighting down there? In the church? Can you please tell me that? I've noticed bruises and the other day I found blood." Wringing. Skin flakes. "And is that man drunk or on drugs?" I raise my hands to try and calm him down. Palms open, non-threatening. "The church cannot be held—"

"I know, responsible. The church cannot be held responsible. Please Father, calm down. Everything is under control. There's no problem. Trust me." I'm not sure if I'm lying. If I am, it must be worse than normal because I'm doing it to a priest.

"I would like to," he says. Fingernails pick at cuticles. I can hear them. "Do you have any idea what could happen to the church if anything goes amiss? The results would be disastrous." He fidgets and makes small jerking motions with his arms and hands. But I manage to calm him down a little. Provide, protection, security. These are all good words to use when trying to convince someone to sign a policy. Or talk them off a ledge. They're soothing. Comforting. They put people at ease. I learnt that in the introductory seminar on my first day as an insurance salesman. "By the way," he says, as he's closing the door behind me. "I wasn't sure if I should mention it or not." He avoids making eye contact. Hides half his face behind the chipped door. "I'm sure it's nothing but," he pauses and sighs. Resigned. "A gold crucifix has gone missing from the rectory." He pauses. Lets it sink in. I know what he's really saying. "But I'm sure it will turn up."

"I'm sure it will, Father. These are good people. And they're very thankful to both you and to the church." They aren't thieves simply because they're poor. That's what runs through my mind. That's what Frosty would say. Try convincing someone else of that though.

The lock slides shut behind me.

Later, Frosty lays on his bedroll staring blankly at the ceiling. There's something different about him. Over the past few weeks Frosty's fever had gone. He moves without pain. The chill in his abdomen is slowly being replaced with a 98.6 degree ball of fire. Capillaries under the skin of his cheeks are pink again. He looks different than he did when we first met. The expression on his face has changed too.

I find Rosalind sitting by herself in the churchyard. She's still shaking. The scene she witnessed inside was like a mirror into her past. That's exactly how it all started for her. Slamming her head against the wall. That same sound. Everything rushes back. Her unforgivable sin.

"I don't know what to do. I don't know how to save them. I don't know how to save myself." The moisture on her cheeks reflects the light from the orange sodium lamp.

I speak in the softest voice I can push out. Like sonic cotton. "Maybe you don't have to save the whole world."

She won't accept that. "Yes I do." Sodium orange streaks down her cheeks.

In one of his sermons, Father Price had said that his greatest goal was to show people God's love for them. There was hope. People have value and they can overcome trials in their life. God wants them to. He was rooting for you. I remember seeing Rosalind listening intently to every word that came out of his mouth. Like each one of them was small salvation. He convinced her. The next week he told us that we were all abandoned.

"You can overcome this. God wants you to," I say. Even though I'm not so sure I believe it. "He's on your side." I put my hand in the small of her back. The ring she wears on her right hand hurts when she hits me. Chips a tooth.

"I'm sorry," she says. "Can you forgive me?"

I always forgive her.

She says she feels like Job. Everything was taken away from him. His children, his health, his money. Why her? She doesn't understand. I tell her that God ends up rewarding Job's obedience during his travails and restores his health and doubles his original riches. He even fathers another seven more sons and three more daughters.

Yeah, she says, but his other children are still dead.

||

The rusty tin can has a nice roll of bills in it for a change. Rosalind counts them one by one and divides them into piles according to their denomination. "Thank God. But where on Earth did all of this come from?"

"Angel donor," Frosty says, chewing on a piece of dried meat. "Someone who really cares. Truly and deeply." He looks like the Cheshire Cat sitting there with that stupid grin on his face. Looking up at me. You could probably count every tooth in his head. "Sold their Porsche."

She slips the folded paper into her pocket. "This is really going to go a long way. How wonderful." But she keeps looking over. Out of the corner of her eye. She doesn't want to ask. But she wants to ask. Gathering her things she says goodbye. "Would anyone like to come with me?"

"Tony, why don't you go and help her carry all of that stuff she's gonna buy," Frosty says, before anyone else can get a word in.

I take my stack of paperwork and slip it into a plastic shopping bag. As I lift it the seam tears and the entire thing splits open, scattering the paper all over the basement. Frosty laughs. He laughs so hard that he starts to cough uncontrollably, making this irritating guttural noise to clear his throat, he spits onto the plate in front of him. "Excuse me," he says, wiping his mouth.

I kneel down and start trying to make sense of the now disparate sheets of paper on the floor. It's going to take forever. All of that work. "It's not funny. How am I supposed to sort all of this out now?"

"Is it important?"

"Of course it's important."

Frosty gets up from his chair. "You still don't get it do you?" He kneels next to me. "None of this stuff has anything to do with what's important in the world."

"I wouldn't have to do this if you hadn't taken my briefcase you know."

"And we wouldn't be getting fed tonight either." He watches me grab at the sheets. "Look at you! You're right on the verge of something bigger than yourself and you just let it get lost in paperwork like everyone else." He grabs the back of my head and shoves me into the small pile that I started. He rubs my face in it. I push against him but he snakes his arm around my neck and starts to squeeze. Tony's dog, Gertrude, starts to bark. "You're a fraud," he says. "You're nothing but a fraud."

I can feel my airway constricting. I try to talk but nothing comes out of my mouth except spit. He slips onto my back. Drapes his right forearm across my neck and places his left hand on the back of my head.

The dog barks.

"Nice transition," Birddog says. "See, told you it works well didn't I?"

His breath is hot against my ear. Spewing millions of bacteria down the canal where they'll take root. Absorbing their nutrients directly from my skin. Multiplying in the dark places where no one can see them.

"What do you want?" he says.

I try to say, "Let me go."

"What do you want?"

I squirm but it's no use.

His breath is moist. Bacteria love moisture. So do piranhas. Mosquitoes.

"In every story there is a protagonist. Every protagonist has to have a goal. You're the protagonist in your own story. What do you want? What is your goal?"

He squeezes a little harder.

"Are you repenting because Price told you that you should? To impress God? To get into heaven? Do you still want something for yourself out of all of this?" He gets even closer to my ear and whispers. "Do you want to fuck Rosalind the haphephobic? Good luck with that by the way." I try to suck some air into my lungs. What makes it in isn't enough though.

"If you wrap your legs around his torso it'll make it harder for him to buck you off," Birddog says. "Go ahead, try it."

"You pretend to be one of us. You pretend to be invested. But at the end of the day, you're still obsessed with making your little bit of money. With having your nice house, fancy car, and flashy little briefcase." Frosty switches to the left side. "But let me ask you something, what good are they to you now? Huh? Now that you can't breathe?" The dark soles of Frosty's shoes leave more streaks across the floor. He puts all of his weight on me. "Do you understand what I'm trying to teach you? All of that stuff is useless to you right now. At this moment. So, stop being so selfish. Stop thinking about yourself for a change."

Feeling good about our actions motivates giving. Not the pure altruism of the action. People are more likely to give when they think that it will make them feel better, or provide them with social leverage. It's not our fault. Any feel good sensation is driven by the brain's reward system. It's all biology. Get your little shot of dopamine. For some, it's the fear of God. A desire to get into heaven. Either way, you get something out of it.

"Do you give to charity when no one's looking? When you can't write it off your taxes?" The sweat beads off of my forehead and lands on the paper, smearing the ink of the signature on the dotted line. The dog keeps barking. "Could someone shut that thing up?"

People don't give to charity. They're sold on charities.

The people who do the marketing for charities know something. So did Stalin. Putting a specific face on an abstract problem opens hearts and wallets. Stalin once said that one death was a tragedy. A million is merely a statistic. Quantifying the scope of a disaster or a particular problem or a group of people lowers giving.

Please help. The devastation is unparalleled. Things are pretty tight right now, they say. My charity had a specific face. It's pressed up against my left ear. Grinding into it. Breaking down the cartilage. The other faces watch in stunned silence. We're in slow motion. If enough fluid builds up the ear can be permanently deformed. Cauliflower. That's what Birddog says.

By Frosty's definition it's pretty much impossible for anyone to be truly altruistic. Except maybe himself. Maybe he's right. My charity flexes his bicep and constricts my airway. His charities watch. "You're still selfish," he says. "Don't just give to get. Give yourself. Wholly. Yourself is the only thing that you have to give that actually means anything." He squeezes. "So stop fighting and just give it. Now." I pull on his forearm and gasp a quick breath. "You have to take yourself completely out of the equation. Like true love. You ever been in love?" True love is caring more about someone else than you do about yourself. But apparently it doesn't exist. We give love to get love. Dopamine. Orgasms. Even numbers. "God doesn't even love you unconditionally. Remember? You got to be better than him."

I try to flip over onto my back, hoping that the force of impact knocks him loose. Maybe he would hit the back of his head. He spreads his legs, lowers his centre of gravity, and drives my chest into the ground. I lose what little air I had left in my lungs.

The Lord tests the righteous, but his soul hates the wicked and the one who loves violence. Psalm 11:5.

I pull on his arm. Try to breath.

"Take yourself out of the equation. Just give it all."

My body is the powdered gelatin that they add to Jello to keep it together. It jiggles when you move it. Just add water. And bacteria. I stop resisting. Go limp. He tightens his grip. I can't breathe. He tightens his grip even more.

"That's it," he says into my ear.

He lets go a second before I choke out. I try to gasp for air but my throat is constricted.

"Slowly," he says. "Take it easy."

He helps me to my feet. Drapes my arm around his shoulder.

"Do you get it?" he says. "Now, do you understand?"

I nod.

"Good. Then we're all ready."

"Ready for what?" My voice is equal parts chainsaw and sandpaper.

"To get to the real work. But, we're going to need a few things first."

Everything gets charged to my credit card. Black pants, black shirts, black gloves. Black leather steel toed boots. Some rope and way too many pairs of handcuffs for anyone to really believe that they were only going to be used for sex. And stationary. It gets stashed under a pile of old boxes in the far corner of the church basement before Rosalind and Tony get back.

"I'm not in the mood for another lecture," Frosty says.

We eat quietly while we're waiting for the sun to set and for Rosalind to leave for work. She works a lot of weekend nights. Saturdays are a particularly busy time for crime scenes. You can't leave blood on the street. Federal regulations deem all bodily fluids to be biohazards. Any blood or tissue left at a crime scene is considered a potential source of infection. And in any violent death there are inevitably fluids to be cleaned up. Usually around the area where the body was found. Sometimes there's a trail of it leading down the hallway or through the alley. That kind of thing. She hated suicides. When a person cuts their wrists or shoots themselves in the head there's tons of blood. Each drop of which has to be treated as if it were carrying some blood borne pathogen. It takes forever to clean. The easiest calls, she said, was someone who's been shot in the chest because the lungs suck all the blood in.

Cleaning up a decomposing body, or a decomp, could be worse than a shooting or stabbing, Rosalind says. A body that's been deceased for days, weeks, or even months undergoes some changes. After death the body swells. Organs digest themselves. Insects move in. The skin liquefies. It's not pretty to look at but nothing compares to the smell. It's partly the result of ammonia being released during decomposition. You have to track down and burn the maggots that are filled with blood. They could be carrying pathogens.

"It's awful," she says.

My molars try to cut through a thick piece of fat that's being really stubborn. But I refuse to waste the calories. "Could we talk about this after we're done eating, maybe?" I give up and swallow the piece whole and hope that I don't choke.

She sighs, looking down at the food she's barely touched. "A person deserves more than that."

"Yes they do," Frosty says.

The small tinny TV speaker squawks as the expert panel on the news wraps up this week's special report on crime and the homeless population. The panel, with their impossibly white smiles, discuss the problem live via satellite. They say that at least one homeless person dies each month as a result of the disturbing new trend of 'bum bashing'. Many more are badly injured. It's like bell bottoms, miniskirts or neon t-shirts. There's an upsurge because it's popular. The expert panel says that they're being perpetrated by upper middle class youths under the influence, imitating each other.

Rosalind switches the TV off. "Don't watch too much of that boys, it'll rot your brain. Then I'll have to clean it up." She gathers her things. "I have to go," she says. "Can someone please take care of the dishes? God bless you all."

Frosty waves his hand and two people get up and start to clean.

Birddog walks me through some choke holds in the fading light of the evening. I know all about choke holds now. B.C.T. he calls it. Basic combat training. He says that if someone swings at you with a bat or a stick, the best thing to do is to rush forward, not backwards like your instincts will tell you to do. The point of force at the end of the bat is what you have to worry about. Don't give em' the opportunity. Come up under the chin. Eyes, ears, nose or throat. Don't forget about the groin. Grab it if you have to, he says.

We travel through an old sewer tunnel and pop out next to a pile of garbage under a burnt out street lamp.

It's cold out but that doesn't stop the entire city from coming alive. Every bar is full to capacity or lined up out the door. The party spills out onto the streets. A river of humanity winds itself down the sidewalks and through the alleyways. People scream and laugh. Music echoes around the wet gray buildings. Suits, ties, shiny shoes, and even shinier cars. Disposable income gets disposed of quickly here. Hands grab for it and pull it out of pockets. It gets eaten. Drank. Some of it is lost or wasted. It doesn't matter though. It's a reward for a week spent in cubicles or in offices or in meetings. I've forgotten what it's like. We linger on street corners or out of sight in the shadows of the back alleys, taking it all in.

Frosty spits. His eyebrows push together as he watches the bodies pass in front of him. "Must be nice," he says. "To have all that money to just blow. Must be nice." He paces slowly, in small circles. Puts his hands into his pockets and then takes them out again. He's anxious. He's looking for a fight. This is a popular area for homeless to come down to on the weekend. There's usually a lot of leftovers at the end of the night up for grabs. There's a cluster of pins on Frosty's map right where we're standing. We stay where it's the darkest and wait. It doesn't take long.

Just like Birddog taught him, Frosty moves forward to avoid the point of force. The end of the pole has nothing to hit. He twists it out of the guy's hand and drives the steel sole of his new boot through the knee. His friends run. They're not laughing anymore. Frosty elbows him across the jaw and then hits him hard in the temple as he falls to the pavement. We surprised them as they were stumbling through the space between two trendy hotspots. It's a short cut that a lot of people use and it's a place where you can almost always find something edible in the dumpster. The drunks started off just pushing the homeless man they found there. Calling him names and laughing. Shoving his face into the garbage he was sorting through. But when they didn't get the rise that they wanted, one of them picked up a loose piece of metal and brought it over his head. That's when Frosty sprung. Knuckles slamming against temples and kidneys. Handcuffs come out of his pocket and he ties the semi-conscious asshole tight to the piping along the side of the building.

The homeless man he saved steps up and takes Frosty by the shoulder. "Thank you," he says.

Before we get the hell out of there, Frosty takes out a folded piece of paper and sticks it into the semi-conscious guy's pocket. One last shot to the head for good luck. Then we're gone.

In between two walls that are plastered in graffiti, I fall to the ground and then I twist my body and wrap my leg around this guy's neck. He's a lot bigger than me. Younger and stronger and probably doesn't feel anything because of the tequila pumping through most of his body. He pulls against me but I stop him long enough for Birddog to kick him in the ribs and for Frosty to put him in a half-nelson. Paddy walks up and hits him in the stomach as hard as he can. The kid slumps to the ground gasping for breath. He's wearing a leather jacket that could feed us for a week and a thick gold chain around his neck. Paddy goes to take them both but Frosty stops him. That's not the way they're going to play this out.

He pulls out the handcuffs and puts them on so tight that the hands start to turn blue. A folded piece of paper slips into the pocket. The woman we saved takes Frosty by the hand. "Thank you." Then we disappear down a manhole and through a poorly lit access corridor. Lights flicker when traffic drives overhead.

We trudge through the inch of water that's settled on the ground. I rub my side. There's going to be a bruise there tomorrow. Frosty slaps me on the shoulder. "Atta boy," he says. "Now we're getting someplace." He starts to laugh. It's a genuine belly laugh. "I told you. Didn't I tell you? Together we're strong. Together, we can do anything."

The next morning, sprawled across the front page of the newspaper in bold black lettering is the word 'VIGILANTE!' Seems police are now on the lookout for person or persons responsible for at least two assaults in the downtown core that seem to be related. Any information regarding these crimes can be submitted anonymously through the police help line or through the official website. There's no mention of the people we saved.

Night time, moving through the narrow space between two slimy brick walls, we appear like a hoard of angry bees. Frosty isn't even the first one to swing this time. Birddog, Lucas, and James take down two guys that were pouring gasoline over a homeless man sleeping rough. They handcuff their arms and legs to each other and Frosty slips notes into each of their pockets before they get tossed in with the rest of the trash. Paddy asks if we should douse them with their own gasoline? Who's got a match?

"They're just kids," I say.

"Sure don't act like it."

Frosty's attitude is contagious. It spreads through all of us. Each victory intensifies it. It's fuel. The group eats it up in handfuls too big to fit into their own mouths.

In the club district, we get there too late. It looks like the body's been dragged behind the dumpster and left there. Contorted. Unconscious. Bleeding a lot and swollen. We watch as the paramedic says it's a code three into his radio. Then they load up the dirty twisted form into the back of the ambulance and speed off with the lights and sirens going full bore. They leave all the bags of cans and blankets behind. He won't even have a name. They'll call him John Doe. The investigation ends almost as soon as it starts and Rosalind shows up with rubber gloves and buckets. Ammonia and sodium peroxide. Just another Saturday night.

In the tunnel underneath, Frosty tenses up and punches the wall. "Jesus! We should have been there. We should have stopped it." I walk next to him through the dark passageway. The look in his eye is hidden by deep shadows. But I know it's there. I open my mouth but there's nothing to say. Nothing that will make anything better. Nothing that will put his soul at ease. He can say all the Hail Marys he wants. "Did you see his face?" The image plays over and over in his mind. Like a skipping record.

We start splitting up into two groups to cover more ground. I went with Frosty. Birddog and Tony took the others. We find Olive sleeping in a doorway down an alley behind a restaurant. Her lip is cut. The biggest rat I've ever seen sits next to her and eats something that's not identifiable. It's not even afraid of people anymore. Olive cowers and slides into the corner. We have to coax her out like a timid dog. Holding our hands out and rubbing our fingers together as though we have something to eat or something interesting to smell. Maybe a treat. She raises her chin and cocks her head to the side. We pick her up and help her to her feet. She tries to walk but she has a heavy limp so we wrap her arms around our shoulders and carry her along. "Thank you," she says. We take her back to the church basement and Frosty gives her his own bed for the night.

Now, the expert panel is talking about something different. The Vigilante. They each have their own theories. One of them says that resorting to intimidation or violence to resolve disputes or seek redress demonstrates citizens' lack of trust in their formal or informal justice system's ability to effectively enforce codified laws and procedures. They say that they can't condone vigilante justice. It undermines the letter of the law. The fabric of our whole society. No private citizen has the right. They all agree with somber bows of their heads. Coming up right after the break, they have, in their possession, one of the notes left behind by the vigilante. What does he have to say? Don't touch that dial.

At least we're good for ratings.

"Is your hand cut?" Rosalind asks Frosty. "Your knuckle is all torn."

"It's nothing," he says, and tries to hide it with his other hand. "Just scraped it, that's all. No big deal."

She reaches down to grab it but catches herself at the last second and retracts. I see a white bracelet slip out of her sleeve. It has black writing on it and a bar code. She turns her eyes away from me and pushes it back up her arm.

The woman on TV unfolds the piece of paper. The note, she says in a dry matter of fact voice, identifies the victim as the attacker in an episode of vagrant violence. The instigator of a vicious attack perpetrated against the most vulnerable members of society. However, no charges have been laid. The vigilante goes on to promise that they will put a stop to these senseless attacks permanently. That's fascinating Joanne, the other one says. Thank you Tom, the language contained within the note is too colorful to quote from verbatim, but you understand the gist of it. Back after these messages.

"Whoever is doing all that is just spreading the evil. Not fighting it," Rosalind says. "The only way to change the world is through kindness and compassion." Her voice is soft and defeated. She looks down at us. "Pray for and love your enemies. That's from the book of Luke." She exhales and sits. She stares blankly at her own hands. "Can someone else take care of making dinner tonight? I'm just too tired." I take her home and get her to bed. Through half closed eyes she purses her lips together and says, "I'm fighting another losing battle aren't I? There's no way to win."

I want to stroke the hair back from her forehead but I keep my hands on my lap. "The important thing is that you're fighting."

Her lips stretch just a little bit. "I wish there was time to finish," she says, turning her head and closing her eyes the rest of the way. She's asleep in seconds.

In the basement of the Holy Name, Frosty preaches his own gospel. "The only way to change the world is through violence," he says. "That's how it's always happened. It's called revolution."

It's two a.m. Some guy is on his knees under a dim yellow light hanging from a bare brick wall. Frosty punches him at the base of his skull. He falls forward and his head bounces off the greasy pavement, knocking him out. We drag him to a corner and pile him on top of his friends. Handcuff them to the rusty bars that cover the old metal door. Frosty looks over to Diggs lying next to the pile of garbage. He leans in to hit the limp body at his feet again but I grab his arm and pull him back. "He's had enough." Frosty doesn't say anything. He just looks at me like he wants to hit me too. "Let's get out of here," I say. We help Diggs to his feet while Frosty throws another letter onto the pile of bruised humanity. Diggs is a shaken up and bleeding from a cut on his cheek. We have to carry him most of the way back to the church where we meet up with the second patrol. Frosty pulls the key for the door out of his pocket and lets everyone into the basement.

Frosty and Birddog make routes for everyone to watch. Each patrol has its own turf to cover on any given night. Checkpoints and schedules. Military precision. It becomes a routine. Muscle memory. Frosty orders us to try and wake anyone we find sleeping. To make sure they're still alive. People deserve more dignity in death than to rot in an alley. They should be buried face up. Not mopped up, or absorbed with a sponge and washed away with ammonia.

When the weekend hit, we'd be out most of the night.

A lot of other things started to bug Frosty.

"Look at this fuck. Taking two parking spots to protect his precious fucking car. This is just the kind of fuck that teaches his asshole kids that they're better than everybody else cause they're rich." The full moon reflects off the hood of a car that probably costs as much as a small house. Lucas spits on the door handle. "There'd be a lot more to go around if these rich assholes didn't scoop it all up from everybody else. If they spread it around. Who even needs a car this expensive?"

Frosty kicks the driver's side door and leaves a size ten dent in it. "Piece of shit," he says, and spits. The alarm goes off but that doesn't stop the other guys from joining in. They laugh when they knock the rearview mirrors off, and they almost double over when Lucas takes a piece of loose asphalt and smashes the front windshield with it. "These pricks think they're so entitled to everything," Frosty says. They always want a little bit more. They always take a little bit more. Problem is, there's only so much to go around.

When you ask the average person what they would do if they were rich they usually respond with "I'd quit my job." But the people who get rich never do.

"Guys, we better get the hell out of here," I say. The alarm echoes across the streets. The lights flash.

Frosty snorts. That snort of derision. Then he tries to kick out the headlight.

"Look, you've ruined it already. Isn't that enough? Now let's get the hell out of here before we're arrested."

Frosty doesn't run away, like every fiber of my being is telling me to do. He walks away. This kind of thing is happening more and more. If Frosty can't find someone to save he has to find something expensive to destroy. With our numbers growing we split into a third patrol. I go with Frosty, Paddy, James, Lucas and Gibbs. Birddog takes Puppy, Colby and Violet. Tony takes Socks,

Diggs and Olive. We start going out more often. Covering more ground.

One night Frosty gets back to the church covered in blood.

12

Rosalind says that you can use meat tenderizer to get bloodstains out of fabric. You make a fifty-fifty paste with cold water and let it sit for fifteen minutes. You can also use ammonia but it sometimes discolors whatever it is you're trying to clean. For the concrete floor you dab the blood with cold water then cover the surface with a thin layer of sodium peroxide powder. It's highly toxic so don't breath any in. You don't want any coming into contact with your skin either so wear rubber gloves. This will also prevent contact with any pathogen that might be in the blood. Sprinkle the layer of sodium peroxide with a mist of water. Do this carefully, it's toxic. Let it sit for a few minutes then rinse the surface with clean water. It's very important that you do this thoroughly. If it remains on the surface the acid used for the bloodstain removal can still continue to etch through the concrete. Scrub the surface vigorously then coat it with vinegar to neutralize the remaining sodium peroxide. Rinse with water.

That knowledge ends up coming in handy.

Frosty slashes the tires of a BMW.

"I didn't know we were carrying knives now," I say. He doesn't answer. He just keeps looking straight ahead as we wind through the back alley maze. It's raining a little bit. Just enough to make it uncomfortable to be outside. It covers everything with a fine mist. Gives everything a halo. The loose pebbles and garbage crunches under our feet. Distant voices from the club strip reach us whenever there's a gust of wind. We see the shadow first. Its lines are crisp against the pale gray of the brick wall. Someone's standing there, holding something over their head.

We're already too late. He drops the cinder block on an old army green coat. Picks it up. Drops it again. One side of it is a deep red that almost looks black in this light. Frosty explodes. He charges in and shoves the guy against the wall. He hits hard but the guy still manages to knee Frosty in the stomach. Then he pulls out a knife and slashes across Frosty's abdomen. He doesn't let up. The tip lashes out. Up, down. Side to side. I run up behind him but he turns and slashes my forearm. This is real. I step back. The skin on my arm feels like it's been set on fire. Blood pools under the hand I'm holding it with. I can feel the warmth spreading.

The guy turns and tries to run but Frosty grabs him by the shoulder and spins him around. He's frantically waving the knife. It catches Frosty in the forearms and hands as he tries to protect himself. The rest of the patrol are frozen. They watch with wide eyes and tense muscles. The blood starts to drip from between my fingers. The harder my heart beats the more of it I lose. They're scared too. Picking fist fights was one thing but having a knife plunged into your chest was something else entirely.

Frosty backs up as the rain starts to come down hard. The sound of it hitting the broken pavement is deafening. It keeps the rest of the world out. The guy advances, making fast jerky motions with the tip of the knife. Frosty ducks to the side and spins around to face him again. From this angle I can see his eyes. I can see the concentration, I can see the hatred, I can see the resolve. It reminds me of a rabid animal. There's no rational thought anymore. He only wants one thing. And he's ready to die in order to get it. He wipes the water and hair from his eyes. It leaves a red streak across his forehead. One arm reaches around to his back. The guy takes advantage and lunges in. Frosty twists his body. The puddle beneath him explodes outwards as the two of them go down clutching at each other. Falling rain creates a haze over the ground. It envelops them like a blanket. A dark mass fumbles underneath. It rolls to one side and spins. Then it stops and there's nothing else in the alley except for the sound of the pounding rain.

The next morning the church basement smells like ammonia and vinegar. With just a splash of meat tenderizer. Father Price paces back and forth. Wring, wring. Skin flakes. Sign of the cross. "One resident in particular has been very vocal," he says. His voice tremors. It's almost unnoticeable if you weren't listening for it.

"The resident directly across from the church yard is very concerned about this. And frankly, so am I." The fury that wants to burst out of his chest, the one God's helping him to contain, is directed solely at me. I stand there, alone, being chastised by the Lord's earthly representative. Rosalind is gone. The rest scattered when they heard footsteps on the stairs. "What was going on out there last night that would cause such a commotion? What on God's green Earth?" Then, he stops pacing. His voice levels out. Like he just got dealt the last card of a royal flush. "And why was there blood outside?"

In the pouring rain we pulled Frosty out from underneath the motionless body. His arms and hands were covered in blood. The knife fell out of his hand and the sound it made when it hit the pavement was drowned out by the falling rain. His feet hung limp behind him while we wrapped his arms around our shoulders and dragged him off. The heavy rain concealed us. We moved between the buildings. Keeping to the dark spots. The guys knew them all. Every dark corner of the city. They navigated fluidly through the ink. Keeping us hidden. Invisible again. We pulled Frosty through the church yard. But when we got to the chipped metal door around back of the church, it was locked and we couldn't find the key.

"What exactly happed out there last night?" Father Price is accusing me of something. He says that helping the homeless is more than a matter of just opening doors. It would be nice if it were but it's a significant commitment. It requires more than just space. It requires people. It's a full time job. One that maybe we weren't up for. "So? What happened? Why is all that blood out there?"

I'm caught off guard. My mind shuffles through a list of adjectives and verbs. The only one that comes out of my mouth, though, is, "Nothing." That's technically a pronoun, I think.

He starts to pace again. The wringing of his hands goes into overdrive. "Well, this is completely unacceptable."

The rain never let up. Our panicked voices cut through it and bounced around the church yard. To a house that sat right in front of it. When Lucas finally broke into the church and opened the door for us, we fell into it like a biomass of king crab. Tripping over each other. The blood smeared across the floor and the counter. It pooled around the drain in the middle of the floor. We bandaged the slashes in our skin as best as we could. The bloody clothes were thrown out. People got to work. Ammonia, vinegar, meat tenderizer.

Hours later Rosalind showed up. She raised her chin and smelled the stagnant air of the basement. She didn't say anything. She didn't have to. Reaching into the small red purse that hung from her shoulder, she pulled out a key. She found it while cleaning up the remains of a double homicide downtown. She placed it on the table and slid it towards me. Tears streaking down her cheeks. She didn't even wipe them off anymore. "I lied for you," she says. Then she turned around and walked away.

Father Price says, "The road to hell is truly paved with good intentions. Hell is filled with good meaning but heaven is filled with good works. Keep that in your heart." He starts to walk away. "And I'm still unable to find the crucifix."

I turn my eyes towards the floor. "I'm sure it will turn up." Indeed, he says. The locks slides shut. The footsteps fade away.

The police say that a lot of blood was washed away by the heavy rain so it's hard to reconstruct exactly what happened in the alley. They'd appreciate any leads. Call this toll free number if you know anything regarding this horrific crime. Be a good Samaritan. Two bodies were found. One was a John Doe. The other was a nineteen year old kid from an affluent upper middle class family. His parents were in tears on the news. They want to see justice done. He was a good boy. Had his whole life ahead of him. He wanted to become a doctor. Police found the bloody cinderblock and two knives on the scene. They're on the lookout for a third person of interest. "Although confirmation does not exists, in the form of a letter that the perpetrator would leave behind, we have strong reason to believe that this crime was committed by the same individual who is responsible for numerous other cases of assault and vigilante justice throughout our city." The flashbulbs go off. The police chief stands behind the podium with a stern expression on his face. He points at the cameras. Let the professionals handle this, he says. We're here to serve and protect. "Private citizens must not take it upon themselves to enforce the law. If you see something, call the police."

'An eye for an eye, a tooth for a tooth, a hand for a hand and a foot for a foot.' It said so in the Bible. Exodus 21:24.

Outside, a group of local residents are talking to some news cameras. We haven't exactly gone unnoticed lately. They want the homeless people gone. They've been putting pressure on their city councilor. It's an election year. "This probably isn't an ideal place for vulnerable individuals to be," they say. "We're afraid that the residents of the shelter are going to fall prey to a lot of illegal activity that exists not far from here." They're concerned for the helpless. How nice. I've never seen a bigger pile of bullshit in my life.

The guy I talked to before stands in front of them all. He's the one with the house right in front of the churchyard. "We're concerned for our kids. A lot of these people have mental issues. It's just not safe. There are a lot of families in this neighborhood. We have to think about the children."

I'm there with Paddy, Lucas, Gibbs, and Olive. We watch the proceedings while we clean the blood from the outside of the door. Paddy spits. "I guess they don't like having us around then."

"I don't know about you guys, but I stink," Gibbs says. "I wouldn't want me around either." We laugh.

The guy waving his cup of hazelnut coffee looks right into the camera. "They don't stay in the church. They leave. They're... around." God forbid. "The community simply doesn't have the resources they need. There isn't even a public washroom available. Where should they go during the day? They should be housed properly at the community shelter." Fifteen blocks away. That raises the average price of a home in this area by at least ten percent.

Judge not, that you not be judged. For with the judgment you pronounce you will be judged and with the measure you use it will be measured to you.

"Frosty's right," Paddy says. "It's us against them. They'll get what they want, at our expense. Just like they always do. How is he doing?"

"He'll be okay," I say. "Just needs a few days rest. He really should have went to the hospital."

"He can't even afford to eat." Paddy buries his face into the palms of his dirty hands with the black finger tips. "I swear," he says, "I'll never be scared, like I was that night, ever again." Lucas, Gibbs, and Olive agree. "He took me in, made me stand up straight for a change. And I went and let him down. That's not going to happen again." Lucas, Gibbs, and Olive agree. "I'll be there for him. I swear."

"Don't worry," I say. "He'll be alright. And, look, maybe you should make yourselves a little scarce right now." The crowd is starting to chant something. The news cameras are pointing at us. "I have to go finish up some work. I'll be back later on tonight."

Stamp.

"These all seem to be in order," Mr. Howard says as if he's looked every policy over personally. He obviously didn't or else he would have noticed the thirteen extra policies that I slipped into the middle of the pile. Right where I knew they would go unnoticed. He slaps the stack against his desk to square them all up and then calls his assistant over to collect them.

Stamp.

"What happened to you?"

The yellow lining around my eyes from the fading bruises make it look like I have jaundice.

"Don't worry, it's not contagious."

I had taken out policies on everyone living in the basement of the Holy Name. If anything happened to any of our group RDC Holdings would still make money from the COLI and their leader, Frosty, the beneficiary of the RDC Holdings employee policy, could distribute the payout as he saw fit. It might get the rest of them off the streets. It would take a serious audit for anyone to catch it. I feel good about this. For once in my life I feel like I'm doing something meaningful through the work I do.

Stamp.

They're listed as administrative assistants. Low salary jobs. Nobody would notice. I give them the address of the church on Bain Ave.

Stamp.

I'm counting. That's the one.

"Is that what you carry your paperwork in?"

"Yeah."

His eyebrows twitch. "Anyway, have you thought anymore about what we talked about? About you coming to work directly for us?" He points at the plastic bag that's balled up in my hand. "Maybe get you something nicer to carry your work around in." He snorts. That snort of derision. "This is a start anyway." He slides an envelope across his desk. It's a check. And it's not small. "A consultant fee. For all your help. More on the way, once we run through the rest of these policies." He leans back in his chair. "Have security escort you out."

I weave through the crowds singing, chanting, sleeping, cooking, screaming, and bathing in the giant fountain that's in the square at the base of the crystal phallus. They don't reach out at me this time. Because I look as if I don't belong. My suit is stained and wrinkled. My hair is oily and it sticks out in every which direction.

I'm holding a crumpled up plastic bag in my hand. They scream at the rich people behind all that glass. They throw anything they can get their hands on. They want the world to be fair. They're fighting for it. The mood is tense. The people are angry.

Back at the church, the street's lined with fire trucks and cop cars. Flashing red and blue lights. People in uniform walking fast and asking a lot of questions, taking note of everything that they hear with little yellow pencils into little folded leather pads. A thick gray haze hangs in the air. It smells like scotch. Single malt. The house directly across from the churchyard is leveled to ashes. What's left still smolders as the fire department douses it with water. It's easy for me to slip by unnoticed.

In the church basement everybody's gone. Everything's gone. Except for the trash. Father Price is scooping it into big green bags. He's wearing the rubber gloves that Rosalind used to scrub the floors down before we had moved anybody in. He looks at me with half open eyes. Shrugs his shoulders.

"You didn't," I say.

"I wasn't given much of a choice." He keeps looking down at his work. "The situation was getting quite out of hand." It's amazing how devout people can be when their religion doesn't ask anything from them. Frosty is right. The only way to really be a part of anything was to give everything to it and expect nothing in return. Now the black clothes with the white collar seems to suit him more. We had eaten the apple and we were now exiled because of it. Back out into the untamed wild to beg for loose change and freeze to death. Out of the garden forever.

Residents in the area had contacted their city councilor. It's an election year so he sends over an inspector who determines that the church is a fifty-year-old public safety building that's not up to code. It's going to take ten thousand dollars to get it to a level that's appropriate for people to sleep in there overnight. Then the insurance company chimes in. They said that their policy would not protect the parish in the case of a lawsuit because housing the homeless does not fall into the realm of normal church activity. They weren't even allowed on the property at certain times of day.

"We could have lost the church. There was no other way." He says this as he picks up an old pair of socks that were left behind and places them into the bag. "And I don't think that any of them really appreciated what we were doing for them. They wouldn't even attend service." He ties the bag closed and tosses it into a pile with the rest of them. "That wasn't a lot to ask."

"But if anyone has the world's goods and sees his brother in need, yet closes his heart against him, how does God's love abide in him?" That's what I say.

"The gospel of John," he says, and looks down, "that doesn't really apply in this situation I'm afraid."

It never does.

Just like that, they're all back on the streets. Huddled over grates. Diving through dumpsters. Getting cinder blocks thrown on their heads. It happens that fast. In a week, nobody will even remember they were even here.

I knock on Rosalind's door. There's no answer. Her neighbor says that she's in the hospital for another round of chemotherapy. The cancer kept coming back. It was relentless.

There wasn't much time.

When I track her down and sit next to her bed she sighs and says that she wished God had made her a lesbian. Men had been the cause of everything bad in her life. And to top it all off she's probably going to hell soon. "That's why I had to leave," she says. "There's just no more time." Every last minute had to be spent making up for it. For losing her faith. The heart monitor beeps. The IV drips. The rosary she clutches in her hands leaves little purple bruises across her skin. She doesn't want to talk about it. The stiff hospital sheets sound like balled up paper when she rolls over to look out of the window. She still had hate in her heart and wanted it gone before the end. I can't help myself. I tell her everything. Confess it all. Everything. I have to do it to clean my soul.

Forgive me father for I have sinned.

She never wants to see me again.

13

It's easy to fall back into old habits. Even if you didn't like them much in the first place. I sit at a desk at work and drink coffee from a paper cup, cold calling people who don't need what I'm selling. I arrange stacks of papers into simple geometric shapes. Hand people pens. Sign here. I sit on the couch alone and watch TV. Tables are meant for even numbers. I sit on the cold toilet seat at three a.m. trying to push out a non-existent bowel obstruction. Sometimes I walk. I walk our old routes, but I haven't seen anybody in weeks. Ever since that night in the basement at the Church of the Holy Name. I've checked the usual spots. It's like they sailed off the end of the earth without me. Man the braces.

'No man shall be able to stand before you all the days of your life, so I will be with you.' Joshua something, verse something, something. I should have expected it.

The off-ramp near the highway. The subway station. The back alley just after last call. There's a size ten footprint in the dirt next to the dumpster. A sign written on a piece of cardboard box. Crumbs from a dog treat. It's like I'm always one step behind them. They're on the move. Jumping in between the dark spots. They know them all. The police stepped up their presence since they found the two bodies in the alley. They fly overhead in helicopters. Looking down at the sleeping city with infrared and thermal cameras. The city had recently passed new by-laws. It was now illegal to sleep outdoors or in vehicles, lie down, share food, or camp in any public spaces. There were curfews in the parks. They wanted people off the streets at night. Frosty used to say that he was forced to break the new laws that kept cropping up. That he had no other choice. He said that society turned him into a criminal so that they could arrest him and get him off their nice clean streets. It worked. I couldn't find them anywhere.

My boss talks to me about something that he says requires my immediate attention. He's been trying to sort this out with me for a long time. I think. I've been avoiding him. Most relationships don't last, they say. It's the norm. A universal human experience. People are in your life one day and then the next they're not. The divorce rate is something like fifty percent. The best thing to do is to stop thinking about them. Living well is the best revenge, they say. He shuffles through some papers. Holds something up for me to look at. I nod.

"I see." It's an automatic response. Something you say so that the person talking to you will think that you're paying attention.

But that part of the brain that kicks in when your eyes glaze over and you find yourself standing in a room for no particular purpose keeps asking: After all that? Rewind, repeat. After all that? Rewind, repeat. You have that feeling in your stomach. Like you're constantly falling. How could you?

Abandoned even by God. It's no wonder.

"So you should head down there and look into it." He folds the paper that he's holding in half and sets it on top of the 'outgoing' pile on the corner of his desk. "I know I can count on you to take care of that." He changed his cologne and he obviously wanted everybody to notice.

"Right away," I say, but I have no idea what he's talking about.

"I'm sure that Mr. Howard will give you everything you need."

The bag with my paperwork in it rips open as I weave my way through the crowds of people that have now set up camp at the base of the gleaming dick. It seems bigger than it did before. Like it's been aroused by all the attention it's getting. The papers scatter in the wind. It's hopeless. I let them all go.

The megaphone squeals that the eighty-five richest billionaires on the planet have as much money as the three point five billion poorest. The one percent pretty much own everything. And it's only getting worse. If current trends continue, the one percent will own more than fifty percent of the world's wealth by next year. The crowd erupts. The guy screaming into the megaphone holds it up the way a weightlifter displays the iron plates for just a moment before dropping them to the ground. One foot forward. Back straight.

This was the center of the protests for this particular city. This cluster of buildings was the financial hub. Where all the rich companies and billionaire CEOs set up shop. Mr. Howard's office overlooked it all. The huddled masses. It's happening all over the world now. A coalition of over fifty charities and different organizations mobilized the protests across the globe. It's making headlines. Panels of experts discuss it on the news. It's a growing trend, they say. Like bell bottoms or neon clothing. People are getting fed up as the gap between the rich and poor keeps growing and swallowing them up whole. They camp out in the financial districts. Storm buildings. Some of them break windows and set fire to the occasional car. They chant. Hold up signs.

"Down with the one percent!" people yell.

Cheers. Clapping.

"Ninety-nine percent against the one percent!" Megaphones. Fists in the air. "They have to pay their share!" The super rich don't pay taxes. One billionaire was quoted saying: 'We don't pay taxes. Only the little people pay taxes.' They don't give anything. But they take everything. It's painted everywhere throughout the crowd.

The police make a line in front of the revolving doors that I had to get through. They're carrying clear Plexiglas shields and they wear helmets. Black Kevlar vests with POLICE printed on the chest in bold white letters. They carry pepper spray and there's a high pressure water hose on standby. The crowd inches towards them. Occasionally one of them gets too close and takes a clear Plexiglas shield to the face.

Someone stops me and wants me to sign something. A petition started in the pages of a notebook. They want a Robin Hood tax initiated to address the growing wealth inequality. "The money from financial transaction taxes could be used for social programs for the rest of us," the smelly guy says. Education, health care, affordable housing. Preferably in safe, up and coming neighborhoods. The protesters want them implemented globally but will settle for regionally or unilaterally by individual nations.

"We need a fair and substantial contribution by the financial sector. A sizeable transfer of wealth to the needy," they say, through the megaphone. "One person doesn't need all that money. Not when it could help so many others."

It's written on their leaflets. There's pictures of families feeding their children rotten food. Bold red type. Exclamation marks. Fists in the air. They want to tax a wide range of asset classes. The sale of stocks, bonds, commodities, unit trusts, mutual funds, and derivatives like futures and options. I read that some asshole spent $95,000 on a four pound white truffle that looked more like a turd than anything edible. How many hungry people could that have fed? Everybody says that if the super rich dropped a hundred dollar bill, they'd actually lose money by taking the time to stop and pick it up. Time is money.

I look at the spaces in between the bodies. Trying to find a familiar face. Frosty talked about the protests. He called them brothers in arms. I weave my way through the entire encampment but I don't see any signs of him or anyone else. I walk around again. Nothing. A government representative with a microphone says that a financial transactions tax would reduce the total volume traded with negative consequences for employment. The few people listening to him boo. He says it could lead to job losses in the non-financial sector as well. He called it the multiplier effect.

Boooooooooooooooo.

The economy would go back into recession and the problem would get worse.

Booooooooooooooooo!

They use big words to describe the problem hoping that people would resign to something they didn't understand. Acquisition indigestion. Asset valuation reserve. Capitulation and collaborative consumption. Everything has a fancy name now to make it seem more benign. Even bathroom tissue, dental appliances and occasional irregularity.

It would equate to an overall loss of tax revenue, he says. Social programs would suffer.

Boooooooooooooooo!

I finally get through. The hard soles of my shoes clicking against the Italian marble floor is all I can hear as soon as the door closes behind me. The human cacophony, just a few feet away through the soundproof plate glass floor to ceiling windows, seems like it's on another planet now. No expense was spared.

Mr. Howard looks me up and down. "You look like shit," he says, and snorts. That snort of derision. "You need a new suit." He walks around his desk and eases into the leather chair with a sigh of satisfaction. "Maybe try doing something with your hair." Then, he takes off his glasses and rubs the bridge of his nose between his thumb and forefinger. He's lost a bundle, he tells me. And he's not very happy about it. He speaks slowly. Methodically. Explains everything that's happened. The logic was to buy shares in the China Life insurance company. Give them a whack of new business in the form of thousands of policies. Watch the shares go up. Make some extra money. Except that's not what happened. China's security regulators decided to crack down on margin trading, he says.

Yadayadayada.

My mind keeps swaying back to the unanswered question. I'm like the dog that gets abandoned in the country when a new baby arrives. The goldfish that gets flushed down the toilet before a family vacation. The clothes you once wore every day that now sit in a donation bin. The expendable element. Life goes on without me.

Shares dropped ten percent, he says. The daily limit. The whole market's down eight. I think he says eight. He talks and talks. I couldn't give a shit.

I should have been listening more closely though.

There are hints of Frosty everywhere I look. In the stories that are printed in the newspaper. Luxury vehicles had been vandalized over the past week. It seems that the perpetrators used thermite along with a fuse made out of dollar store sparkler placed on the exhaust manifold to burn out the engines. The manifold heats up and ignites the sparkler which in turn ignites the thermite which burns through the engine.

You can make thermite out of aluminum and rust. It's easy. And once it's lit there's nothing you can do to put it out. Birddog learned about it in the army. They used thermite hand grenades to destroy cryptographic equipment when there was a danger that it might be captured by enemy troops, he said. The destruction is complete. A classic use of thermite was to disable artillery. Frosty wanted to know more. You can use copper too. It's easy. It burns at over 4500 degrees Fahrenheit so any water that you throw at it will evaporate before it ever makes contact.

"So, you see that we're going to have to do some damage control here. Divert attention. You understand?" Mr. Howard says.

"I see." It's just a thing that you say so that the person talking to you thinks that you're paying attention. It's polite.

I should have been listening more closely.

Some billionaire decided that he'd treat a bunch of homeless people to lunch at the fanciest restaurant in town. Because the best way to spend all of that money is on a publicity stunt. He wants people to know how rich he is. That's why they get the bright red sports cars. A bunch of homeless sat down to crab cakes and wine. Rare steaks. Foisgras. The billionaire announces that he's also going to give everyone present money. Three hundred dollars to help them out. But homeless advocacy groups say that many homeless have drug and alcohol problems and giving them that much cash is the wrong thing to do. So they put a stop to it and collected the money themselves. Twenty cents of every dollar goes to helping people. Administrative costs were a bitch. Our billionaire was trying to get a round of 'We Are The World' started when a chair flew through the picture window at the front of the restaurant. They trashed the place. By the time I get there everybody's gone. Scattered or arrested. The whole restaurant is turned inside out. I can see Frosty's afterimage. He has a knack for getting people angry.

"You're the victims here," he would say, "this is targeted specifically towards you. And it's going to keep getting worse, not better. Unless you fucking do something about it you're going to be erased. Your lives will have meant nothing." He snapped his fingers for dramatic effect. I taught him that too.

"You're dang right it is. Lock and load." Birddog would always follow the H.M.F.I.C. And that's what Frosty had turned into. The Head Mother Fucker In Charge. It's an infantry term. They say the success of a movement depends on the first follower. There's science behind it.

Frosty once punched me in the stomach. I doubled over. "Doesn't feel good does it? So what are you going to do about it?" Life isn't fair but you have the power to make it fair, he said. "You have to hit me back." There's one thing that brings everybody down to the same level. Violence. And he was more than willing to cast the first stone. An eye for an eye, a tooth for a tooth. "You just have to have the guts to do it." Most sensible people go out of their way to avoid a fight.

The whole group believed in him. They followed everything he did. Trusted everything he said. It's easy to do. Make a fist and swing. We'll do it together. He propped them up. Made them feel useful and wanted. Like they were part of something bigger than themselves. Like they were part of a family again. One that I'd been kicked out of.

Mr. Howard talks and talks. I couldn't give a shit.

I should have been listening more closely.

"So we're going to try and get the entire process out of the limelight and grease a few palms. Just remember to stay calm and don't do anything rash. Okay? Okay," he says.

"I see, I mean, okay."

He's pressing his fingertips together as though there's an invisible piece of glass between his hands. Just like I used to do. It helped me get into character. The leather chair doesn't squeak when he shifts his weight. "Before I forget," he says, "here's your check." He slides it across the polished wood of his desk. It's just as big as the first one. "So what do you think?"

I don't really have anything to say. But he keeps staring at me with a look on his face like he just saved my life. My lips are dry. They stick together when I try to open them. What comes out of my mouth is a burst of air followed by a nonsensical low frequency pop. The look on his face doesn't change. "This is great. Thank you very much." I know what's coming next. "I'll have security escort me out."

"That would be great," he says.

Weaving my way through the crowds and tents I think I see Frosty. He's gone in an instant. Was that Tony? Olive? I'm going crazy. There are shadows of people everywhere. In the dark corners. Frosty knows every single one of them. He can move between them and stay invisible.

I end up walking around. Through the crowds. Across the streets and down the alleys. Nobody even notices that I exist. They can't even see me. I'm like a poltergeist. I'll set something down and you'll have no idea how it got there. I walk through the churchyard at the Holy Name. There's still blood smeared across the metal door that leads to the basement. I walk past the place that Rosalind rents. The lights are out. When I finally stumble up to where I live, the cops are waiting for me.

They put me in handcuffs. RDC Holdings, their subsidiaries, and consultants, and who else knows, are all under investigation for insurance fraud and I'm heavily involved. The CEO of the Jianchi Daodl Corporation reported an accident and made out with bags of money from the insurance claim before anyone found out that the people who died didn't even exist. They see that I've been paid recently by RDC Holdings. As an insurance consultant. I've recently paid my bills with that money. My mortgage. So they're taking my home.

14

The State Vs. 50 Cambridge Av.

That's what the papers say.

My condo's been charged with a crime. Not me. Not yet. But my condo has. Because payments towards the unit were made with money from questionable circumstances. Namely a massive insurance scandal originating from the offices of RDC Holdings. They're not available for comment at this time though.

If the police suspect you've committed a crime they arrest you and put you on trial. At the trial you're innocent until proven guilty and prosecutors must prove your guilt beyond a reasonable doubt. But if police suspect that your house was involved in a crime, or benefited from one, they can take it, sell it, and pocket the proceeds to buy that fancy new marguerita machine they've had their eye one. They don't even need to prove you've committed a crime, charge, or even arrest you. It's called civil forfeiture.

"Fight all you want," the cop says, as I thrash my arms, "you'll just end up in jail. And right now this place doesn't belong to you. I'll ask you one more time, can I have the keys?" He holds out his hand. I spit in it. Now I'm charged with assault.

We've been conditioned to bow down to uniforms. Like some sort of Pavlovian dog. Stop. Freeze. Put your hands up. Ding, ding. Wipe your mouth. You're drooling. Flashing red and blue lights keep everybody in line. It's the Milgram experiment all over again. I'm not falling for it anymore. He wipes his hand on his pants. Then another one grabs me from behind and wrenches my arm around my back. The cold metal handcuffs press against my wrist. I sit on a hard wooden bench while my lawyer talks to me through the bars.

It's going to be a tough ride, he says. The house is guilty until proven innocent. The onus is on me to prove it's clean. I paid my mortgage with the consultant fee from RDC Holdings. Tried to get a little ahead. That's what we're taught to do. Only one percent of seized property is ever returned to their former owner. Most people weren't even charged with a crime. Policing for profit. They're going to sell my condo and keep the money. And there's nothing you can do about it.

"I'll do what I can," the lawyer says. "But I'm not sure it'll amount to much." He takes out a pad and pen. "So where should I send my invoice now that you're moving?"

The police, the ones who serve and protect, are getting greedy. An amendment to the law that governs the revenue, that's what they call it, of civil forfeiture now entitles all branches of law enforcement to a portion of the net proceeds of forfeitures they help make. As a result, the amount of money sucked out of peoples pockets by the boys in blue shot up by 1,400%. The State vs. one pearl necklace. The State vs. one Gold crucifix. The State vs. $17,500.00. The State vs. 50 Cambridge Av. You can't make this stuff up. The burden of proof is on the owner not the police. And they don't make it easy. They can spend the money on whatever they want. New toys, professional development in Hawaii, or booze for the Christmas party. It doesn't matter. I'm fucked. That's what my lawyer says the next time I see him. He also says that he can't do any more work for me until I've settled my bill for services already rendered.

Then I find out I'm fired.

"You look like hell. Where did you spend the night?" my boss says, swiping a lint roller across his suit jacket.

"It's a long story."

He spreads his hands across his desk. The gold tiepin keeps it perfectly straight down the seam of his shirt. It has stripes on it at forty-five degree angles. "I bet it is. But you understand our position. Don't you? This company cannot be associated with any perceived criminal activity. The policy is clear."

"But I haven't been charged with anything."

"Nevertheless. We have to engender an image of trust. Caring. Compassion. For God's sake we sell insurance here. "

Oh, the irony.

"I'm sorry," he says. "But I'm afraid we're going to have to let you go."

It can happen that fast. To anyone.

Financial experts say that you should have at least six months worth of living expenses in the bank, just in case. You never know what can happen. Most people are too busy living beyond their means to think about it. New cars, new technologies, new clothes, and kitschy art to decorate the new house that you can't really afford. Keep six months worth, they say. Just in case. Like everybody else, I didn't. And my credit card is maxed out. My boss doesn't even have to give me severance in this circumstance, so he doesn't. The little money that I have left is gone fast. City living is expensive.

After our last meeting it's no wonder that Father Price cites the insurance clause as the reason that I'm not allowed to stay at the church for the night. It's windy under the Fourth Street Bridge and there's people screaming at each other. I end up walking around all night. I don't sleep a wink. I know from experience that most of the worst crimes in the city happen at night to people living outdoors. Around three in the morning I find a park that's free from the usual drunks and addicts breaking the curfew law. I sit down and take off my shoes. My feet are swollen and moist.

"Hello."

The cop walks by me slowly.

"There's a curfew in effect on all public parks."

"I'm sorry I…"

"You're going to have to move along."

At least he doesn't catch me with my eyes closed.

The protest downtown runs around the clock. The people don't ever leave. They occupy the same space, they say. They pitch tents and cook food. The city had to bring in a bunch of portable toilets so that the surrounding pockets of vegetation, and all that lovely corporate art, would stay clean of human waste. I end up huddled around a small coal grill next to some guy that smells like rotten avocado. He gives me a piece of jerky to eat. I'm pretty sure it's homemade. Definitely homemade.

"We have to stand up for ourselves," he goes off, "stick together. Show them that we won't be ignored any more. There's power in numbers. Did you know that the top one percent own forty percent of the nation's wealth? What are the rest of us supposed to do?"

I stare into the dying embers of the coal, trying to chew the jerky just soft enough to swallow it down in one big gulp.

"And did you know that the top one percent have only five percent of the nation's personal debt? It's all these rich guys, getting richer thanks to our backs. We'll show them though. We have to exercise our political power. Together. That's what this is all about."

It scratches my throat on the way down but it takes the hunger pains away for a minute.

The moisture in the air condenses in the early morning hours leaving everything slightly damp. Then the sun comes up. The world starts its daily routine once again. Dogs are walked. Jobs are done. Errands are run. People start spending. It's what makes the world go 'round.

I haven't slept in something like thirty hours. I'm seeing things. Mostly birds. It looks like there's a lot of birds in the sky all the time. My hair is greasy. It sticks to my scalp in plumes letting everybody know that I'll be bald soon. My tie is rolled up in my pocket. I push my way to the front doors of the building but the police and security won't let me inside to see Mr. Howard. They say, "Sorry sir, you have to move along." I say, "But I'm employed by RDC Holdings." They say, "Sorry sir, you have to move along." One of them plays with the pepper spray that's clipped to his belt.

One little bump in the road. Or one big bump. I can only think of two things right now. Sleep and food.

"First of all, you get yourself a sleeping bag. However you have to," Frosty said. He told me that was the most important thing about living rough. However you have to. It's getting harder and harder, but the best places to sleep are in public. It's safer. And try to sleep during the day. If you're going to sleep rough at night, try to find others that are doing the same thing. But make sure they're not drunk, high, or crazy. Rooftops were good for getting a little shut eye. But most of the time they were hard to come by. Stay away from abandoned buildings. They're dangerous.

I walk aimlessly around a grocery store looking for free samples. I've walked through these shiny white aisles a thousand times, raising my hand and saying 'no thank you' to people wearing paper hats and offering a taste of cinnamon roll, Mediterranean chicken, or some strong smelling cheese that came on the end of a long stick. They're all gone today. The one time I would have happily said, 'yes, don't mind if I do,' and nibbled on the flaky dry crust of a small quiche tart. You can find them in the freezer aisle. My clothes are wrinkled and stained. My hair is greasy and matted to my head. It's not long before I'm escorted out of the building by security. Sir, if you're not going to buy anything you'll have to vacate the premises.

Move along sir. No loitering.

The soles of my shoes skim the concrete. I don't have the energy to lift them up all the way anymore. I plod along like one of those zombies you see in the movies. Staring straight ahead. Swaying from side to side. The occasional grunt. People steal glances and keep moving. There's obviously something wrong with that guy. Is he drunk? It's still early in the morning. Hardly any time has passed. Like it just decided to freeze all of a sudden. It's too tired to keep moving forward. Just like me.

The automatic doors open and I slip inside the lobby of a hotel unnoticed. There's a public computer so guests can stay connected while they're traveling. It's a relic. Most people carry around computers in their front pockets now. But it still works. There's nothing in my inbox except an invoice from my lawyer that has a star next to it. I try a last ditch effort. Givemesomemoney.com. A large donation was made a couple of days ago. But, the money's already been taken out. Frosty.

"Excuse me sir? Are you a guest registered here at the hotel?" Security escorts me out. I need to sleep.

15

There's a latch on the inside of the grating that you can unhook with a little piece of bent metal if you jiggle it. It's hard to find in the dark. I slip through. It's cold and damp but at least it's private. My socks will never dry down here and the cold air stings my bare feet. I roll out the sleeping bag that I stole from some guy at the protest while he was busy screaming some slogan. Get one however you can. That's what Frosty said. It's red and the tag says that it's rated to minus thirty. I'm starving but I can't bring myself to do anything about it yet. I've thought about it a lot though. Thought about begging. Hunger is a very humbling thing. I could do it just long enough to get something to eat. Just long enough. That's all I need. I could make a sign. Route through a dumpster. It's humiliating. Humbling. I wish I were invisible. I might as well be down here.

The ends of my toes are light purple.

When I go looking for food I get kicked in the ribs and my back stomped on. I spit out blood onto the oily pavement. It smears against the sleeve of my jacket. The cuff of my shirt. You don't even have the energy to run after not eating for a couple of days.

The fight is over some moldy fruit. He says the dumpster is theirs. There's only one of him. They owned it and everything in it, he says. He coughs a lot. There's scratch marks all over his forearms and neck. He hops inside the dumpster and closes the lid. I can hear him talking to nobody inside.

When the sun comes up I start walking. I have no destination. I just walk. I need something to eat. The faces around me look angry. Like they're happy I got what I deserved. An eye for an eye, a tooth for a tooth. I formulate a plan. My first instinct is to tell the long-winded story.

"I'm sorry sir, I hate to bother you but…"

But nobody ever wants to hear that. That's what Frosty said. They don't even slow down. They look at their phones, shrug their shoulders, or just raise their hands to your face. The more compassionate ones would say, sorry. I managed to sleep for a couple of hours in the tunnel, wrapped in the sleeping bag with my knees pressed against my chest. Someone could steal it if they happened down there while I'm gone but I can't carry it around all day. I need some food. Frosty told me that you have to stake out the best places to find food. You have to check them often. And be thorough. But be careful, it's more than likely that they'll be someone else there scoping it out too, and things can get pretty territorial.

They own this dumpster. And everything in it. You can't think straight.

"Move along," the cop says. No loitering.

He stands there and watches me leave. Watches me until I've rounded the corner. The sides of my abdomen feel like someone is twisting knives into them. My hands are cemented to my gut. I'm almost doubled over. At this point the decision is easy. "Spare some change for something to eat?" Short and sweet and to the point. It keeps the humiliation down to a minimum. Reduces the amount of contact. With any luck they forget your face after two steps. Or once they walk by the next guy. But there wasn't a next guy. I've only seen two other people living on the street in the past couple of days. They're both completely out of their minds. I hear word that the shelters are half empty nowadays so I decide to check one out. I figure that it will at least keep me out of sight. The rumors are true. There's barely anyone there. I grab a quick meal and check the place out. The people who are there are not the kind of people that you want to sleep next to. They reek of urine and spend most of their time wandering the halls screaming. One of them pulls out a broken bottle and starts swinging it around. I decide to spent the night in the tunnel instead. At least I'd be left alone there.

The grate's been shut. Someone's been through here. My sleeping bag is gone. I should have taken the time to hide it better.

It's quiet. The only thing I hear for awhile is the steady drip of water that falls from the pipes on the ceiling. Where I should have hidden it. Like Frosty used to do. I almost fall asleep for a second. My head bobs and I almost drift off but something keeps me awake. A noise. There are voices that echo down the smooth concrete walls. They're getting closer.

It's cold. There's blood on my clothes and I'm shivering. There's a low rumble in the distance every couple of minutes when the subway goes by. The footsteps are here. They're right in front of me. Only the tips of their noses poke out of the deep shadows cast by the flickering overhead light as they turn and look my way. They slow down, look, but they don't stop. The same thing happens a few hours later when they come back. They're carrying something this time. At least they leave me alone.

Move along says the cop. Get a job says the businessman.

A new by-law passed in city council makes it illegal to ask for anything of value of another human being in and around tourist attractions. They say it's a law designed to protect tourists from mistreatment. Also next to a bus stop, public bathroom, train station, taxi stand, or any time after dark.

Move along says the cop.

I walk. I walk all over the city. With no place in particular in mind. I don't care anymore. I want to be selling insurance. I miss stacking the papers. Passing the pen. I want to be in my office. It was warm inside and you could get free coffee down the hall and drink it out of a paper cup. Sometimes there were doughnuts. Lunch orders and happy hour. TGIF. I want to go home and order a pizza. I want to drive, go to the movies, have a drink. I want to be sitting in my heated bathroom at three in the morning. Hind sight is twenty-twenty.

The only place on the street where I'm welcome is the protest. They'll take any warm body they can get. Hundreds of people are camped out now. Shouting slogans around the clock. Harassing workers. The city orders them to vacate the premises. If they don't, they'll be forcefully removed. The people say democracy has failed and that government is no longer representative of the majority. This is an outrage. A few of them push. They're quickly pushed back. I hang around for most of the day. Sometimes you can score a little bite to eat. There's a sense of community here. A togetherness. But at night I head back underground to be alone. A few more people pass through the tunnel again. They look at me but they don't stop.

Move along.

This is my spot.

Get a job.

Chants, slogans, slim pickings. Down with the one percent.

The next day is exactly the same as the one before it.

At night when I flip open the latch my sleeping bag is back and there's a plastic bag with some bread in it on the ground. It's quiet and still so I manage to get a few hours of sleep. The sleep is heavy and thick. Just what I needed. It doesn't last though.

"This isn't a good place to make camp man." The tip of a nose pokes out of the deep shadows that hide the rest of his face. "Are you tweaking?" he asks. "Are you a tweaker?" He snaps his fingers. Up, down, left, right. He stands over me and crosses his arms.

The dirt on my hands smears against the hard crust of the bread. I hold it to my chest so that he can't reach out and grab it. I hold it tight to my own heart like it's pumping the blood through my arms.

"Well, are you on something?" he says.

I don't want this. I'm afraid of him. Of what he might do. The unknown. The basement of the church seems like a paradise lost. Clean. Warm. Dry. Familiar. We were all together. Sharing stories and helping each other out. One time the guys told me that they'd never follow somebody who promises to help them. They've each learned from experience how that usually goes. Come with us. We'll help you. Tony said that he was once robbed out of sixty cents because someone needed bus fare. They kicked him in the kneecap so he couldn't run after them. He smiled when he thought those days were behind him. He said 'thank you' and went to sleep knowing that he'd wake up the next day. Then we ate the apple. It's human nature. We were hungry. Now this guy is standing in front of me and I don't know why.

Socks said that he was once offered five dollars by someone if he would allow them to kick him in the balls.

"You should come with me man," the nose says. He holds out his hand. Rubs his fingertips together. Like he's trying to coax a scared dog out from behind the refrigerator. Like he's trying to lull a baby to sleep. Talk a kitten off a ledge.

Socks said 'no' but they kicked him anyway and didn't even leave him the fin.

I look up at the nose, clutching the dirty bread. Crumbs on my shirt that I was saving for later fall off and land on the ground. They absorb the water around them and double in size.

"I can help you," he says. "You should come with me. I'm just like you. We're stronger if we stick together brother. There's a place I can take you."

"No thanks."

"I can help you."

Sure you can.

You're taught from a young age not to trust strangers. Don't talk to them. The man in the run down panel van with no windows doesn't really have candy. You haven't really already won a million dollars. Hitchhikers will chop your head off and then ditch the rest of your body somewhere out in the dessert if you pick them up.

You hear about it all the time. Humanity's an ugly brand of creature. Just ask any priest.

But every time you leave your little nest you have to trust in strangers. We trust that the pilot isn't drunk and that he really knows how to fly the plane. That the car will stop at the red light. That the guy in the black trench coat isn't going to pull out an AK-47 and empty a clip into all the shoppers in the frozen food aisle of the grocery store. That the dishwasher at our local restaurant isn't going to rub the forks all over his balls, and that the people holding all of your money aren't going to piss it away and then piss all over you.

It's a calculated risk. Still. I'll take my chances alone.

Move along. No loitering. This is our spot.

He reaches out to help me up. I press backwards until the concrete pushes back and I can't go any further. He raises his hands and shows me his palms. "Okay, man. It's okay. I'm not going to hurt you. I'm here to help you. Make sure you're alright." I can smell his breath. It mixes in with the odor that wafts from his underarms when he raises them. It smells different from the odor that wafts from mine. I want this guy to go away. I don't trust him. He can see it on my face and takes two steps back, still keeping his hands up. "I understand," he says. "Been there. I'll be back to check up on you. Don't be afraid the next time you see me. Cause you will." As his body disappears into the shadows further down the tunnel, he stops and turns his head. "You are just as important as anyone else," he says.

About an hour later, as I'm about to fall asleep, the tunnel is flooded with voices. Could be a maintenance crew or something. Broken water main. Or maybe that guy came back with some friends. I hide my stuff deep in the piping overhead, just like Frosty used to do, and slip out. The last thing that I want is for someone to realize I'm living down here and secure the grate so that I can't open it again.

So I walk. The night's cool and I have nowhere to go so I head down to the business district. It's pure chaos. The city is making good on their threat to break up the protest. The police swarm. Dressed in full body armor. Carrying riot shields and pepper spray. Billy clubs. Those who don't leave peacefully are herded up, handcuffed, and thrown in a temporary detention center that they made by stringing some heavy-duty fencing around a parking lot. People are screaming as pure capsaicin is sprayed into their eyes and they're dragged off. Some people fight back. They have a right to be there, the people scream. It's public property. Not tonight it isn't. A line of them get thrown to the ground by a high pressure water hose manned by four people in uniform. It says, 'to serve and protect' on their shoulders. People stream past me going every which way. I get hit and fall to the ground. When I look up two pairs of chunky leather boots are coming my way. I get to my feet and run. It doesn't matter where.

I end up in an alley. But I'm not alone. I find this out when a pair of arms wraps around me from behind. I throw my hips forward and mash with the blade edge of my hands. Just like Birddog taught me how to do. The arms let go, but I catch a few knuckles across the jaw that drop me. I can smell the booze on them. I would have been better off taking my chances with the cops at the protest. But I'm cornered in this alley now. They laugh. I try to run but my feet get kicked out from under me. There's four of them.

"This is for your troubles," one of them says, as he throws pennies at the back of my head. They all start to laugh.

"Hey, we can use this!" another one of them says.

I'm turtled on the ground. Trying to protect my head with my forearms. Then I get hit across the spine with something hard and I'm underwater. Floating in a pool of acid rain. It burns everything. The flesh off my bones. The will from my spirit. My face scrapes the ground. The small rocks and random particulate on the ground grind into my skin. I spit the blood out from my mouth. It's hard to breathe.

"Who the fuck are you?" one of them says.

I feel someone trip over me and fall. I can hear, over the ringing in my ears, that more people are here. But I can't bring myself to uncover my face. They're thrashing around the alley. The sound of shoes sliding against the grainy asphalt. Someone gets hit. Someone goes down. A piece of wood falls to the ground. Someone screams. Someone tries to run away. "Come here you fuck!" a raspy voice chokes. Not so tough now are you? Some kind of liquid sprays against my forearms and hands. It's thick and warm. Then it's quiet.

"You can get up now," a voice says. "It's okay. They're gone."

Someone kneels down beside me and moves my arms away from my head.

"Are you okay? Don't worry, you're safe now brother."

Never talk to strangers, my mother used to say.

"Let me help you up."

Under the orange glow of the sodium lamps I recognize the guy from the tunnel. I recognize the smell. Can you walk? I wipe the blood and sweat from my eyes. My ears ring. Three more people huddle around. How is he? I don't know. I recognize one of them. It's Frosty.

Then I pass out.

16

It's pitch black. The kind of darkness that's so absolute you think you've gone blind. Like your eyes have been dug right out of your skull and are on your bedside table in a glass of warm water to keep them moist. But they're not. I can feel my eyelids scraping against them when I blink. I'm not deaf either. The dried up blood in my nostrils whistles when I breathe. For a moment it's calming. Vast. Endless. Free from the chaos of illumination. Light is short. It needs constant nurturing to be sustained. Darkness is. I'm at the beginning.

Then panic sets in.

I can't see my hand but I know it's there, resting against the coarse material of the thin mattress that I'm lying on. I can't see it but I know it's there. The particleboard wall that gives me a splinter when I run my fingertips along it. It's quiet. But the silence isn't as absolute as the nothingness that stretches out endlessly from my pupil. There's a low rumble in the distance. Something's moving outside. Something's breathing inside.

It moves when I sit up.

When the light hits the back of my eye it's too much. Everything goes white. The chaos returns. It takes a second to adjust so that I can see the bare bulb pushing back the ink into the corners of the room.

"You look like shit."

Shapes start to take form. Blurry afterimages. I can see something moving. It's long and it looks like there's a hand on the end of it. My head pounds and my body throbs. Undeniable proof that I'm still alive and that this isn't the first level of hell. Which is good, cause I didn't have any change for the boat ride.

"You really look like shit." Frosty's face comes into focus. He's smiling. His teeth look like little black beetles all lined up perfectly in a row. He spits.

Part of me wants to drive the palm of my hand up through the bottom of his nose like Birddog taught me to do in basic. It drives the cartilage up into the brain. Part of me wants to smile and throw my arms around him.

"Where am I?"

He dusts off my jacket. Licks his thumb and wipes a smear of blood off my cheek.

Ow.

"Been through the ringer have you? Out on your own?" Something like that? 'No man shall be able to stand before you all the days of your life, so I will be with you.' Joshua something, verse something, something. "Now you really get it," he says. "Now, you don't just think you do. Welcome aboard. Don't worry, you're safe here with us."

I'm a yellow jacket.

"Where is here?"

He drapes his arm over my shoulder.

Ow.

"I'll show you."

We're underground. Living like ants or cockroaches or centipedes. Someplace moist and warm enough to start laying eggs for the colony. Potato bugs under boxes. People move around everywhere. I can see the shadows they cast in the dim yellow light. I can hear their voices. There's dirt under my feet but everything else gradually recedes into black. Once my eyes fully adjust, I see it.

"You've been busy," I say.

"You don't know the half of it."

It's a city. His own underground colony. Populated with everyone who didn't have a home anywhere else. He's the mayor. Their father. The general. Whatever you want to call it. There's little particleboard shacks peppered everywhere. Put together with whatever they could get their hands on. Scraps of wood and cinderblocks. Old plastic signs offering goods and services. Tiny pockets of light in the ink, like stars on a clear night. The rest of civilization is someplace else. They don't exist down here. Not even the alien archeologists that will visit in ten thousand years and start digging around will find a trace of this place. They won't have any theories about how we lived. What our social dynamics were like. Mating rituals. Not even God could see us down here.

"I found a safe place. Nobody bothers us here," Frosty says. "You're safe now too. From all the rest of society who thinks you're shit." He spreads his arms open. "Not bad eh?" He laughs a genuine laugh. Like a proud father watching his child take their first steps.

They found this place by following a group of feral cats. Deep under the city, where not even one photon of light from the outside world bounced around, a tunnel that was once used for freight trains. It was closed in the nineteen seventies and no one had been down there ever since. Except the cats. They colonized the dark side of the moon. Dug a hole and laid some eggs. Just like ants did.

"We could survive a nuclear war down here," he says.

He set the earth on its foundations, so that it should never be moved...

Where did I hear that? It doesn't matter anymore.

Frosty gathered as many homeless as he could and brought them down into the tunnel. Into the Marianas trench. They built houses with whatever they could scavenge or steal. Warped particle board. Plywood. Cinderblocks. In between the piles of trash spread across the dirt. A neighborhood. They tapped into the electrical grid. The water lines. There's so many of them. Each milling about with a distinct purpose. They're organized. Organized society implies government. Citizenship. Fidelity to the just and natural service of citizens is communal righteousness. They all serve it. Government implies a leader.

Living by Frosty's rules. No drugs. No booze. They needed clear heads, he said, to get done what they needed to get done. They obey his every command. Each one of them has a specific job. A specific purpose. It becomes their habit. Their ritual. They're all cogs in an intricate machine who's function only Frosty knows. For now anyway. We would all come to know just what it was that he had in mind eventually. By that time though, the machine was already in full swing. It's momentum pushing us forward. And there was no turning back. We trusted him. Believed in him. He saved us all.

"Down here, we don't compete with each other anymore," Frosty says, "we work together. Look after each other. For the greater good. The bigger picture. It's a true community in every sense of the word."

Communal righteousness. I can see it in everything they do. Hello neighbor, some of them say. Beautiful day isn't it? How can you tell down here? They help each other get things done. Build each other's houses and share what little things that they have.

Everything that needs to get done, gets done. The foragers come back from their rounds with bags of food from all the best spots around the city. Someone builds. Someone cleans. Someone cooks. The new arrivals are in charge of maintaining the latrines. Frosty gives orders to Birddog. Birddog sends them down the line to Tony and Paddy. It gets diluted through the colony from there. A pheromone trail for the rest to follow. The special forces missions are classified. They do this every day. He drills it into them. Communal good. Specific tasks. Sit, kneel, stand when the bells rings. Drool a little.

In one of the shacks they're grinding aluminum cans with a fine power sander that's siphoning electricity from a small half bare wire that's tapped into the grid.

"You mix it with powdered rust in an 8:3 ratio and you have thermite."

"I know," I say. "I remember."

"Pretty cool eh?" Frosty smiles. A real smile. Not just something you did as a social convention. "All you need after that is something that burns hot enough to ignite it."

"I know."

A dollar store sparkler would do. On the exhaust manifold of a Mercedes-Benz S-Class. You can use copper powder for an explosive mixture if you want too. Birddog learned about it in the army. They used thermite hand grenades to destroy cryptographic equipment when there was a danger that it might be captured by enemy troops. Now he looks up from his work and laughs. "That one really scares the shit out of them," he says. "Nice shiny car ain't worth shit anymore."

It's a class war. And they're on the offensive.

Frosty says that down there, in the dark, where no one can find them, they're free. They weren't shackled by society's conventions anymore. Free to build. Free to grow. Free to start new lives. Free to be themselves. They're safe. They're invisible. By choice this time. Life liberty and the pursuit of whatever. They're free to live. To prepare for the time of reckoning.

Where have I heard that before?

"It's going to be a hell of a thing," Frosty says. "Wait till you see it. You'll love it too. Especially now." He laughs and slaps me on the back. It hurts like hell and I taste blood in my mouth. "Now that you're one of us."

I spit on the ground. It's full of red particulate.

A group of us goes topside after dark. The rich neighborhood. The really rich neighborhood. We split into two units so that we can cover more ground. Over fences and through estates. Watch out for motion detectors and listen for dogs. If you're seen, go underground. You can get back to home base through the intricate network of tunnels that were so filthy no rich guy would ever think of climbing down into them. They connect the entire city. Except in one spot where the pipes from the new water treatment plant cross. We hide behind a group of shrubs that are trimmed to look like animals. I have my head next to an elephant's ass.

The house in front of us is bigger than most public parks. "If there's a top," Frosty says, "then there has to be a bottom. One percent owns most of the shit on the planet. They're at the top. Us, we're at the bottom." One percent of the population are homeless. Frosty reaches into his bag and pulls out an electrical extension cord that's cut and frayed at one end. There's no moon out tonight. The darkness is thick. Almost like we're still underground. We move around the estate and creep up to the side of the house. "We're bringing them down. All that nice, expensive shit. I'm going to take it all away from them. It'll be worthless." He plugs one end of the cord into an exterior outlet. We run it to the door and he attaches the bare leads on the other end to the metal plate and door knob. The next morning when whoever tries to leave the house they'll get a shock that would wake up Abraham Lincoln. We run wires to window frames, garage doors, aluminum siding. Then we're gone.

Frosty says that he's going to take everything they love and turn it against them.

Thermite on the exhaust manifold of their brand new luxury car with built in seat warmers and dual wishbone suspension. The explosive kind. By the end of the week they'll be too afraid to even sit in a car. Do it enough times and it becomes conditioning. Just like that dog.

"I'm going to make them scared of just about everything they're dying to go out and buy."

It's perfect.

The good stuff's inside the houses. Socks was an electrical engineer before he got sick and went bankrupt trying to keep himself alive. He pops the box open like it's not even locked and cuts a wire. I'm the lookout. Lucas works at the window. In about thirty seconds we slip inside the mansion.

You can soak tobacco in water overnight. Then strain it into a jar through a porous towel. Once it sits for a while the water will evaporate and leave you with pure nicotine. Four or five drops in a cup of coffee is enough to kill someone. A few into the bottle of single malt should be just right to cause nausea, palpitations, maybe even arrest. Frosty leaves a folded up note in between the bottles that they'll be sure to find next time they go to pour a drink. They're arranged by year and probably cost the average person's salary for six months. I ask him what it says. "Three of these bottles could kill you." He laughs. "Good luck."

"I thought that you were just going to make them sick."

"I did. But three of the bottles *could* kill them. Maybe. Could is an abstract quantity."

We put magnesium strips into the cigars in a box of Cohiba Behikes. Once it ignites you can't put it out. You have to sit there and watch it burn your thousand dollar cigar to nothing.

Frosty says it's that rich mentality that keeps the rest of us divided. You're really wearing those shoes? That jacket? That's so last year. Get some new clothes will you? My kid uses the expensive macaroni to make art with. What does yours use? The generic kind? The money spent on pointless extravagance could effectively end poverty the world over. We all have a right to exist. We all have a right to what the world has to offer. We're not garbage. That one percent is going to learn that the hard way. On our way back home our laughter echoes through the tunnels that are so filthy no rich guy would ever climb down into them.

Sometimes Frosty leaves notes behind even though we didn't do anything. This apple has a razor blade in it. If you turn this key, it will explode. Something's been added to your chocolate cake. Can you guess what it is? He does it just to get them to throw away perfectly good things. They pile them to the curb. We pick them up the next night.

"That one percent dominates the lobbying for federal and state policies. They tell you how to live. Now we've turned the tables. We'll tell them how to live."

The bigger the TV the better. We take a large sheet of smoothly cut aluminum foil and tape it in front of the screen. Turning the

TV on and off repeatedly builds up a static charge and turns the area between the screen and the metal into a giant capacitor. Now they have to stare at an aluminum sheet instead of an ultra high definition OLED screen because they'll be too afraid to take it off after what happened the first time. The more expensive something is the more completely it will be destroyed. The more cushy it makes your life, the more it's going to hurt you.

We're fire ants nibbling at the toes of those holding the magnifying glass to our hill. We crawl all over their safe gated neighborhoods while they sleep and they have no idea how we got in there. Or how to get rid of us. We stick to the dark places because we knew them all. They were scared shitless.

Frosty laughs when we get back, sometime towards dawn. "Hope you had as much fun as I did. You're one of us now. You're part of the hoard. Welcome home."

Entry number five.

17

Frosty tells me that that no one had given Muhammad Ali a chance against George Foreman in 1974. When Ali took the belt. Foreman was a powerhouse. Nobody had lasted more than three rounds against him. After the second bell Ali starts to cower against the ropes. Foreman pounds as fast and as hard as he can, not realizing that the elastic ropes are absorbing most of the force. Ali taunts him. I thought you could hit George. Is that all you have George? George you disappoint me. George hits harder. By the fifth round Foreman was worn out. And by the eighth he was knocked out.

"Strategy can make power irrelevant," Frosty says, "look at what happened in Vietnam. Our brains work just as good as theirs do. We can outthink them."

Our methods are crude but they're having a major effect. Nobody knows who we are, or where we come from. Shadows on security cameras. Then, your perfectly manicured shrubs cut to look like mythological figures are on fire, and the pool in the back yard is filled with human shit. We pollute their safe little nests and there's nothing they can do to stop us. They're afraid to go to sleep at night. Afraid to stay awake. So they lobby the city. The counselors. They pass a motion to beef up police presence in the affected areas. It has no effect. The police don't know the terrain like we do. Strategy. To them the streets are a beat. To us they're home. After a while, people complain that public safety in other parts of the city is being put at risk to keep the wealthy safe. It's not fair. Crime is up twenty percent in lower income neighborhoods. Counselors get letters. It's an election year. Do they focus on the voter or do they pay for the campaign? That's politics for you. There are news stories. It's an outrage. If the wealthy want more protection let them pay for it themselves, the middle says. They can certainly afford it.

Divide and conquer. Isolate and invade.

The poor say, fuck em'.

"That's how we used to do it," Birddog says, "destabilize the area. That's 101. Frag grenades help a lot too."

Public outcry wins. Privately hired security starts making rounds through the extra wide streets and the immaculately landscaped yards with our message, mostly profane, burned into them with fertilizer. Statues of fat kids holding harps and pissing into fountains filled with perchloric acid. Alliance Security have white cars with orange stripes on the side and their employees carry batons and pepper spray cause they're not legally allowed to carry guns. They say things like, 'evening 'ma'am,' and tip their hats as they pass by Stepford wives walking their tiny battery powered dogs. We're there too. Right where they can't see us. They have no idea how close we are. We're watching everything.

At night we walk in silence. Single file through the tunnels and pop out through a maintenance hatch. We're gone just as fast as we arrive. Before anyone even knows we're there. They find out when they wake up though. We even hit the local golf course with as much vinegar as we can get our hands on. Which is a lot. So much for taking their minds off it with a nice round of eighteen.

Underground, in Frosty's shack, there's a wad of cash and a gun.

We become photophobic. Living underground all day. Coming out at night for supplies or to carry out the missions that Frosty has planned. Foragers go for food. A group wanders the streets for any potential new recruits. Another hits construction sites for new building materials. One for essential hardware. The special ops team climb through the heating system of one of those big box stores to steal some black clothing. A splinter group breaks off and hits the sporting goods department. In the morning we're all over the news. But they have no idea who we are and no idea how to stop us. The police chief says that every possible precaution is being taken, but they can't catch us. We know the streets. Every inch of them. They're our home. The anchors on the news say that due to certain similarities they believe the crimes to be perpetrated by the same vigilante that was committing violent acts in the alleys.

But, due to the scope of the new crimes, it is very likely that these are being executed by more than one individual.

Downtown the protesters are alive and well living in the parking lot prisons put up to confine them. Barbed wire and fences. Each of them has a number. It's well lit, even in the middle of the night, so that they can be watched over at all times. The police are allowed to detain them indefinitely without even laying charges. The motion passed in city council when they refused to leave the financial district. They still scream. They still chant. Brothers in arms. They're winning public support. It's an election year too. That's where we go after dark. We need a diversion. But there's a stop that we have to make first.

One city counselor proposes raising the property tax on the most expensive houses in the city. He says that the extra money could be used to fund social programs. There isn't enough affordable housing. Public pools are closing. The library is underfunded. It's a landslide victory for the opposition. Practically every counselor was getting campaign contributions in the election from the same people the tax was aimed at. By keeping the councilors in their pockets, they could essentially create policy for the city. That's how it works. They get what they want.

We break into city hall from the underground parking lot.

Phase two.

"We take the power away by neutralizing their support system," Frosty says. He read it in the library before he started getting kicked out for, he made invisible quotation marks in the air with his fingers, smelling like a toilet.

"That's how we used to do it," Birddog says.

Destroy supply routes. Infrastructure. It not only makes it harder to get things done, it turns people against you. They no longer feel protected. Privileged. We're going to send them a message. The plan is to trash the offices of the councilors with deep pockets. We're going to leave the same message here. We're going to take away their privilege. We're going to make them scared. One of them is working late. We spring out from behind the cubicle dividers in the hallway and pin him down to a desk. He's so scared he shits himself.

"You know," Frosty says, "I think this city is a pretty great place to live. Don't you think councilman? We've got restaurants, museums, plenty of parking. It's really a great place to live." Emphasizing 'really' and 'great'. Spit bubbles form in the corners of the councilman's mouth as he tries desperately to suck in enough air to feed his clogged heart. He manages to shake his head. Yes. Yes it is. His cheeks are red, his forehead is sweaty. "But only if you're rich," Frosty says.

His caramel teeth hover above the councilman's nose and slowly, methodically, he explains to the esteemed councilman that somewhere down the line the institution that was supposed to serve the people had forgotten all about them. The esteemed councilman struggles but we put all of our weight onto his arms and legs to keep him pinned down. His fat stomach heaves upwards, straining the buttons on his shirt. Obesity is a big problem in this country. But only if you have the money to feed it. We're supposed to be a community, Frosty says. But we're not. We're supposed to look out for one another. But we don't. There's supposed to be compassion. Wasn't there? Wasn't that the whole point? But there isn't.

"Oh, now you're listening?" Frosty cups the palm of his hand over the councilman's ear. "There should be equality for everyone. But there isn't."

We're equal now though. At this very minute. There's one thing that makes everyone equal. Everyone in the world. Frosty pulls out a knife and brushes it gently against the esteemed councilman's neck to scare the hell out of him. We don't have a problem with this. It works really well. Besides, losing everything makes you angry. Living underground makes you hard. Hiding makes you hated. Being hated makes you hate back. Equally. We don't feel sorry for him.

"You haven't been doing your duty councilman."

We're doing ours. Earning our citizenship. All of us. Like a bee colony. At this very minute, while Frosty holds a knife to the esteemed councilman's face, booby traps are being set. Cars are being tampered with. Houses are being broken into. Alliance Security doubles their price to patrol due to the number of incidents encountered by its employees. The damage done to their patrol cars. The injury reports filed. They say that pricing is a complex and multifaceted process. They say that unforeseeable circumstances have doubled the cost of providing reliable service. They say that they must raise prices to offset the increasing costs of maintaining their infrastructure and work force to current industry standards. The residents accuse them of not honoring their contracts. They accuse them of price gouging. Of taking advantage of them to make more money.

The people are surprisingly unsympathetic. Even though they spend their entire lives emulating the affluent. On the news they say things like, 'the rich can afford it,' or, 'they can just hire someone to take care of it.' If the poor knew who Frosty was they'd hoist him onto their shoulders and parade him through the public square.

"I think they deserve it," one woman says.

Guerrilla warfare campaigns always have strong ties to the people, according to Birddog. It must coincide with their aspirations. You need sympathy, co-operation, and sometimes assistance. Che Guevara once said that the guerrilla fighter is a social reformer, that he takes up arms responding to the angry protest of the people against their oppressors, and that he fights in order to change the social system that keeps all his unarmed brothers in ignominy and misery.

Frosty paraphrases. "Fuck 'em."

The funny thing is: everybody wants to be rich. There isn't one person alive on the planet today that would turn down the opportunity. It's in our nature. But everybody wants to get rid of the rich. Wipe the slate clean. So they'll have a fighting chance to get there first the next time around. If there were no rich, they could aspire to something else. Maybe take up finger painting. The organ. For now they're going to buy the knock off jacket and hope that nobody notices. Stand next to someone else's expensive car and then post the picture on whatever social media they're into at the moment. Everybody's living the life. Rolling in it. Making it rain.

The offices are turned inside out. It looks as though a hurricane ran through the entire floor. Frosty says, "This is just an introduction. Let's get out of here. We still have more to do tonight." On our way out he folds another note into an origami duck and leaves it on the mayor's desk.

The esteemed councilman lies there gurgling.

Outside we split up in two groups to attack this from different sides. In case one of us fails there's a redundancy. Birddog calls it Operation Omega. It has a nice ring to it.

We open up the chain link fence with razor wire around the top in the downtown parking lot and set all of the arrested protesters free. Misdirection. They scatter everywhere like insects under a magnifying glass. The cops scramble to catch them. They run back and forth swinging their little clubs. Shouting orders that no one obeys. There's a lot of swearing. They manage to catch a few but most of them get away.

"That ought to keep them busy for a while," Frosty says, as we slip beneath the asphalt. "A while is all we'll need."

The esteemed councilman dies of a heart attack after we've gone. They find him there the next morning. Sprawled out on the desk, lying in his own shit. Doctors say that at the moment of death the sphincter muscles relax and the bowels are evacuated. It's perfectly natural. The marks on his body tell another story though and the mayor says that they will not take this act of terrorism lying down. The people responsible will be found and brought to justice. A new campaign promise. It's an election year.

"This is serious now," I say to Frosty.

"It's always been serious. Anyway, we didn't kill him. The fat bastard killed himself. I wish I could afford to eat myself to death. Wouldn't that be nice?"

"Two people are dead now."

"I know." He frowns.

"Two people."

"I know, but it wasn't our fault. Either one of them." He shoves past me.

When I get back to the shack we call home, I find the money and the gun. Frosty says that after the big donation was made to the cyber begging thing, he withdrew it and hid it. But he wasn't going to spend it. He didn't want to spoil anyone. People have to learn how to be self-sufficient. They can't rely on the charity of others anymore. On donations. Good will. It's unsustainable. He's keeping it for an emergency.

"What kind of emergency?"

He doesn't answer.

So what's the gun for?

"It's for an emergency."

I hop over a fence and run through a backyard. Over another fence, through a shrub, and down a manhole that the shrub's put there to hide. The two guards chasing me run right past. But I'm only a diversion. While they're chasing me, another group loosens the lugs on their tires on their cars. Six blocks later they fall off and Alliance Security ups their prices to compensate. Their services get scaled back. Birddog taught Frosty all about it from his time overseas. You make it look like you're coming from the east, then you attack from the west. Attack the hollow, not the solid. Attack. Withdraw when the enemy advances. Harass them when they stop. Attack when they're tired. Pursue them when they withdraw. Be the guerilla. The cops are busy trying to run down all of the people that we set free, so we're operating unobstructed. The security companies are having a hard time finding new employees after some of them quit. The authorities still have no idea who's behind this wave of terrorism. That's what they call it. Terrorism. Frosty gives them a hint. That's our mission tonight. Another message. In red paint. All over houses, cars, corporate headquarters, and the art in the square. Spread with gasoline and burning bright in fields. In red paint. Everywhere. We are the one percent.

18

There's always something dripping underground. The leftover. The waste. It all finds its way down here eventually. Through the cracks. Along the pipes. It travels slowly but eventually the ground opens up and it falls onto the dirt. You get used to it. After a while you come to expect it. You want to hear it. The methodical ticking is calming. Almost like a lullaby. We sleep under an onyx sky while the world above us scrambles to make sense of what's happening to their tidy, perfectly planned environments. There's talk of curfews. More police. The national guard. Nobody knows who they're dealing with. Where they're coming from. How they're getting there. They bring in consultants. The consultants wear suits. They bill by the hour and drive nice cars that they park underground so that they won't get scratched.

"The best thing about these assholes is that they've never had to do anything for themselves. So, they have no idea how," Frosty says. "We've always had to do things for ourselves. We have a leg up."

B.O.H.I.C.A, Birddog says, and laughs. Bend Over Here It Comes Again. Only the soldiers on the winning side tended to use that military acronym. He's enjoying it just as much as the rest of us. Seeing them scared. Seeing them scramble. All of the security and convenience money can buy isn't worth anything anymore. They take their kids out of school. Keep them inside. Don't touch anything. Some of them leave town to stay with relatives or in country homes. And Frosty isn't even finished yet. Only he knows the next phase, though. The head motherfucker in charge.

In the dark, underneath the world, we're a living organism. Consuming any nutrient that we can feed on. Anything that comes dripping down our way. We grow new blood vessels to support ourselves. Like big fat tumors. Each person is in charge of a specific piece of it. It's structured. It becomes ritual. Everybody down here becomes the same. They became uniform. Homogenous.

One thing makes everyone equal.

One thing.

In the sunlight above us, the consultants in suits quote Sun Tzu and Machiavelli. It sounds impressive. Like they might actually be worth the invoice that the city will receive when this is all over. They say that swift action is needed. A committee is assembled to come at this from every possible angle. They sit around a large table and eat gourmet sandwiches for lunch and talk about how they really shouldn't have that extra piece of dessert. It goes straight to your thighs. They drink lots of coffee. The specialty café in the lobby cleans up making triple soy no foam lattes. At the end of the day one of them says: "Maybe we should hire more cops." Then they collect their pay checks. "Maybe we should bring in the national guard." Bonuses all around.

Frosty says if you get arrested you're on your own. That thing about all for one and one for all doesn't apply here anymore. We can't afford it. There's too much at stake. Most of us don't have an identity to tarnish anyway. We're not in the system. Society forgot about us when we fell down. We're simply stepped over on the way up the stairs now. You're either a fuck up or eventually you're going to want something. We slip through the cracks, along the pipes, and splash down on the dirt. Pooled together. Congealed in the primordial ooze and spontaneously forming complex polymers from abiotically generated monomers. We reproduce. Strands of DNA make exact replicas of themselves. We eventually use our front fins to crawl out of the water. The rest is history.

We want to stay invisible. Nobody can know we're here. Watch your back whenever you come and go. We are the shadows. We only exist until someone points a flashlight at us.

Birddog and Tony ask for my help. They open up a few boxes of shotgun shells, some thumbtacks, and pull out a heavy drill.

"What the hell is all this for?" I say.

Birddog holds up a shotgun shell. It's red and it has a gold ring around the bottom where all of the gun power is packed.

"Protection," he says. "An early warning system. Learned about it when I was in the middle east. You need good hard ground to make it work though. Something packed and dry. Cement is perfect."

"What are you going to do with that?" I'm not sure if I want to know.

Birddog says that it's non lethal. It might take off a couple of toes. Maybe some of the foot. We have the right to defend ourselves. Frosty says so.

We drill holes into the concrete around any point of entrance. Just big enough to fit a shotgun shell into it and just deep enough so that the top sticks out about a millimeter or so. Then we shave a thumbtack down and put it at the bottom of the hole and place the shell inside. Now, if someone steps on it, the primer on the shell will be triggered by the thumbtack and it will go off. The buckshot will probably take most of the foot with it.

"We have a right to be safe," Birddog says.

"Our lives matter too," Tony says.

Down in the ant colony, I hear Paddy say, "If they come up behind you, stick your hips out and hit them in the balls with the blade edge of your hand." Ok. Good. Let's try it again. Apply pressure upwards until it pops. He's passing down the knowledge to the new recruits. They practice it over and over again until it becomes muscle memory. I hear someone I don't know say, "We have a right to protect ourselves." When the dinner bell rings, they all file in an orderly fashion and take their place in line. They patiently wait their turn without pushing, shoving, or screaming. Military precision.

"This is our home," someone says in the darkness. "No one is going to take it away from us. I don't care if I have to hurt someone to protect it. I will."

Everybody's on high alert because a shoal were followed into the tunnels a few nights before. They don't know who it was or why. But everyone in the colony knows the tunnels. When they hear footsteps echoing behind them, they double back, split them up. Cut the power to the lights. Turn them around. Soon, there are no footsteps behind. But it leaves everyone on edge. We have to protect our home. It's our right. Now there're shotgun shells drilled into the concrete that stick out about a millimeter or so. If they get stepped on, they'll explode outward and take a foot with them.

"If we lose our territory we lose the war," Frosty says. He uses that word more and more often now. War. He gets other people to start using it too. He rallies people behind it and they love him for it. He's given them a home. He's given them a community where they weren't relegated to begging and pleading for charity. Stepped over and ridiculed. Where they're useful. Wanted and safe. And most importantly, he gives all of them a purpose.

He's given all of that to me, too.

I walk by a few people standing in front of a fire burning in a trash can. "Money doesn't buy you your humanity," one of them says. The others agree. They look at me. I nod. You bite the toes, you bite the elbow, I'll take the chin. The piranhas formulate their plan of attack. They psych themselves up for it so when the moment comes they'll be ready. Together we're strong, one of them says. We matter too.

Frosty often makes the rounds through the camp. Moving back and forth between the pockets of light. You're not garbage, he says. We're all in this together. We can make it work. We're a family. But you have to give yourself fully to the cause. Give without reciprocation. One of the most truly altruistic animals is the vampire bat, he says. If one of them fails to find a victim in the night it will lock mouths with a successful hunter who will then regurgitate blood. He read that in the library before he was kicked out for smelling like the drainage valve of an outhouse. Be the bat, he says. You do this for the greater good. Your lives will mean something.

Startled fish. Overbites. Drones, workers, vampires, yellow jackets. Whatever. They've gotten used to the idea of being forgotten. Erased. This is hope. A legacy. What everybody wants. To matter. The more often you repeat it the more it sticks in your brain.

"Cut the head off of the snake and the rest will just fall away," people say. The snake is the rich one percent. The other one percent. The head of that snake was the money. Ours was a war of decapitation.

The same things echo through the different cells in my brain. Like that dog that starts to salivate whenever it hears a bell. I sit in front of a fire by myself while some clear liquid drips onto my forehead from somewhere up in space. I don't even notice it anymore. Above it all, in the sunlight, the people who matter are formulating a defense plan. The chief of police says there's going to be a crackdown. This is a very serious matter. We cannot stand idly by while some members of our community are terrorized. They still haven't figured it out. He slams his hands against the podium for effect and says that they have to take care of each other. This is their city. The room erupts in applause. The expert panel on the news says that it's a serious matter. They repeat it. A serious matter. Our specialized consultants are examining the problem from every conceivable angle. The report should come any week now. They want turkey for lunch tomorrow. But not Mark, he's a vegetarian. "These acts of vandalism are a clear affront to democratic capitalist society," they say, "specifically targeting our captains of industry."

Captains of industry. Frosty spits. Birddog spits too. So does Tony. "Robber Barons is more like it." He read that in the library before he got kicked out for potentially spreading lice to other patrons. He says captains of industry don't exist anymore. They all died out after the great depression. It's everyman for himself. I read an article in the paper about a guy that was so rich it would take him two hundred and eighteen years to spend all of his money at a rate of one million dollars a day.

"How much is enough?" Frosty says. The shadows standing in the firelight in front of him nod silently at first. Then a low rumble of voices starts to spread from figure to figure. Then there's fists in the air. "How much can you sit on while the rest of the world starves?" Now the low rumble becomes a high pitched buzz.

Turns out we're not the only ones asking those questions either.

The financial district was vandalized the night before. Windows were smashed. Cars were lit on fire. Graffiti. Two people are reportedly arrested. We do a head count. Everybody's here. We do it again. Everybody's here. Police say that the suspects are in custody and are awaiting a court date.

"Was it you?" Frosty asks me.

"I thought it was you."

"I didn't do it."

Everybody else says, neither did they.

"If none of us did it," Tony says, "then who do you think did?"

Down with the one percent. Equality for all. We are the 99%. Painted over everything. Scratched into the glass. Keyed into aluminum.

250

This is perfect.

Guerrilla warfare must coincide with the aspirations of the people. You need sympathy, co-operation, and sometimes assistance. Pass me that stick of gunpowder will you? You can't blow up a house with gunpowder. We went from being the joke of society, the stuff stuck to the bottom of a shoe, to something else. I half expect a fifty-seventh ribbon of support and awareness to be added to the list. Maybe purple? Nobody knows who we are. Where we come from. But they're starting to know why. And they're starting to jump onto the wagon.

But, how far are we going to go? How far is far enough?

All of these things cross my mind as I stare into the flames that hungrily lick the sides of the trash can. My small pocket of light is peaceful. The darkness around me gives it a tranquility. But it doesn't last. It never does. I hear shuffling feet. Someone giving orders. I can't see what it is through the nothing. Something falls, someone shouts. I try my best to ignore it but the hand that falls onto my shoulder pulls me through the ink and forces me to engage.

"You're gonna want to come and see this," Frosty says.

It's hard to see what Frosty's showing me because the candles are almost burnt down to the nub. The ink wraps itself around everything it can get its hands around. We're taught to fear the darkness when we're young. It must have something to do with evolution. Almost everything does. But it's all wrong. Light is short. Darkness is. It was here at the beginning. It will be here at the end. There's someone lying still in the small particle board shack. She shifts slightly in the bed when I walk in.

A patrol found her on the street. It took three people to carry her down here. Her red jacket stained a rust colored brown. Mix it with aluminum powder to get thermite. Frosty kneels beside her bed. He knows better than to touch though. We feed her water. Her hair is gone. Her lips are blue. They curl up almost imperceptibly when she turns her head and sees us. You'd have never noticed it unless you were looking for it.

Rosalind's insurance claim had been rejected. They said that her cancer was a preexisting condition. I've heard that one before. The form letter that the insurance company sends out in these cases was still in the front pocket of her jacket. I notice the logo in the top right hand corner. It's from my old company. She's left penniless. Evicted. Alone. Eventually invisible.

It looks as though she's wearing one of those skeleton costumes that are all the rage in October. The black ones with the white bones. You can see the outlines of tibias, ulnas, scapula, and clavicle. She melts into the blankets. The candles flicker. The ink drips in. It'll be there at the end. It will always be there at the end. The last thing anyone sees. My hand trembles. She purses her lips together like she's going to say something but no sound comes out.

Softly, I make one of my own. Shhhhhhh. It almost sounds like the ocean. The organs in my chest sink into the ground. Just like they had when I lost her the first time.

She'd wandered out into the street, and with her last bit of energy she found what looked to be as good a place as any to lie down and die. Someplace she'd at least be found. Buried face up.

Frosty stands up and leaves. I can't see the expression on his face through the dark shadows that are setting in but I know it's there. I'm probably making it too.

So there are two things that make everyone equal.

19

"This is an emergency," I say to Frosty, "this is exactly what you said the money was for."

He says that the money won't change anything for her. It's too late for that. He says it's not enough to be a significant help to her. He has to keep it. He says using it to make one person comfortable would be like throwing it all away.

"But it can help some," I say. "You're the one who always talks about compassion."

He shoves me against the wall and says that the money is better spent helping the most people it possibly can. He says it would be irresponsible of him to spend it all on one person. He says that the best thing we can do for Rosalind is to take care of her down here. Make her as comfortable as we can. And then make sure that she has a proper funeral.

"This is no place for someone in her condition to be," I say.

He doesn't budge. He never does. He can't.

"This is no place for anyone to be."

There's no changing his mind. His resolve is the fuel that keeps everything around us going. Friction will eventually slow down any moving object on Earth unless you apply some kind of external force to it. He's that external force for us. Pushing us all further along. Rocket fuel. Twenty-five thousand miles per hour and into orbit. We leave so many things unfinished in our lives, he says. "It wouldn't have been for nothing. Her life I mean. She helped me start all of this. She's like, our mother." Like she had babies without conceiving. Hail Mary full of grace.

I drape some more blankets over her when she starts to shiver. It's perpetually moist down here. Drip. It gets into your bones. Drip. She turns her head. The blue vein in her temple pulsates. I forgive you, she says. Drip.

"You kind of have to don't you?"

She smiles.

Outside I can hear the same people talking about the same things. The game is rigged, they say. We've been lied to, they say. It's time to demand real democracy. The only way to get it is by taking out the people making up all of the rules. Keeping us in our place. It's only one percent. Practically nothing. The will of the many has been subordinated to the will of the few. We need new rules. His message is spreading. Taking on a life of its own. DNA. Cut the head off and the body falls away. Unless you're a cockroach. If you tear the head off of a cockroach it will eventually die of starvation because it has no way of eating. Eventually.

"Why is everyone talking like that?" Rosalind says.

"Don't worry about it," I say, "we're going to take care of it."

"Take care of what?"

"Everything." I tilt a glass of water towards her mouth and she drinks.

Outside, a patrol returns from setting fire to some offices in the glass penis. Hit them at home. Hit them at work. If there's no safe place for us, there'd be no safe place for them either. People cheer when they bring back artifacts that once sat on those polished wooden desks way up there, looking down on everyone else. They kick them along the muddy ground to each other like soccer players.

Rosalind drinks until her throat backs up and she coughs. "What are they doing out there?" she says.

"Helping."

"Helping who?"

"Everybody."

I hear Frosty's voice. "We are also the few, it's time that something bent for us." They all cheer together in one loud chorus. Dr. Frankenstein pieced together and entire organism from disparate parts. Now the organism grows if you fed it. It has babies. And it fights back if you attack it. "Did you know that there's a waiting list at the rich cemetery? They want to lord over us even after their dead."

"Do you really believe that?" Rosalind says.

I honestly don't even know anymore.

She raises an arm with the skin practically falling off it. You can see the outline of the bone in her forearm. It trembles as she moves it through the air. Swings it over, and rests it on my hand. It's cold. "You can't change the world with violence," she says. "Because it ends up being the same old place that it's always been. You can only change it with love." She coughs. I wipe the spit from the corners of her mouth.

"But we can change things, together," Frosty says outside. The worker bees applaud.

The meek shall inherit the earth. Matthew 5:5.

She sighs and more spit bubbles push their way out of her mouth. I ask her if there's anything that I can do for her. Anything at all. Name it. Yes there is, she says. There is.

It's daytime but Frosty and I go topside anyway. The light is blinding. My eyes water. They burn. The lids want to close. They want to protect the organ but I force them open. The sun just hangs there. Full and radiant like it's suspended by a string. The sky around it is a bright clear blue. Blue. I miss blue. The chaos is deafening. People walk past us yelling into cell phones. Car horns honk. There's music coming out of every open window. Every open door. Everything's moving. Towards, away. Nothing is static. You can't count on it. The activity makes it hard to think straight. The moment a thought starts to form in your head something tears it away and pushes you along. No loitering, it says. Move along now. But I can't forget about why we're here. We're here because there's a white cloth on the table beside Rosalind's bed. A crucifix, two blessed candles, some holy water, a glass of drinking water, a spoon and some cotton. Everything is ready to go.

The heavy oak door crashes behind us like a thunderclap. It echoes across the hard wooden pews and the stained glass windows. It's almost amplified as it moves around the empty Holy Name. The architects thought of everything. Someone starts playing the organ.

We find Father Price in the rectory. He's practicing his sermon for next Sunday. "Paul says that the one who is strong in the faith, and therefore understands that he is free from legalistic constraints in disputable matters, must not look down on those who don't believe they have such freedom. He also says that those who are weak in the faith and therefore feel that they must follow certain rules, must not condemn those who do not follow their rules." He clears his throat and looks at himself in the mirror. Then he sees us standing behind him.

He says, no. Absolutely not. "I'm terribly sorry to hear about poor Rosalind's affliction, and I will pray for her." But he's not following us down there. He says 'no' again. I remind him that it's a mortal sin to deprive a sick person of Extreme Unction. The Last

Rites. A mortal sin. Those are the worst kind. Father Price says, yes. Yes, he'll go. I say, thank you Father. And I actually mean it.

Frosty takes out a long piece of black cloth. "This is for our protection," he says, trying to slip it over Father Price's eyes.

"I'm not sure that I'm very comfortable with this."

I pull at Frosty's hand. "I think we can do away with the blind fold. He is a priest after all. We can trust him."

"He's already sold us out once before."

Father Price objects. "That was a matter of legality and the place of the church to…"

"We didn't steal a crucifix. He knows it too. We were set up. Isn't that right?"

Father Price stutters.

"We're not doing this for us," I say.

"Fine." Frosty takes the Bible from Father Price's hands. "But you have to swear to keep our secret. You have to swear on your God." He takes Father Price's right hand and places it directly in the middle of the large golden cross that's printed on the cover. "Do it." Frosty could be very persuasive. We lead Father Price through the underground maze. He takes out a small black handkerchief and wipes it across his forehead every hundred paces or so. Makes the sign of the cross on his chest and whispers prayers under his breath. At least I think they're prayers. When the wall splits open and everything is dark, and we're looking down at the small pocket of humanity settled right around the first circle of hell, Frosty says, "These are the people that really need your help."

Frosty points them out one by one as we walk past the small pools of light and make our way to the last shack on the left side of the old unused train tracks. "But these people don't have nice clothes to show off every Sunday."

I light a candle. Like Rosalind wanted. Father Price takes it from my hand. "Everything is ready." He nods and goes inside the small makeshift structure where Rosalind lies. He'll prepare her soul. Ease her fear. Now she'll get the confession she deserves. Her absolution from sin by the penance she's already done. The first sacrament in the series. I can hear the voices inside. "Forgive me Father for I have sinned," she says.

Frosty paces. He spits. It gets lost in the darkness. "What a waste of time." He doesn't want to believe in a God. Not after what he's been through. How can something that's supposed to be all wise, gentle, and loving be capricious enough to create a world so full of pain and injustice? And to top it all off, he says, we have to spend our lives on our knees thanking him for it. Bone cancer in children. Tsunamis. Killer bees. Once you get rid of Him life becomes simpler. Pure. He starts to walk away. "What did God ever do for her?" It's a rhetorical question.

The alien archeologists dig. They mostly find bones and plastic. Rubber. Glass. Concrete foundations. It looks as though they fashioned these primitive tools out of indigenous metals. They communicate telepathically. The world is quiet again. I think it's meant to fire small projectiles, one of them says. What could be the use of that? They scratch their heads and catalogue it. Nobody will remember what we used to fight about. What made us fall in love. The sound we made when we laughed. Or cried. Except maybe God. The verdict is still out on that one.

Inside, I can hear Father Price. As I walk through the valley of the shadow of death, I fear no evil, for you are with me.

I wait outside until Father Price tries to push the door open. The moisture down here makes the old wood swell and warp. I pull from the other side. It takes a few tugs. He wipes the oil from his hands using the small black handkerchief. The skin on his face is the kind of white that you can only achieve by buying that powerful bleaching detergent they advertise on late night television. "It is done. May God rest her soul in peace." He picks at his fingernails with the cloth. "But, she should really be under medical supervision."

"You're preaching to the choir." Without that money, this is all we can do. Inside the candle lit shack Rosalind turns to face me. Her lips curl upwards. "Thank you," she says. You're welcome. I run my palm across her scalp. She looks up and says, kiss me. She trembles. Her lips are cold and dry. It's quiet and dark. Light is impermanence. It's the darkness that was here before. It'll be the only thing left one day too. I close my eyes. We're the only two people on Earth for one moment.

Everybody else is busy getting ready for phase three.

Frosty hands out folded up pieces of paper to a few of the guys. "You're each going to take three people with you. So pick people you can count on." Birddog asks if he should make some napalm? Or maybe some nitroglycerin? It's simple he says. E.A.P. Easy as pie. "You didn't say that in the army."

Frosty distributes rope, duct tape, plastic ties. Paper tubes packed full of gunpowder with fuses made from soaking string in a mixture of potassium nitrate and granulated sugar. Each inch buys you thirty seconds. Make sure to wear gloves, he says. Actually, it doesn't matter. You barely exist anyway. You're practically a ghost. A poltergeist. Poltergeists can move objects in the real world. They can pinch. Bite. Trip. Hit. They're invisible. Just like us. Poltergeist are said to haunt specific people rather than specific locations. Just like we're going to go.

Her lips are soft and fragile. I can feel the cracks in them and the spots where the skin has started to flake off a little bit.

Outside, Father Price says, "Excuse me? Excuse me?" I can hear his feet shuffling. "Excuse me."

"What do you want?" Frosty says.

"How do you, or rather, how do I, how would I go about getting home?"

"Why do you want to go home? These are the people that really need your help Father. Isn't this good work too? You could be like our Friar Tuck. Just don't make any booze."

"I'll take him back up," I say. Frosty looks over.

Somewhere, farther in the dark, there's a stir. Move! People yell. Hurry up! Feet shuffle. Heavy breathing. Get him down here! Oh shit. Oh shit. Over there. Lie him down.

They say at the end of your life you regret the things you didn't do.

"What's going on out there?" Rosalind whispers.

I speak softly. Like I'm trying to talk a kitten off a ledge. "Don't worry. It's all okay. It's all going to be okay." She looks back at me through glossy eyes. They slowly disappear as the candles burn out and the darkness becomes complete. "I'm sorry," she says. For everything. For not being able to trust you. I wish we had more time. So do I. Maybe I can buy some.

"Promise me one thing," she says.

20

The hole in the ground is three feet by nine feet and six feet deep. The perfect size for a body. Across the unused rail tracks that divide the entire tunnel in half. The side that we don't use. The burial is simple. We don't pull the brain out of the nose with a hook. There's no drying out of the organs and putting them in canopic jars. No filling it with sand. No wrapping it in bandages. We just put him in the hole. We don't even have a box. But he's buried face up. A small wooden cross is planted in the ground just above his head. Frosty allowed it. He even let Father Price say a few words.

"As I walk through the valley of the shadow of death, I fear no evil, for you are with me."

The hole in Tony's chest isn't even that big. Probably less than an inch. The inside of it is just as dark as the unused corners of our underground tunnel. The wound seems insignificant. Like there's no way something so small could do anything more than maybe itch a little bit. You have holes that big all over your body. But your ears, nose, and butthole don't kill you. It had took three people to carry him. By the time they got down here, he was dead.

After a lunch of rotisserie chicken and salad, Mark had the eggplant parmesan, the expert consultants published their recommendations. They were implemented immediately by a bunch of terrified people who had no idea how to do anything for themselves. The paper work went through. The budget was approved. The vote was unanimous.

There was nothing revolutionary in the report. Nothing to justify the enormous bill. Increase police presence in affected areas. The power to arrest without probable cause. Search and seizure. Yada, yada, yada. Typical ways that people in power exercise it. Except one especially bright vegetarian had proposed a new kind of deterrent. They would broadcast it on every television channel. Take out billboards and ads in all the newspapers. Start a word of mouth campaign so that every citizen in the city would know that the use of deadly force, if necessary, is being authorized to deal with any instance which law enforcement deems to be contrary to the public good. These acts of assault and vandalism will not be tolerated in our civilized society.

We don't get television or newspapers where we are. I had no idea how far we'd come.

The store that Tony and his crew had been sent to that night was on a street that had been heavily vandalized by some of the freed protesters. There was paint everywhere. Windows were smashed in and replaced with wooden covers that were clumsily nailed into the wall around the window frames. We are the something, something, they said. Down with the one percent. Equality for all. Things like that usually made the job easier. But thanks to the new mandate, there was an increased police presence there. They hid quietly in the shadows that we usually use to protect ourselves.

"What was all that noise about?" Rosalind asks.

"It's nothing," I say. "You don't have to worry about it." She doesn't need anything else pushing downwards on her soul.

Frosty sorts through bags that are covered in blood. Tony's blood. "Did you get everything? Everything on the list?"

Everything.

Good. His life wasn't in vain then. It was worth something now. He died for a cause. Something bigger than himself. He made a difference. Now he can start to implement the plan. Frosty wants to go over everything one last time. To make sure that all the possible kinks are worked out ahead of time. Once it's finished they'd be taken care of. "I hope you're all ready," he says. "You're going to have to do some things that you're not going to want to. But it'll be over soon, and it'll be worth it in the end." They believe in him. They trust him. I'm starting to wonder.

"What are you planning?" I ask.

"You'll know, when you need to know."

"Three people are dead now. Or haven't you been counting? Tony is dead for God's sake. What did he die for?"

"You'll see." He spits. "They'll pay for it."

"How far are we going to go? How far is far enough?"

"Why don't you ask Tony? Now, shut up and come on."

There's one other person he wants to make sure is taken care of. She'd taken care of him once. He owes it to her. I owe it to her too.

When they brought Rosalind down into the ink I noticed the logo in the top right hand corner of the page that was sticking out of the front pocket of her stained jacket. Assurance Insurance. The form was signed by my old boss. He's terrified when he opens his front door and Frosty hits him in the face with the butt of his gun.

"You brought a gun?"

"It's an emergency."

Frosty drags him into the house and throws his bleeding head down into the middle of the living room. Right in front of his wife and kids. They scream. She holds her hands in front of the kid's eyes. "Now, this is what you're going to do," Frosty starts. Got it? Answer me, Lewis. Do you understand? He kicks him in the ribs. The dirt on our shoes stains the white carpet. So does the blood. My Boss is still wearing the gray suit that he had on that day at work. The red tie is still around his neck. He wears it even at home. He has to set an example for the little ones. You have to make an impression starting at a very young age. He snivels and coughs. Reaches his hands out as if that'll do anything if a bullet flies out of the barrel. Th-th-th-th-th-there's nothing I can do, he says. The form is already filed. She has to write a letter of appeal for the case to be reopened. Please, please don't hurt us. Frosty looks at me for confirmation. I nod. "You're going to get that letter then," Frosty says, "and when you get it you're going to stamp it on through. Understand?" Appeals happen a level up, Lewis says. He has nothing to do with them. Is this true? It's true. The process can take years. She'll be dead by then.

The whole process is designed to screw the insignificant masses and make a little bit more money. Until the insignificant decide to screw you back. Lewis keeps looking at me. His pupils are dilated. He takes frantic breaths. He reaches for my foot. Leaving five trails of dark rust across the white rug. I kick it away. How much is your bonus going to be this year Lewis? Tell me, is it worth anything now? Right now? You can have your job back, he says. All of your policies were transferred to me. They're all still active. A big account. You can come back, he says. You can have everything back.

I kick him in the stomach.

"Ever heard that saying, an eye for an eye? A tooth for a tooth? A hand for a hand?" Frosty says. "Cause I have. It's in the Bible."

Frosty puts the gun to his temple. The wife screams. The kids cry.

Frosty cocks the hammer back.

Please no, Lewis says. Screaming. Crying.

"Have you?"

It's a scare tactic. A damn good one too. He'll fold. First thing in the morning, Lewis is going to push the paperwork through. If there's anyone in the world that deserves it, it's her. Now she might have what she wants most. A little more time. All of this is worth it.

Frosty spits as we walk through the inch of water that settled in the corridor leading downwards. "You really scared the shit out of him," I say. "He thought you were going to kill him."

He looks over at me with a blank expression. The skin on his face just hangs there. It bounces up and down a little with each step that he takes.

"Wait, were you going to kill him? What the hell? You never said anything about killing him. Three people are already dead! Killing people doesn't make things even. Doesn't make things fair." Jesus.

"He gets a bonus and she dies. In what kind of world is that fair?"

Rosalind says the world is what we make it.

Her policy is going to be honored. Fully. With Father Price as the beneficiary. If not, we know where Lewis lives. And what a lovely family he has. Don't bother trying to call the cops. They can't help you. Lewis whimpered. Cried. Agreed. Just please don't kill me, he said.

"What is this?" Frosty looks at a streak of blood that's smeared across the wall. It marks our path. Tony's lungs had sucked in most of the blood but there was still a trail in the tunnels that anyone could follow. When we get back he sends a crew out to hit it with sodium peroxide, vinegar, and water. Like Rosalind used to do. Don't let it touch your skin. These tunnels can't be marked in any way. Nobody that comes down here can be able to find out where we go. Understand? That's very important.

"Who do you expect will be coming down here?" someone says.

Frosty doesn't answer.

Nobody else knows about it, but Tony had given us a lot more than just the guns and the ammunition that his crew stole, on the night that he was shot. I made sure of that when I was sitting across the desk from Mr. Howard on the forty-second floor. His life would be worth something. I have the paperwork to prove it.

Sitting in a particleboard shack I shake the hell out of an old pen to get the ink to pool at the tip. I fill out the insurance forms. Digging Tony up and dragging his body to the hospital to get a death certificate isn't even an option so I'm calling in some favors.

Besides an explosion, the best way to fake your own death is to die tropical. Many public servants in small developing nations will pretty much do anything for a buck. Somewhere, within sight of an endless white sands beach a phone rings. Death by drowning seems legitimate. Shark attack? Too exotic. It doesn't take long to come to terms. "I'm holding the money right now. I'll wire it immediately," I say, into the phone line that's filled with static. He'll email a copy and send the original to the embassy in Malabo. I have the necessary documentation within hours and I start the life insurance claim. Employees of RDC Holdings death benefits triple in case of accidental or violent death. This would be more than enough money to take care of a lot of people and replace the money that I took from Frosty to make it happen.

"Where have you been?" Frosty asks in the shack later that night. Or was it day? It didn't really matter anymore.

Just to get some air, I say.

Some air eh?

Yeah, some air.

He gives me a long look before sticking a gun in my hand. "Here, it's almost time."

"Time for what exactly? Why do I need a gun?"

Birddog moves down the line of waiting drones and hands each of them one of the pistols that Tony's raiding party managed to steal from the vandalized sporting goods store before he was shot in the chest. "How many of you have ever fired a gun before? Show of hands."

When loading your pistol hold it in your strong hand and drop your elbows to your rib cage. Insert a magazine firmly into the well.

Don't slam it. The palm of your hand should seat the mag solidly in place.

No one raises their hands. "That's what I expected," he says. "Well, we're about to change all that."

It's heavier than I thought it would be.

"Why do we need to know how to work a gun?" Lucas says.

Frosty spits. "In case of an emergency. You have the right to protect yourselves."

"Against what?"

Rotate the pistol with your strong hand. With the other, grab the slide and pull it forcefully to the rear and let it go. Let the recoil spring drive the slide home and chamber a round.

"Promise me one thing," Rosalind had said.

If your pistol goes 'click' instead of 'boom' tap the base of the magazine with the palm of your support hand to make sure that it's seated properly. An unseated mag is a common culprit. Only tap it once.

"I promise," I had said.

Grab the slide and rack it hard to the rear. This allows the extractor/ejector combination to clear out the chamber and the slide to pick up a fresh round.

There's a special place in hell for hypocrites.

All hands rise when Birddog finishes and asks, "Any questions?"

D.E.H. That's what his superiors would tell Birddog before sending him on a mission. Don't Expect Help. That's what he says to the people standing in front of him now dressed in black shirts, black pants, and black boots. It's everyman for himself again. You have to know these things ahead of time. Try it again. Do it again. If you fuck up you could compromise the entire mission.

Rope. Duct tape. Plastic ties. Envelopes. Guns.

Father Price wants to leave but Frosty won't let him.

"I'll take him topside," I say. "I'll even blindfold him if it makes you feel any better."

"We're at a critical juncture. We can't afford any strays right now."

"You're just going to keep him hostage?" I ask.

"And who do you think he's going to run to the minute he gets topside? Huh?" He shoves me harder than I would have expected. I stumble backwards and almost fall. "You really think that he's only going to tell God when he kneels down next to bed for his nightly prayers? Why don't you use that head of yours for what it was really intended to do and think." He puts a piece of rope in my hand. "Here."

That's not how it was supposed to be, I say.

Nothing ever is, he says. "Look around. Do you think this is how it was supposed to be? Is this how we were supposed to live?"

Her lips were cold and dry. Just in case, she said. Just in case.

Father Price gets to his feet and starts running. He doesn't get very far before he trips in the darkness and practically knocks himself out. The darkness takes a little getting used to but you eventually adapt. He gets thrown roughly into an old chair that has rusty nails sticking out of it in every direction. "When I am afraid, I put my trust in you. In God, whose word I praise, in God I trust. I shall not be afraid. What can flesh do to me?" He says this over and over again like a record skipping.

Take the rope and form two opposing loops. One overhand, one underhand. Stack the right loop on top of the left. Reach through the top loop and grab the right side of the lower loop. Reach through the lower loop and grab the left side of the upper loop. Holding the ends, pull to create the handcuff knot.

Father Price is tied to a chair and we're all going to hell.

Frosty laughs and slaps him on the shoulder. "See, now you're being helpful." He hands out little pieces of rope to everyone standing around. "You're going to have to be able to do this yourselves, at least one person in each group has to know this. Try it on each other."

I loosen the knot around Father Price's hands. "You didn't need to tie it this tight."

"What's your point?"

Even though it's cool in the underground, Rosalind's hair is slightly moist from the sweat. We have her covered in anything that

274

we can spare to keep her warm. She rests her hand on the back of my head. Just in case she went to hell, Rosalind says. In hell there's only anger and sadness. One last time. One more kiss. One more moment of closeness. With someone she can trust. With someone she could maybe even love. Just in case she goes to hell and she's lost forever. For all of eternity. She wants to feel close to something tactile again. One last time. The warmth. I wrap my arms around her.

"I'll be back as soon I can," I say, "You rest."

"Where are you going?"

"We're going to help people."

"You can only change the world with love," she says.

Frosty folds a piece of paper and puts it in his pocket. One last message. "Is everybody ready? It's now or never." I have a gun tucked into the waist of my pants. A bag full of duct tape, ammunition, and rope. I also have a target. This is it, I tell myself. After this, it's over. There's just a little bit more to do. We can't stop now. We've come this far. Caesar has crossed the Rubicon. Alea iacta est.

The die is cast.

It's easy to follow along with Milgram talking into your ear. The voice is soft and melodic. It tells you the things that you need to hear. That you want to hear. They did scientific experiments about it in the sixties. Before it was illegal to screw with somebody's head.

Please continue.

The experiment requires that you continue.

It is absolutely essential that you continue.

You have no other choice, you must go on.

"Wait till we get to the other side," Frosty says. "It'll be like paradise. Not a worry in the world. You'll see. Trust me."

"Lock and load!" Birddog says. "I can't wait to get started."

The success of a movement all depends on the first follower.

"We can do this together," they say. "We can do anything together. Change the world." It's almost like a dull chant. Like a ritual.

Frosty points to me and says, "You're with me."

We head out through the dark tunnels in single file.

Rope. Duct tape. Plastic ties. Folded up notes in our front pockets. Guns.

21

Phase three.

Nobody says anything as we make our way through the underground. We all know what we have to do and there's no reason to talk about it. Groups splinter off in different directions the further through the subterranean maze we get. Covering the city with our web. Soon, there's just three of us walking in silence. Asbestos flakes flutter down from the ceiling when traffic drives by overhead.

"You have to follow your instructions to the letter. To the letter," Frosty said, handing out paper. "You know what to do with these. You've all been briefed."

I haven't been briefed. Why haven't I been briefed?

"The success of the entire mission relies on every single part of it working together. We're a team. Different parts of the same machine. Do whatever you have to, just get it done. Got it?" He looked over at me. "You're with me," he said.

We synchronized our stolen watches. Mine was gold. I hated it cause the metal watchband always pulled at the hair on my wrist. We grabbed our stolen weapons.

We each become that one little cog that regulates the timing for the next step up, which turns the rotor, that swings the arm, that chops the head off of somebody twenty fuckin' miles away. Just like Birddog said. It's funny how that happens.

Please continue, Milgram says.

The experiment requires that you continue.

It is absolutely essential that you continue.

You have no other choice, you must go on.

"Wait till we get to the other side," Frosty says. "It'll be like paradise. Not a worry in the world. You'll see. Trust me."

Frosty leads the line of us through the tunnels. He's the head of the snake. He walks with a purpose. An authority. I walk behind him. We're all doing exactly what we've been told to do. We're acting how we've been told we have to act. People have a propensity to obey what they perceive as authority. Because once people accept the right of an authority to direct their actions they relinquish responsibility to them. Even as adults we still obey our parents. Anyone wearing chevrons. Epaulets with gold rope around them and tassels. It's just easier that way. Leave the thinking to someone else.

'Let every person be subject to the governing authorities. For there is no authority except from God, and those that exist have been instituted by God.' Romans 13:1.

This idea isn't new.

Now there's three of us left. The lights flicker when the subway goes by. Water seeps through the cracks onto the dirt below. There's a dab of blood on the wall that never got cleaned up. We turn a corner. Down the dark passageway there's a yellow light shinning. There's a shadow. Something's moving down there. Frosty stops me and puts his hands on my shoulders. He smiles. There's little dark streaks between his teeth. Blood that's seeped into the cracks from the gingivitis on his gums.

"I have a present for you," he says. "You're going to love this."

The duct tape sounds like an injured animal when Frosty pulls a long piece off the roll and starts wrapping it around Mr. Howard, to keep the tubes packed with gunpowder in place around his chest.

Diggs says, "You can't use that. They'll be nothing left to identify the body with. It'll be like tomato soup. Kind of defeats the purpose."

Identify the body?

Mr. Howard looks at me through the blood and the sweat that's dripping over his eyes. Please, they say. Help me. You know me. You can't do this. I'm a human being for God's sake. Frosty knows the look too. His eyes had been saying it for most of his life. But they didn't say it anymore.

"Can't we blow something up?"

Mr. Howard pisses himself.

This is happening in every corner of the city. Stolen watches are synchronized. The time is right now.

"My present to you," Frosty says. "The guy that took everything away."

He's just one of many. The richest people in the city are being rounded up. That small percent. Tied to chairs using the handcuff knot, and beaten with fists or the butt ends of guns. We're waiting outside their homes when they walked to the curb to put out the garbage. There's someone hiding in the back seat of their car when they finish work. They're pulled into the alleyway coming out of the store they stopped into to pick up some milk on the way home. Their expensive cars are left idling on the street. Place your right forearm across the neck and wrap it around your left arm which is perpendicular with the hand resting on the back of the head. Choke them out. Pull them against the car seat with a knife to the throat. They won't move. Point your gun at them and say, "Let's go." They've never had to do anything for themselves. They won't know what else to do.

Drag them underground where no one will hear them pleading. Negotiating. Weeping. Break a few fingers. A few ribs. The jaw is always a nice one. It shuts them up fast. They offer you money. As much as you want, they say. Tape this note to their chest before you kill them. But put it somewhere that the bullet won't travel through. It's important that the message stays intact. The message is everything.

They breathe heavily and sweat. "Whatever they're paying you I'll double it," they say.

"I'll give you anything you want," they say.

"I have children," they say.

"Please."

It all falls on deaf ears. This is the mission. Phase three. Redistribute the wealth. Show everybody else what happens to hoarders. Scare them into doing the right thing. We're just following orders. The ends justify the means. The good of the many outweigh the good of the few. That's what everybody tells themselves.

"Go ahead. Hit him," Frosty says. "I know you want to."

Please, I'll do anything, he tries to say.

Frosty opens up his cheek with the same ring that he took off Mr. Howard's finger. It looked like a class ring. Harvard or Yale or something like that. Actually wearing them is terribly pretentious. Unless you're trying to prove something.

"Shut up."

I haven't hit him yet.

"What are you waiting for?" Frosty says. "Do you know what this guy did to you? Did you know that he turned you in? The only reason that he gave you that money in the first place was so that you'd be the scapegoat and he'd walk away scot-free and rich. This guy took everything away from you. Aren't you angry? Don't you want revenge? Go ahead. Do it. What are you waiting for?" The tape leaves adhesive all over Mr. Howard's suit. It's ruined. He doesn't even care. "He beat you down. You were the tramp in the dark alley. He turned you into a statistic. Now, you can return the favor."

Fifty percent of all statistics are made up.

Frosty spits. Red flakes and bubbles. "I thought you'd be happy." He pulls the gun out from the waist of my pants. "He threw you under the bus. Then it was business as usual. Like you never even existed. You were chewed up and spit out. And for what? A little bit of extra money that he didn't even really need. That's what."

Mr. Howard's eyes widen. He takes a sharp breath. It's serious now. It's always been serious to Frosty.

Rotate the pistol with your strong hand. With the other grab the slide and pull it forcefully to the rear and let it go. Let the recoil spring drive the slide home and chamber a round.

"I promise," I had said to Rosalind.

Frosty puts the gun in my hand. He slaps it into my palm and curls my fingers around the grip. Looking at Mr. Howard, I want to do it. That prick. That asshole. That greedy fucking asshole that took everything away. I want to do it. But I don't.

"Point the gun at him. Go ahead."

No.

"Point it at him."

No.

"You never said anything about killing people."

"I told everybody that they'd have to do something that they didn't want to do. We all agreed. Now. Do. Your. Part."

He took everything from you. Forced you to live in the dirt, underground like a dog. He ruined your life. He took your home away. He made you into this. Into the homeless person that's now holding a gun and pointing it at someone else. He made you into a murderer. "You have to do it if you want to be saved," Frosty says. "You can't get back up until you've gone all the way down to the bottom."

I realize that I'm squeezing it as hard as I can.

"Point the gun at him," Frosty says. His voice becomes a drone in the back of my mind. "That was his plan all along. Did you think he was really impressed? Did you think that he was really trying to help you? He was never your friend. He was never your colleague. He was just using you. You were a screwdriver. A box cutter. A simple tool. And when he didn't need you anymore he threw you away." Mr. Howard's face has streaks of blood across it. His eyes plead with me. His short, sharp breaths sound like a panting animal. The sweat beads on his skin.

Frosty used to say that everybody's life mattered. Rich or not. That was the whole point. He lied. And this gun wasn't just supposed to be a scare tactic.

"Come on! The prodigal son is right here." Frosty paces and scratches the back of his neck. "You know, most people get it all wrong. They think that the word 'prodigal' is something good. The prodigal son returns. They say it like it's a compliment. But it's really an insult. You know what it means? It means, wasteful. But he returns. And they take him back. Because the farther away you go, the more God wants you back. Funny eh?" He raises my arm. "But not us, we're not taking him back. We're going farther. Now, point the gun at him. Go all the way." He points at Mr. Howard. "The prodigal son is here waiting for you. God wants us back. Make him want it even more."

Life isn't about money. And there's only one way to change the world.

"Your life gets ruined and they go to the bank. In what kind of world is that fair? In what kind of world can they get away with that?" The world is what we make of it.

No. I won't.

Now, I feel the coldness of the barrel against my temple. My head tilts. Frosty had saved Diggs. He had rescued Diggs from beatings, starvation, and sickness. Kept him safe. Diggs owed him. His life. Everything. Now, Diggs is just following orders. His orders are to make me shoot. Or to shoot me. His hand shakes a little. I can feel the barrel pull at my skin. He pushes hard and cocks the hammer back. That's what they do in movies to signify that they're ready to do it. They're totally committed.

"Just do it," Diggs says. "Please. I don't want to hurt you."

"I saved you too, you know." I lift my arm. The barrel trembles.

Please.

Shut up.

I promise.

Shut up.

Frosty rips the last tubes of gunpowder off of Mr. Howard's chest and tapes a handwritten letter to it. "When you shoot, make sure that you don't hit the note, okay? It's important that the message survive."

I'm not going to shoot. "You've made your point. Look at him. He pissed himself he's so scared. You've said what you wanted to say. Nobody has to die."

"Unfortunately, yes he does. The ten richest people in the city are going to die tonight. That pesky percent. Their money is going to be spread around. We're going to even things out. Then, if the others don't hear that message, the next ten are going to die. And then the ten after that. Until all of that money is doing what it's supposed to be doing and people aren't hungry or freezing anymore. Until there's no one living on the streets or in the sewers.

You can be a part of that. This is your moment of truth. This is your big chance." To be truly altruistic. To give yourself fully to others and ask for nothing in return. To give to us instead of taking from us. Isn't that right? Didn't you take? You did. Even if you didn't know you did.

There's still a gun against my temple. Enough of this, shoot him. It makes perfect sense. He fucked up your life. So you shot him. Isn't that right? It's a logical explanation. Do it for us. Do it for me.

He hits me with the butt of his gun.

What are you waiting for?

He checks his watch and sighs. Diggs is shaking so much that the end of the gun can barely find my temple. Tears run down his face. "Fine," Frosty says. He tells Diggs to get lost. He can handle it from here.

"Give yourself fully. Let go. Light is short anyway."

Darkness is.

I'm a screw driver. A box cutter.

"Let's try something different. I know you love her," he says. "And right now there's a gun resting right between her eyes. The priest too, but I know that doesn't bother you as much. Everybody has a part to play. Everybody has something to give. Whatever you think about us means nothing anymore. It's about the people not the person. I'm just as happy if they're collateral damage. But they don't have to be. Up to you."

Mr. Howard's eyes are wide. His pants are wet. His frantic breathing sounds like a tissue stuck inside of a vacuum cleaner.

Frosty hits me again. Then kicks me in the stomach while I'm on all fours. The gun slides out of my hand and into the corner. I do that thing that's in every horror movie where the guy tries to crawl away knowing that he can't get more than a few feet before the chainsaw starts digging into his back.

This is happening in nine other places.

But something else is happening at the same time. Something that only Frosty and a few others know about. Something they kept secret. The new life is going to start tonight. Down here. In these dirty tunnels. Frosty realizes that he can be better than equal. But, for once in his life, he's going to need something from somebody.

He'd found my paperwork while he was scouring my things, looking for the missing money that I took to bribe the official into signing Tony's insurance policy. He'd found all the rest of them too. Thirteen others. The policies that I had slipped into the stack at RDC Holdings to take care of the people at the church if something ever happened. He knew whose names they were under. Knew who the beneficiary was. The benefits triple in case of accidental or violent death. The police had already gotten an anonymous tip and found Brock's body slumped over in a dumpster. Covered in moldy food and blood. That would be two big insurance checks on the way. Two wasn't going to be enough for what he had planned. He needs more.

22

"He was going to kill me. He's going to kill all of us," Olive says.

She clutches my arm as we run down the tunnel. Drone voices echo behind us. Their footsteps bounce off every smooth concrete surface underneath the city. This is a dead end. This is where the pipes for the water treatment plant divide the tunnel. There's nowhere else to go. He's getting closer. I can hear his footsteps in the water.

"You're going to pull that trigger weather your conscious or not," Frosty said, while I was on the ground, "They're going to find your prints on that gun. You owe us that much."

Mr. Howard breathed heavy. He tried to loosen the rope around his wrists.

Frosty's breath was hot in my ear. At first I was pissed off, he said. "When I found out the money was gone. Then I figured it out. I guess I should thank you. Everybody should thank you. You've given us a new life."

It was for the greater good, I said. I took the money to bribe the official. To file Tony's insurance claim. To help everybody. So his death would mean something. The check that's on the way can take care of a lot of people.

"And more of those checks can help even more people."

I inched along the ground with Frosty standing over me. He kicked me again. Placed his foot on the back of my neck and pushed my chin into the floor. The oil smeared against my face and mixed in with the blood.

The past means nothing. We must continue forward. The experiment requires that you continue. It's for the greater good. We've come this far.

But Milgram's experiment didn't work on everybody.

I grabbed his ankle and spun onto my back and I kicked him hard between the legs. I drove a foot through his right knee and it buckled and I'm running through the tunnels. Mr. Howard is on his own and I couldn't care less. His screams fade with each corner that I turn until they're gone completely.

The underground is alive tonight. Voices echo from every direction. Gunshots. The time is now. The dust that took years to settle fills the air. Stirred to life again by the shuffling feet around every corner. The cloud grows. Skin flakes and hair. Concrete and dirt. I can't help but cough. Two yellow jackets approach. They nod their heads as I shuffle by.

Is it done?

It's done.

Thank you, they say. Thank you.

I round the corner. Then another. Pick up the pace. Frosty's voice echoes behind me. My boots splash up the few inches of water running along the ground, giving me away. I think my rib is cracked or broken. Every breath feels like a knife twisting into my side. I run. I run head first into Olive. Thank God, she says. Tears streaming down her cheeks. They were going to kill me. She grabs hold of my arm. Don't leave me. We have to get out of here. We run. There's only one way out now. The pipes for the water treatment plant cross here. He'll be able to follow us.

"Something about giving ourselves to the greater good," Olive says, panting. "He kept saying it over and over. Make our lives worth something. Help the most. Selfless giving. The rest were all going to die." Phase three is leveling the playing field. Spreading the money around where it's actually needed. Two birds with one stone. Now it looks like there's really three birds. And we're one of them. Paddy, James, Puppy, Lucas, Olive, Socks, Gibbs, Colby, Brock, Violet, Tony, Birddog. Everyone that I had taken out an insurance policy for through RDC Holdings while we were at the church. They're all going to die tonight too. If they're not dead already. And Frosty is going to get rich. Brock was already taken care of. So was Tony. A new existence awaits. One that isn't in the sewer. One that's above ground with everybody else. Benefits triple in case of accidental or violent death. He's going to take the rest of them away. Start over again with a bankroll. Sacrifice the few for the needs of the many. He's justified in his actions. Their lives will mean something. They will have a legacy. Everything's coming together.

Justified. That word doesn't pop into the microphone when you say it. Even torture is justified as a source of useful information. Obliteration bombing is justified as a way to shorten a war. The greatest happiness for the greatest number measures right and wrong. It makes it okay. According to some. It only makes sense if you're on the right side of it though. Rosalind wouldn't think so.

"We have to get out of here," Olive says.

There's only one way out. We have to move the manhole and go topside. No matter how hard I push it doesn't budge. It's been sealed shut. Shit.

Boots splash through water. His voice bounces around a corner. It's getting louder. "There's nowhere to go now," it says. "We're going to see this through to the end," it says. "We've gone too far to stop now," it says.

I cup my hands together and Olive puts her foot into it. I push hard on the heel of her shoe and throw her up. She fits into the small space between the pipes and the ceiling. About the width of a rolled up sleeping bag if you forced it in just right. Hide here. "What about you?" she asks. I have to go back for Rosalind. I owe it to her. The footsteps get closer. Frosty rounds the corner and I throw myself into him. The two of us fall into the water that streams by on its way to the underground. Every breath sends a bolt of electricity across the left side of my body. He elbows me in the jaw then forces my face into the few inches of water. He holds me down until my lungs feel like they're filled with Tabasco sauce. Until the moment my body almost inhales by instinct, before pulling me out. I gasp. Electricity. I can't get enough in. He grabs me by my collar and drags me back to where some other drones are waiting.

"Who were you talking to?"

"You can't kill them," I say. "They're our family. Your family. You said it yourself, it's just money. You can't throw them away like garbage. You saved them in the first place!"

Don't you see? he says. They're going to help a lot of people. Right now they might as well not even exist. But after they don't anymore, after they give themselves, their lives will have had meaning. They'll leave something behind. A legacy that will last. It will all have been worth it. For the greater good. They will always be remembered.

Thank you, the drones say.

"You can be a part of that new life. As soon as you get out of jail that is. You see, someone has to take the rap. But don't worry, the sentence will be light. You were coerced. Damn these violent protesters. They ruin everything." He smiles.

I spit at his feet. It's filled with globs of red particulate.

"You're a fucking fraud," I say. "You call everybody else a fraud and you're just as bad as all of them."

He grabs me by the neck and slams me against the wall.

"What did you say?"

"Fucking fraud. You know there's a policy out on you too. You've seen it. Benefits triple in case of accidental or violent death. You know that too. I don't see you lining up to take one for the team. Take a bullet. Give yourself fully. What a load of shit you selfish fucking fraud."

He presses the barrel of the gun against my forehead.

Who do you think will take care of these people? he says, spitting in my face. "You? Spineless shit. Rosalind? Just like the good old days? She'll be dead. And then what? Huh? Then who's going to give a shit?"

Thank you, the drones say. We will remember you.

He tilts his head down and angles his eyes upwards. It adds gravity. I taught him that.

"You're just like him," I say, "going around asking everybody to devote themselves to something bigger. Asking them to make the sacrifice you're not willing to make yourself. To believe in a better world. But you won't do it yourself. Everything is selfish. Peace of mind. Money. Paradise. Bullshit."

Say three Hail Mary's and sign here.

He grits his teeth and cocks the hammer. "I'm sorry to hear you say that. Good thing there's always plan B."

Thank you. We will remember you.

"TARFU."

It stands for Things Are Really Fucked Up. It's a military term.

Now, Frosty has a gun pressed against his head. The hammer cocks.

"Isn't that right?" Birddog says. "Things are really fucked up. All of a sudden, shit got real." Birddog hits him twice with the butt end of the pistol then picks him up and sticks the barrel into his ear, pinning him to the wall. "Then it turns out, it was you."

Birddog was going to do it. The note was stuck to the rich guy's chest. He was tied up and Birddog had his forehead lined up in his sights. He was going to do it. He was so deeply entrenched in the inner workings of Frosty's machine that it all seemed perfectly logical to him. But his time in the service had taught him something else besides how to break bones. It taught him how to survive. He developed an uncanny knack for hearing sounds associated with the manipulation of firearms. He heard the guy behind him pull a gun out. Heard the hammer cock back. And he knew, from the shadow on the wall, exactly where it was pointed.

"You get on outta here," Birddog says to me, with Frosty pinned to the wall at the end of his gun. "This ain't going to be pleasant." He presses it harder when two drones inch forward.

She'll be safe where she is. I leave Olive in the pipes and sprint through the tunnels taking a quick left or right whenever I hear voices up ahead. I should have taken a gun with me. Stepping off the concrete, onto the dirt, I make my way down the steep hill that takes me to track level. Where all the particle board shacks sit. Cinder blocks. Old cardboard signs advertising good and services. The new utopia. There's hardly anyone left in our underground city. They're all out in the tunnels doing their part tonight. I get to the warped particleboard door that has Rosalind and Father Price behind it. Somebody else is in there too. Holding them hostage with a gun. Frosty's seen to it.

There's this thing that people do in movies where they throw a rock or something at the door, and when the person inside comes out to investigate they knock them out or tie them up and make off with the loot. That didn't work in this case. I hear Rosalind scream. There's a thud. The door gets pushed open. Father Price looks me in the eye and says, "Forgive me father for I have sinned," when he comes out of the shack with Rosalind wrapped around his shoulder, a club in one hand, and blood spattered on his chin. I ask him about the whole turn the other cheek thing.

"Behold, I have given you authority to tread on serpents and scorpions and over all the power of the enemy," he says. "Luke 10:19."

This time, I take the gun.

Rosalind is walking on the few inches of water that rushes past her feet. Just like Jesus once did. Slung across the both of us, we try and move her through the tunnel as fast as we can. Her feet lurch forward feebly and just graze the surface. But there's an intensity in her stare. A determination. Two drones round the corner. They're just following orders for the greater good. They say that bees exhibit altruistic behavior when they commit suicide by stinging to protect the nest. These drones don't. When I point the gun at them they stop dead and throw up their hands. They step back a couple feet. I wave it some more as we slide through and down the next tube. They crank their heads around the corner like rats scoping out a carcass. I pull the trigger and they scatter.

Then, there's an explosion.

23

The dust cloud spews out like a spot light. It finds its way into your eyes and your ears and your lungs. Powdered concrete makes it hard to breathe. It weighs down your chest. A second explosion rocks the tunnels harder than the first one did. The smell of burnt skin and hair mixes together with the particulate in the air. It gets stuck in your mucus membrane and just sits there until you eventually inhale it. Rosalind's toes graze the ground. Her feet lurch forward feebly. We keep pushing through the thick haze even though it's almost impossible to see where we're going.

Bodies move through the tunnels and scatter in every direction. The ant colony has been firebombed by some sadistic kid who's just discovered gasoline and matches. Rats abandoning a sinking ship. Birddog made the nitroglycerin. You have to handle it very carefully. Nitroglycerin explodes if you shake it around. People push past us trying to get out of the tunnels. They shove us into the walls and step on our limbs. All of a sudden it's everyman for themselves. Rosalind says that we should just leave her behind and save ourselves. We keep pulling her forward even through we've been thrown into the inch of water that spins around our bodies.

Someone grabs my arm and pull us to our feet. Through the floating soot I can barely make out Olive's face. And Colby. They pull us along with them. "We have to get out of here," she says. Socks is bloody. Violet is limping and using Colby's shoulder for support. Paddy is coughing uncontrollably but keeps pushing us forward. Olive says that when she left her hiding spot after the first explosion, Frosty was bloody and Birddog slammed his face against the wall before climbing on top of him and pressing the blade edge of his forearm into his neck. She found Paddy still alive and they made a break for it. In the dark tunnels filled with smoke, and the powdered concrete that gets into your lungs, they found Colby, Socks, and Violet. "They were going to kill us," they say. I know. "But they kept thanking us."

Have the insured pull all the triggers. That was the plan. Have them pull the triggers. Hide the guns. Off said insured. When the bodies are dragged out, blame it on the protest masterminds and collect the claim. Benefits triple in case of accidental death. Once you're free and clear, the guns resurface to close the case. Suspects are named and convicted posthumously. The insurance company will want the money back since benefits are null if death occurs during the committing of a crime. But who cares. You're already gone. You barely existed in the first place anyway. And now there's no one looking for you. I have to admit, it's not a bad plan. Everyone thinks Frosty is stupid because of the way he looks. He isn't, but there's one thing he never thought to think about. We're supposedly made in His image.

"You guys have to go," I say.

We round a corner and run head first into the barrel of a gun. The drone holding it shakes. His face is contorted into something that looks more like some old crumpled up clothing than a face. Like he seriously needs to get to a bathroom. The gun in his hand sways back and forth. The dust starts to settle on our shoulders.

"Put your sword back in its place. For all who take the sword will perish by the sword." Father Price steps forward. "The lord tests the righteous, but his soul hates the wicked and the one who loves violence." The gun trembles. "You were not made to kill," Father Price says. "You were made to love." He steps forward again. Passes the barrel and rests his hand gently on the drone's shoulder. Father Price moves around him with the rest of us in tow. "You know this in your heart my son." We're all infants in the eyes of the Lord. We leave him standing there pointing the gun into the darkness.

A right, then another left. Rosalind needs to catch her breath. I look at the scars on Paddy's face. The black fingertips. I look at the bald patch on Olive's head where the hair was been pulled out of her scalp by the root. Colby can only see out of one eye. Violet has little purple dots that run up the inside of her arm. Birddog has red welts that look like he'd been burned with the end of cigar. He hadn't. Tony had a dog that he couldn't bear to live without. In another world, he had a house and credit cards.

"You guys have to get out of here," I say. "Take Rosalind and get out of here."

"No," Paddy says. "We can't do that. We're coming with you." Family. Community. You don't give up on your family or on your community. "We're not alone anymore. That means you're not alone, and they're not alone either." They might still be alive. There's a chance.

Rosalind's head rolls back. The tip of her nose pokes out of the shadows cast by the flickering overhead lights. A white flash runs across the part of her eye where the blue iris used to be.

"Father Price, you have to take her out of here."

"Thy will be done."

I grab him by the shoulder. "Right, left, left, left, right," I say. "Repeat it."

"Right, left, left, left, right."

Say it again.

Right, left, left, left, right.

"There's a latch on the underside of the grate about halfway down. Pull it towards you."

There's a latch on the underside of the grate about halfway down and pull it towards me.

Say it again.

Rosalind's chin rests in the palm of my hand. "I'll be right behind you. I promise."

"Where are you going?"

"To help some people who need it." I take out the gun. This is an insurance policy. Sign here. Father Price won't take it. Rosalind won't take the gun either. I shouldn't be surprised. "Get out of here as fast as you can. We'll meet you back at the Holy Name." Rosalind's blue lips turn up at the corners. Fingers reaching out from the crooks of her eyes. It's beautiful. I knew it, she says. "Hurry. Go."

A few people shove past me as I run through the tunnel. Abandon ship. But I'm running further inside. Then, at the end of a dark tube, I see their two shadows through the dust that's starting to settle. I hear them thrashing in the inch of dirty water. Like an unholy baptism. Frosty has Birddog on the ground with a gun angled down towards Birddog's face. The muscles in my body surge. Finding as good a foothold as I can, I get ready to charge him. I'm going to grab him by the neck and push him into the water. I'm going to throw all of my weight at him and plow him into the wall. Then I'll pick up the gun. Then I'll push it into the skin on his forehead so hard that it leaves a circular indentation. That's what I'm going to do. I can picture it all in my mind. But I don't have the time. Frosty spits. Snorts. That snort of derision. The gun goes 'click' instead of 'boom'.

If your pistol goes 'click' instead of 'boom' tap the base of the magazine with the palm of your support hand to make sure that it's seated properly. An unseated mag is a common culprit. Only tap it once.

Frosty hesitates. That's all the time Birddog needs to get the better of him. He learned it in basic. With a knee pressed against Frosty's chest Birddog grabs the slide and racks it hard to the rear. This allows the extractor/ejector combination to clear out the chamber and the slide to pick up a fresh round. He looks over at me. "Get the hell out of here," he says.

I leave them alone in the dark and the dust.

Lucas is already dead. So is the guy in the navy blue suit with the shiny gold belt buckle tied to a pipe in the corner, next to a small access panel that says: danger 10,000 volts, in bright red lettering. His hand looks like it's holding an invisible apple. There's a note smeared in dirt and blood underneath it. When I find James he still has his hands in the air. The black barrel behind him quivers to the left and to the right of his neck. There's a body off to the side. A crumpled up note shoved into its mouth. And two drones who obviously hadn't realized just what the hell they'd gotten themselves into. Their eyes are wide, and they're trying to open them wider. But they're not searching for something to tear to shreds with their piranha under bites anymore.

"It's over," I say. "Just get the hell out of here." They're gone before I even finish. People rush past the door. Splashing. Shouting.

"Thank you," they say.

After the explosions, the shootings, the electrocution, it's chaos underground. After the explosions, the shootings, the electrocution, the drones have come to realize something. That maybe they're made in His image. That pulling the trigger isn't as easy as they thought it would be. They fall apart. It's everyman for himself. A survival instinct takes over. It has something to do with evolution. Almost everything does.

Right, left, left, left, right. The grate's left open. They made it out. Thank God.

When I pull myself out I expect the fresh air to clear my head, but a thick white cloud burns my eyes the moment it makes contact. It irritates my mucous membrane. That's what tear gas is designed to do. It controls crowds. The white cloud is heavy. It lingers in the air. Slowly lurching by until it's caught in an updraft where it makes circular patterns as it dissipates. I feel like I'm going to cough up my intestines. The entire city block is on fire. Literally.

I make a break for it.

The police walk through the swirling white clouds wearing gas masks. Helmets and matching full body armor. They carry clear Plexiglas shields and batons. Walking side by side, they push back an angry mob of protesters wearing windbreakers and sandals. A few of them shoot rubber bullets at people. They're designed to produce contusions, abrasions, and hematomas. With the occasional bone fracture or abdominal trauma. Nothing serious. They're made from wax now because the rubber had a tendency to bounce uncontrollably.

The protesters throw anything they can get their hands on. Rocks and bottles mostly. Their signs litter the ground, having been abandoned for a more practical weapon. Something with a little more weight behind it. A group of guys wearing black balaclavas smash a store front window and toss a petrol bomb inside. The insurance companies aren't going to like this at all.

"Please disperse," someone yells through a megaphone.

We are the something, something they chant. Equality for everybody. It's the perfect distraction.

Rosalind and Father Price are on their way to the Holy Name. The others wait for me behind a dumpster. "Run away from the chaos," I tell them.

"What about you?" James says.

I'm running into it.

Olive has those big doe eyes. I don't know if it's from the gas or something else. "When will we see you again?"

"I'll find you." She looks at me. "I promise." I spin Paddy around by the elbow as he turns to leave. Keep them safe, I say.

"I promise."

I know I can trust him. They disappear down the alley. I duck out into the floating white cloud of gas and into the street.

The protesters have rallied hundreds of people together. They take over. Marching. Chanting. The more angry ones start setting things on fire. Destroying property to make a point. Throwing cans and rocks, and anything else they could get their hands on. The police converge on the scene for the good of public safety. They douse the entire area with white gas. They hold up riot shields and spray pepper into people's eyes. Handcuff their hands together so that they can't hurt anyone else. The protesters never stop chanting. Even though they're losing ground fast. They throw their bodies in front of the riot shields to protect each other.

Brothers in arms.

There's small pockets in the street where the gas has cleared, or hasn't gotten to yet. I stay down wind but another cloud approaches from behind. I keep moving. One officer clubs me in the shoulder as I run by. Some people rock a police cruiser back and forth and then decide to set it on fire since they can't turn it over. They scream. Please disperse. Fire. Rocks, bottles and rubber bullets made out of wax. Billy clubs, broken bones and bruises. Then I see them.

Father Price and Rosalind are crouched in a recessed entrance way. The gas lurches by but the exhaust from the climate control system overhead keeps it from finding its way into their eyes and throats. She leans against him clutching at his chest. He protects her head with his left hand. They can't move fast enough to make it across the riot safely. By the time I get there I'm hit four times and my intestines are in my throat. I can taste the blood in my mouth.

"Thank God you're here," Father Price says.

We wrap her around our shoulders. Rosalind's toes graze the ground. The white clouds roll by. Megaphones squeal. The flames are consuming half the block. Smoke billows into the night sky. There's broken glass everywhere and the protesters chant together. Arm in arm, and hand in hand.

"If you pour yourself out for the hungry and satisfy the desire of the afflicted, then shall your light rise in the darkness and your gloom be as the noonday," Father Price says.

"Amen to that."

A guy in a red hooded sweatshirt gets clubbed then cuffed. At least it will hide the stains. They drag him away. A woman keels over after getting hit in the groin with a bean bag round. Cuffed and dragged away. The cloud rolls by. People cough and put their hands over their eyes and scream. They vomit down the fronts of their shirts that they have pulled up over their noses. They're cuffed and dragged away. The line of police move forward. Rubber bullets, broken bones and bruises.

Tomorrow on the news they're going to praise the brave men and women of law enforcement who risked their lives to quell this violent protest. Who stood to protect the property and livelihood of businessmen and captains of industry. The police chief says that when people go to a protest wearing goggles and bicycle helmets you know they don't have peaceful intentions. "I wasn't doing anything violent," one woman says, "and a police officer hit me over the head." There are debates. Panels of experts. It's unacceptable they say, at their shiny desks with their slicked back hair and inhumanly white teeth. We'll be right back after this commercial break.

A large group of protesters are trashing a historical building that has recently been converted into a bank. They kick at the front doors. Smash the windows and spray paint the façade. The insurance companies aren't going to like this at all. We slip by as the line moves in. We've almost made it across the street when two officers block our path. Their breath pushes through gas masks. Voices are muffled. They move in.

"He's a priest for God's sake!" I yell.

They move in.

"Get her out of here," I say to Father Price.

As God is my witness, he says.

I throw myself against the plastic shields and push. I manage to gain a couple of feet of ground before one of them reaches around and clubs me over the head. There's no sign of Rosalind and Father Price as they slap the cuffs against my wrist and drag me off. They made it. Thank God. Or the closest thing to him.

When my eyes stop watering I recognize where I am.

The fencing around the parking lot has been reinforced, and there's more officers standing guard. Bright spotlights shine down on us from above. Every few minutes they bring in more people who are clutching their eyes or rubbing their heads and wrists. The protest rages for a full day before the authorities regain some semblance of order. They estimate it's cost millions of dollars. People interviewed on the street by news crews say they support the protesters. Something needs to be done. But nothing ever is. Nothing changes. Life goes on the same as it always has. People go to work. Spend their money on the newest gadgets, or cars, or clothes. On the weekend they get together in even numbered groups sorted by social standing. Some of them manage to jump the queue. Most of them don't. In a couple of weeks the whole thing is forgotten. Someone makes a video of a talking cat. It becomes a viral sensation. It's all people can talk about.

Eventually the bodies are found underground. Unfortunate victims of the violent protests. The police say that the nitroglycerin had exploded accidentally. They could tell because the bodies of protesters had been found all around the blast zone. It made perfect sense. They wanted equality for all so they targeted the richest people to redistribute the wealth. They have forensic evidence. They found notes to prove everything. Nobody will know what really happened. In his final bid, Frosty became invisible again.

Four days later they let me out.

24

Besides dying tropical, the best way to fake your own death is an explosion. Or two. The woman across the desk looks everything over. She stacks the papers together and smacks them against the table to square them all into a tidy pile. Everything seems to be in order, she says.

Benefits triple in case of accidental or violent death.

"Now all I need for you to do is sign here." She hands me a pen.

I sign on the dotted line. The others are in offices just like this, signing papers just like this, and claiming insurance checks. You can't tell who they really are once you clean them up. Comb their hair and give them clean clothes. A briefcase or a tie. They suddenly become trustworthy and nobody asks any questions. The plan is to pool all of the money together. Evenly.

I'm supposed to appear in court in two weeks time to answer for my participation in the violent protest. There's considerable loss of life and millions in damage. Someone has to take the blame. I don't think they'll miss me. Leaving the offices of Assurance Insurance I throw my driver's license into the garbage. I throw the fake one that says I'm related to Joseph Rhodes away too. Frosty. In the event the beneficiary dies the settlement goes to the closest living relative. It all makes perfect sense to the adjuster. Mr. Howard, and everyone with him, were the victims of a heinous crime perpetrated by the terrorist and violent protesters. It's a tragedy. All because of money. What a waste. They say that hindsight is twenty-twenty.

I won't be needing an identity anymore. Either one. By the time they realize their mistake it'll be too late. We'll be gone. The others do the same. Some civil servants will do anything for an extra buck. A little bit more. We're invisible once again. The forgotten. The faceless. We'll never be found but we'll all be buried face up.

Entry number six.

The city declares three days of mourning then it's business as usual. Gaps that are left behind get filled in an instant. The second ten richest people are now the ten richest people, and life goes on.

At the rectory I see that my condo's been sold and that the proceeds have gone to the police pension fund. It's a small article in the paper. Right at the back. Life goes on. Dogs are being walked and their shit's being scooped up in eco-friendly bio-degradable bags and left in the bushes. Jobs are being done. And people run to the bank as soon as their work day ends so that they can get their money working for them. That's what all the financial advisers tell you to do. People hem and haw over what to have for dinner, and splurge on the expensive eleven year old olive oil so that they can impress their friends. They're foodies you know. Very discriminating. Politicians say that they want to uphold the integrity of the office and do well by the people. It's because of the people that they're in office. Without the people, they're nothing. Then the assistant runs to the bank to cash the big check left by the lobbyist, to pass a bill that would tear down the low rent housing on the corner of Jane St. and build condos. This area is being gentrified. Commercials tell everybody to spend their money, so they do. They buy insurance that keeps them poor so they can die rich. And they make car payments on the newest mobile devices while they're stuck in traffic. It can do zero to sixty in three point five seconds. Some new people are born to carry on the cycle. Some people are buried face up.

"Spare some change?"

Move along says the cop.

Get a job says the businessman.

Some things are never going to change.

The alien archeologists dig. The world is quiet again. They have no idea how we lived. Our mating rituals. The sounds that we made when we laughed. Or when we cried. God might. But the verdict is still out on that one. They dig. They mostly find bones and plastic. Rubber. Glass. Concrete foundations. Duct tape preserved in amber.

Entry number seven.

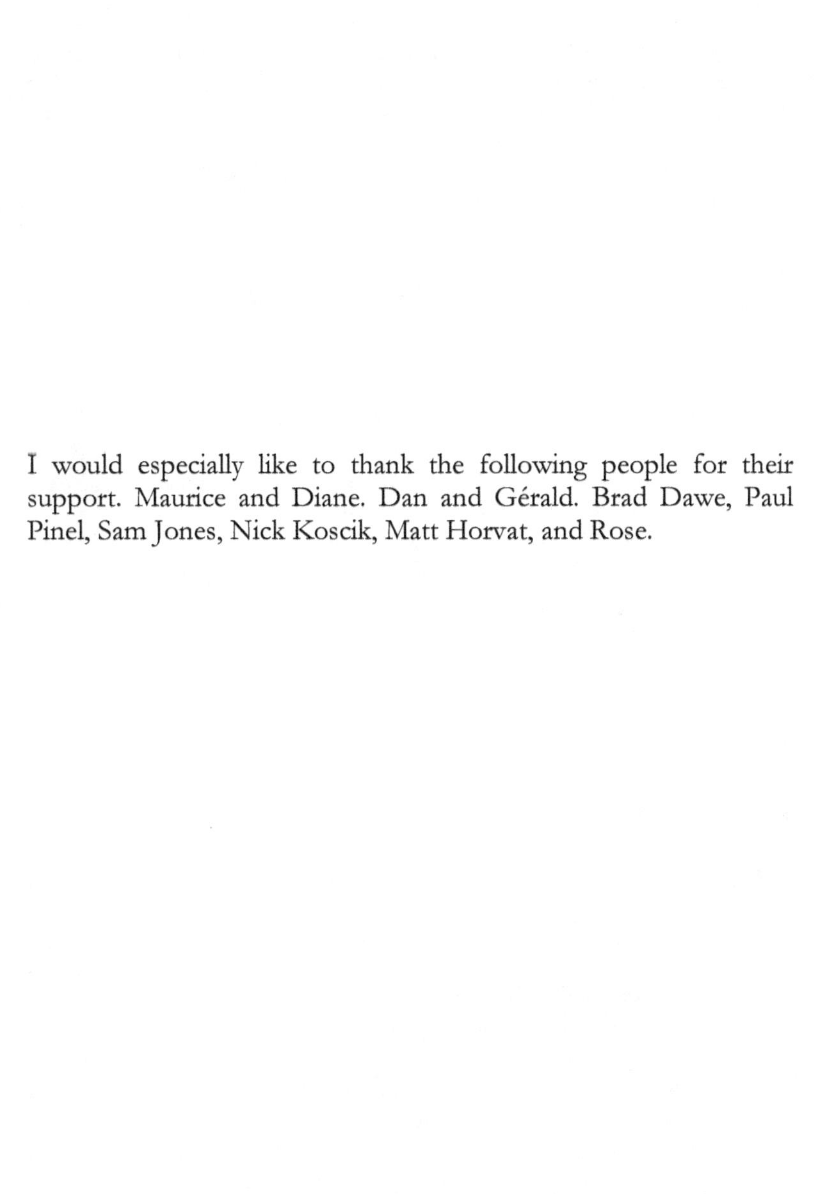

I would especially like to thank the following people for their support. Maurice and Diane. Dan and Gérald. Brad Dawe, Paul Pinel, Sam Jones, Nick Koscik, Matt Horvat, and Rose.

Rick lives in Toronto and also works in film and television.